Maple Candy Christmas

A Christmas In Quebec Novel

Amanda Cook

Contents

A Chilly Reception

"And with a final sprinkling of shredded tinsel, your tree is set for the best Christmas party on the block. Block parties are not just for summer, and especially here in Vancouver with our mild winters and dare I say it, 'temperate climate'. Hosting a block party during the Christmas season makes great sense. Show your neighbours some love! Let your light shine! Bring joy and sparkle to your neighbourhood this Christmas." Evelyn zoomed out and walked around the decorated tree, giving the viewers a panoramic view of the stately blue spruce, dressed in Christmas finery.

"And remember, Christmas is also the season of giving and on behalf of my generous sponsors, we'd like to encourage you to support your local homeless shelter and give the gift of a roof to someone less fortunate this year. The donation window is open, and here in Vancouver we are starting the bidding on our sponsor's pop-up homes, at $5,000.00. Remember, fifty percent of the funds raised by this charity drive will be funnelled directly into building a permanent homeless community cooperative, right here in the heart of Vancouver, on land donated generously by the City of Vancouver and the blessing of the Musqueam, Squamish and Tsleil-Waututh. We acknowledge their ancestral ownership of this precious land."

Evelyn moved a few steps to the right, and centered on a grey, oval shaped shelter that resembled a fabric igloo but with cells that were inflatable by air or water. About every six inches around the circumference of the base of the structure, velcroed loops wrapped around slats of wood, anchoring the structure to a bed of simple wooden pallets. Through a zippered door held open by similar ties, a combination electric cooktop and heat source cast a warm glow around the interior. A kettle whistled merrily, demonstrating the functionality of the solar powered appliance.

"These off grid structures can be used in any setting, even the most remote places in the world. The integrated solar panels on the roof ensure enough power to keep the pod cozy and comfortable even in the harshest of environments, and certainly more than enough comfort for the needs of our great city. If you are local to Vancouver, check out the pop-up in Stanley Park, and while you are at it, take in the beautiful lights of the season.

"Our goal is, as always, to eliminate homelessness everywhere, and with your generous support, we can truly make a difference." She panned a little further to the right, where a tall sign shaped like a Christmas Tree was lit up with a rising silver bar that marked the current donation level. At the top of the tree was a star of Bethlehem, waiting to be lit up once the donations met their goal. "The meter is rising quickly, as your donations pour in. Remember, no donation is too small!

"Share the love and remember your hashtags. I want to see your memories in the making. #homelessgiving #sharetheroof #Christmasviralcharities, and of course me, your host, #Christmaseve #Christmaswithevelyn, #chirstmassnowqueen. See you in the next stream!"

Evelyn smiled a toothy white smile at the camera, blew a kiss to her phone and then clicked the stop button conveniently tucked into the palm of her hand, that automatically added her wrap up theme music and some more hashtags to the feed. The livestream recording button went dark and with a sigh and a muffled groan she arched her back, both hands on the small of her hips as she stretched. It had been a long run of recordings, sometimes only hours apart, some in the middle of the night and in more than one location, however she had chosen her own back yard for this last video in her 'Christmas With The Homeless' series.

She walked over to the gifted shelter and popped her head inside. It was just as cozy as she had said, and there really was one set up in Stanley Park. She intended to donate this one to the cause, but for now, it was a great way to test out the shelter and know for sure that it was a great product to answer the needs of the homeless. She had even slept in it a few times to see how comfortable it really was.

Her locations had ranged all over the city, where ever the homeless could be found, and unfortunately, there were all too many opportunities available to interview the people society had forgotten. She walked over to the cedar deck she had built at the back of the property and mounted the steps to her favourite spot. She'd built a peekaboo window in the middle of the wooden privacy fence, that allowed her an unobstructed view of the city and harbour below. The Lion's Gate bridge stretched off to the right, the lights just coming on as twilight faded to full dark. The grand arches swept through the fiery sky, the bruised blue-grey mountains dominating the skyline.

Reaching over to her right, she opened the door to the mini fridge that sat within convenient reach and pulled out a bottle of wine. It was her favourite, a crisp Sauvignon Blanc with citrus notes, grown in the Okanagan valley. Tipping a generous pour into a long-stemmed wine glass, she sat down in the padded lounge chair, kicking off her heels to watch the sun set. Solar lights, strategically placed in her garden winked on as their sensors registered the failing daylight. She took a slow sip, savouring the refreshing taste of the wine and blinking slowly as she relaxed.

Moments later, she awoke with a start. She had fallen asleep, right arm tucked under her head as she stretched out in the lounger. Her glass sat on the nearby side table, half empty. An angry buzzing was issuing from the pocket of her sweater. With a muffled oath, she pulled her phone from her pocket. The alarm she has set for herself flashed an angry red. "SocialBuzz Gala, 15 minutes."

"Well, grinch me!" Evelyn exclaimed, and jumped to her feet, pushing back her long fall of curly auburn locks. She has slept a good hour, time she was supposed to have spent getting ready for the biggest event of her life. It wasn't every day that you received a request for your attendance at the most exclusive awards ceremony in Canada. Granted, her last six or seven videos had gone viral with over a million views, and her following was steadily climbing, but the competition was fierce. New influencers were popping up all the time and with her quirky Christmas niche, well, it was a very specific audience. Not like those influencers that covered politics, or animal experiences. She was the Snow Queen, an influencer that specialized in Christmas charity events across Canada. That was her thing. And she was proud of it. And of her favourite charities—all were the ones that strove to resolve homelessness.

She picked up her shoes and hiking up her skirt she sprinted for the patio doors of her hillside home. She had taken no more than ten steps when the phone rang. Evelyn tapped the receiver behind her ear, not pausing to look at the call ID. She knew who it would be. "Evelyn

Christmas," she said, a trifle breathless as she leaped up the deck stairs two at a time.

"Eve! Where are you? You were supposed to be meeting me here at the Sky Train station. The train will be here in five minutes."

"I'm so sorry, Natalie! I'm running a bit behind. You go, I will find you at the Paradox."

"You had better hurry! I knew it. I knew I shouldn't have taken the day off. Now you are going to be late for the most important event of your life!"

"You worry too much, Nat. I got this. Now go and save us some good seats and a bottle of good wine. This is a night to celebrate!"

Evelyn hit the end button and raced upstairs, punching in a pick up request in her Uber app as she ran. She quickly showered, then dressed in a slinky red dress she has bought earlier that week, just for this occasion. It was a more daring piece than she usually wore, in her signature red that bared one shoulder, hugging her chest, waist and thighs before ending a good six inches above her knee. Moving to her dressing table, she sat down and quickly arranged her thick hair into an updo that allowed kiss curls to escape and caress the nape of her neck. She wrapped a pearl studded collar around the updo, clasping it at the back in a style reminiscent of the hair bands her grandmother had always loved.

A simple pearl necklace, gold and pearl drop earrings, and a woven gold, green and red bangle completed her ensemble. She slipped her grandmother's engagement ring onto her left ring finger for luck, then put on a pair of strappy golden heels. A quick touch up of blush, eyeliner, mascara and a shade of light red lip stick with a pearl sheen. and she was ready to go. She gave herself the once over in the mirror, then swung a sleeveless cashmere bolero over her shoulders and headed for the door, grabbing up her pearl studded clutch on the side table.

Her phone buzzed again. The uber driver had arrived. She pulled open the rear door and slid into the Acura's plush leather interior.

"The Paradox?" asked the driver in a lilting accent.

"That's correct," she replied.

The driver pulled away from the curb and entered the stream of traffic. Evelyn tapped the SocialBuzz app logo of a cartoon bee holding a cell phone, then pulled up her feed to check on her viewer's reaction to her most recent posting. A cheshire cat grin stretched her lips as she checked the likes. It had been a little over 90 minutes since her post and already she was at 200,000 likes and climbing. She let out a happy giggle and then sent a text to Natalie to let her know she would be there in about fifteen minutes.

The ride to the convention hall was faster than she had expected, as rush hour traffic had given away to the nightly flow of the downtown core. By some miracle, they hit every green light, so that she arrived only ten minutes after she would have had she taken the Sky Train. But what she had gained in time, certainly lightened her pocket book. Still, she had to admit that the short nap had restored her energy levels, so much so that she walked into the hotel lobby with a spring in her step and a sparkle in her eye, eager to participate and enjoy the night's festivities.

She did not initially notice the eyes that followed her as she crossed the lobby. Yet, she did glance around, not exactly looking for anyone, but still, sensing that a pair of eyes were following her. The posh hotel lobby was done up in a modern minimalist style of walnut wood panelling, smooth grey granite tiles and sea blue accents. The dark sky and lights of the surrounding buildings winked through the glass of the atrium's ceiling. But it was the man who reclined on the sofa of the nearby lounging area that caught her eye. It was difficult to gauge his age. Dark blonde hair cut in a carefree surfer style and swept to one side framed a tanned face with stormy blue eyes. But it wasn't his looks that distracted Evelyn. It was the look of total disgust that wreathed his face as he looked at her. She could feel his loathing washing over her in waves, so much so that she stumbled as her heel caught on the edge of the tile transition to carpet. Forced to look away by her near slip, she took her gaze off of the man. She hurried to the doorway, glancing back over her shoulder as she paused before the ballroom. But the man was gone. Quickly, she glanced around the now empty lobby. He was nowhere to be seen.

Shrugging, she put the man out of her mind, as she spied a happier, welcoming face. Natalie rushed up to her and handed her a glass of wine, then tugged her by the elbow. "We are seated over here, see, they have name tags for our assigned seating. Come on, I will introduce you to the others at our table." Natalie looked her up and down and then smiled appreciatively. "You look amazing, Evelyn!"

"Thanks, Nat." Evelyn eyed Natalie's black sequined, belted black dress with equal appreciation. "You clean up pretty well yourself. How did you fight off all the men on the Sky Train?"

"Ah. Well as to that, I pulled out my favourite magazine and started reading where they could read the title." She snickered aloud. "Ten Dating Secrets For Lesbian Lovers". After that, they wouldn't even glance my direction. She smirked. "Come on."

Natalie pulled her along behind her, weaving in and out of the formally set tables filled with attendees. While formal dress was indicated on the invitation, it didn't specify white or black tie, so an eclectic mix of "formal wear" styles were in evidence, based on the age of the person and their interpretation of the term. Evelyn felt the eyes of the crowd following their twisting path to a table near the front of the room.

Seated at the table were six other couples. An elderly man and his wife smiled up in greeting as they arrived, nodding politely. Beside them was a younger woman, possibly their daughter, for the younger woman was a near carbon copy of the older woman's features, only younger and more relaxed. Beside her sat a young man of a similar age, and then as Evelyn's eyes completed the circle of greeting, her smile froze. The last couple consisted of the man who had frowned at her so severely from the lobby. His expression had not changed on iota. She met his gaze briefly before continuing on to his companion, possibly the most beautiful woman she had ever seen in her life. A sculptured face with high cheekbones and almond shaped eyes, framed by long straight blonde hair, and a long slender neck around which a diamond studded necklace sparkled in the lowered light of the overhead chandelier. She gazed solemnly back at them, then turned her gaze away, in a dismissive manner.

"This is my friend, Evelyn Christmas. Evelyn, please meet George and Francesca Cummings, and their daughter Melissa, and her boyfriend Ryan. And this is Nicolas Jollie-Saint and his girlfriend, the actress Sabine Perdue. Everyone, this is my boss and best friend, Evelyn Christmas." Evelyn nodded to each person in turn, blinking towards the end at the cold reception across the table. Unfortunately, the circular configuration of the table placed the unpleasant Nicolas Jollie-Saint at her right elbow. How she wished she had chosen to sit beside the smiling Cummings. Evelyn sat down, taking a large sip of her wine to steady her nerves.

Natalie leaned over and whispered in her ear, "How did you get so lucky, to sit beside Mr. Handsome?" She nudged Evelyn in the ribs. "He's pretty dreamy, don't you think?"

Evelyn rolled her eyes at her assistant, and shrugged. "He looks pretty uptight, to me. Besides, he has that blonde bombshell with him. I am not looking to get my eyes scratched out tonight."

"You know why we are here," whispered Natalie. "This is the place to be and be seen. The people in this room are the super wealthy, the super influential. These are the heavy rollers who can make or break a fundraiser, just by showing up at the door. You NEED to be here."

"I know. Don't worry, I got this."

The doors to the kitchen at the back opened and formally attired wait staff funnelled out of the doors, carrying their first course, which turned out to be a roasted red pepper soup blended into a spicy, creamy concoction that smelled heavenly. Famished after a long day out in the chill December air, Evelyn dug into the soup straight away. A pleasurable sigh escaped her lips as she savoured the soup, feeling the warm tingle spread throughout her body down to her red tipped toes.

"Oh, that was so good!" she exclaimed, putting down her spoon and smiling at everyone around the table. "Exactly the right start to a fantastic dinner."

Francesca smiled, leaning forward to be heard above the buzz of the conversing crowd. "What exactly do you do, my dear?" Her bejewelled fingers flashed as she picked up her glass of wine and took a delicate sip.

"I am a charity gala coordinator. I help charities set up their fundraiser events and then take them to social media like SocialBuzz here, and help get the message out to a much wider audience than traditional radio and print ad marketing, or direct mail, which is almost a thing of the past. Don't get me wrong, there is still an audience there, but to truly expand your reach, you need to be able to connect with people and donors across multiple platforms simultaneously . My company, Christmas Viral Charities, specializes on capitalizing on the good will that is embedded in the Christmas season."

"What a wonderful thing to be doing at such a young age!" said Francesca, eyes sparkling. "I love a good charity event. We are so blessed in this country. We immigrated to Canada when my daughter was just a baby. We had been living in Beirut, but when the bombs started to fall, we fled the country. So many good people there lost their lives. We have never forgotten our humble beginnings. My husband was fortunate to begin working for the central bank and has been a banker all these years." She patted his hand. "We are retired now, but we do love to attend events such as these." She turned her eyes to the man to Evelyn's right, the one she was trying so hard to ignore.

"And what do you do, young man?"

The transformation that came over Nicolas' face was amazing. He smiled at the elderly woman and his eyes softened to something almost human. Evelyn stared, nonplussed. *Who is this camelion?*

"I am the broker of record for one of the largest real estate companies in Vancouver. We specialize in distress sales, bank foreclosure and federal tax-liened properties. Basically, we clean up the mess made by other people, repurpose the properties and sell them at a price point that allows the mortgagees to recover their losses. We are the financial recovery arm of the big banks, you might say." He smiled at George across the table. "A pleasure to meet you again, Mr. Cummings."

George nodded his head in acknowledgement.

Just then, the wait staff returned with their salad course. The soup bowls were whisked day and replaced by a spinach salad with goat cheese and pickled beets and red onions, with a crunchy sunflower crumble on top. Murmurs of appreciation swept the table and they began to eat. The new course was just as tasty as the first and Evelyn happily picked up her fork and began to eat.

The second course was followed by a third, a freshly caught Pacific Salmon steak in an herbed butter on a bed of creamy mushroom risotto, sprinkled with fresh herbs and a lemon beurre blanc. Soft sighs of satisfaction and the light murmur of voices were a pleasant back drop to the stringed quartet playing on a small dais at the side of the room. Overall, the atmosphere was a relaxing one. That is until Evelyn heard the conversation occurring to her right.

Nicolas was shaking his head in a negative fashion and once again frowning with intense dislike at Evelyn. Her eyes widened when they met his stormy blue grey ones, confusion reflected in her own. Once again, she felt the waves of disgust emanating from the man. What was wrong with him?

"This is never going to work," he said to the woman on his right. "I told you this was a waste of time. "She is nothing more than a silly Christmas bauble. All style and no substance. As fake as they come," he said, meeting Evelyn's eyes once more. "I think it's time to leave."

The woman placed a manicured hand on Nicolas' jacketed forearm, caressing it possessively. Sabine's ruby encrusted lips leaned forward as she spoke into Nicholas' ear. "Darling, lets at least stay for dessert. There might be some good speeches to come, too. Let's enjoy the rest of our meal."

Nicholas turned his head and his gaze studied her perfect features. He smiled, squeezing her hand. "You are right, there is no reason for me to allow this woman to destroy our evening." He glanced back at Evelyn, the sneer firmly back in place.

Evelyn's eyes widened and her face flushed with outage. Never had she been so thoroughly dismissed by someone so unlikeable. Snobby. Arrogant. "Scrooge!" She nearly shouted the last word of her train of thought. Natalie put down her fork with a clatter, looking from Evelyn to Nicolas in surprise.

The dessert course arrived, a plum tart in a butter crust with a maple cream chantilly. Evelyn was sure it was wonderful, but she didn't taste a bite. Her evening had been soured by the completely obnoxious person sitting beside her. She turned her back slightly on him, giving him the coldest shoulder she could muster in the warm room.

The dessert plates were cleared and coffee and tea served in large carafes on the table. At a table to the right of the speaking podium a woman got to her feet and approached the microphone.

"Welcome, welcome!" she trilled, her voice flowing over the room and silencing the conversations. "Thank you so much for making time in your busy schedules to attend the 5th annual SocialBuzz awards. This award banquet was created as a way to acknowledge the amazing work of the presenters and influencers, who make a difference in our society every single day. For those of you who do not know me, my name is Tanya Sculley and I am the founder of SocialBuzz. As our name suggests, we are all about providing users with a platform that allows them to reach the most people possible, through text, media posts and video content that is specifically curated by them. Every single day, we have a break out artist that goes viral, and that commands the attention of the world. From pop stars to actors, and even simple country folk, if you have a message and can deliver it well, our audience will gobble it up."

Nicolas yawned, ostensibly loud, his back turned to Evelyn so that all she could see was the wavy fall of blonde hair, just brushing the collar of his navy jacket. His hair was frustratingly perfect, and looked to be incredibly soft. With a start, Evelyn realized where her thoughts were going, and she pointedly looked past the man, to the woman speaking on stage.

"We will begin this evening with the youth awards. This category acknowledges those under the age of sixteen, who have made outstanding content that has gained them an incredible following. First let me bring up Ashley Peters, age 9..."

Nicolas leaned forward and spoke into Sabine's ear. With a nod of her head, she reached under the table and picked up her purse then stood up. Nicolas followed her motion, standing up, then nodded to the seated couple and left the table. Sabine wrapped his left arm in hers, hand possessively placed on his upper arm as she swayed at his side. Evelyn watched them leave the room, a frown on her fact.

"Hey, wake up!" said Natalie, giving her a shove to break Evelyn's eye contact with Nicolas's retreating back. "What's with you, tonight?"

Evelyn shook her head, trying to clear her thoughts. Why was she allowing this complete stranger to get under her skin?

"I don't know. Stupid really, to be worried about that old Scrooge." Dismissing the man, she turned back to the podium to watch the next set of awards be handed out, clapping politely to acknowledge their accomplishments.

"The next award is for the most viral video of 2025, as judged by the number of views, shares and likes across all influencers. We are excited to tell you that this is a totally new influencer to our ranks, and this person has literally exploded on SocialBuzz, bring in no less than 10 million views over the last three months, with a staggering three million views happening just today. We here at SocialBuzz are buzzing with excitement, to introduce you to our Golden Buzz award recipient for 2025... Ms. Evelyn Christmas!"

Applause exploded and cheers rang out as Natalie gave the stunned Evelyn another shove. "It's you!' she screamed, as Evelyn got to her feet. Shocked, heart racing, she waved at the people around her, who were now standing and applauding. She pasted on her showtime smile, hiding the nerves that raced through her body, making her flush. The hostess, Tanya, waved at her to come join her on the stage.

Evelyn walked on shaking legs up the short steps to the raised platform and joined her in front of the microphone.

"We are honoured to have you here with us this evening," said Tanya. "Your work on behalf of the homeless of Vancouver is unrivaled in the world of charity. Your video monologue of only a few hours ago has already surpassed three million views and donations are pouring in from all across the country. We are receiving inquiries from the mayors of other big cities in Canada, and also from the USA and Europe, who have watched your platform and your vision, and wish to speak to you about creating similar campaigns to address the homeless needs in their communities. You serve as an inspiration to all us, and a beacon of hope for a kinder, gentler world. This is why you are our grand prize winner and this years SocialBuzz Gold Winner. We will donate $1,000,000 to the charity of your choice. I don't think we have to look far to know which one that will be!"

The crowd roared their approval, and called "Speech! Speech!"

Smiling, Evelyn stepped up in front of the mike. "Thank you. Thank you." she waited for the voices to die down before continuing. "I know this may sound strange, but I am actually speechless. Speechless with shock at this award, speechless with pride in my community. speechless with joy at your support of our homeless neighbours, brothers and sisters. No one should be homeless. Not for any reason. It is a sign of a civilized nation when they care enough about their neighbours and friends to share and support people through the hard times. We all have them. But for the grace of God, any of us could find ourselves in that situation. I know this because I was one of them. Homeless. Scared. Hungry. And in those deepest, darkest times, you feel like *no one cares*. I vowed then and there, that if I ever found my way out of my situation, I would make it my life's mission to solve this one very solvable aspect of modern-day society. Erase homelessness everywhere. I want to thank my assistant, Natalie, for all of her support, and her parents, who passed away a few years ago, for taking me in off the street, and for giving me the chance to climb out of the hole, and become whole once again. Thank you all, for your love and support. We truly couldn't have done this without you all. God bless."

The roar sounded once again as everyone rose to their feet, clapping and whistling. Evelyn waved once again, and stepped back to have her photo taken with Tanya and the rest of the SocialBuzz movers and shakers. As she smiled for the camera, she thought she saw movement in the doorway at the back of the hall. The door closed silently and all was still.

The Next Gig

Natalie shouldered open the door, purse strung over one shoulder and her arms full of bundled mail. She closed the door behind her with her foot, shook her head to divest her hair of the clinging drops of rain, then kicked off her short leather boots before staggering into the sitting room where Evelyn sat hunched over her laptop, typing. A cooling cup of coffee rested by her left elbow.

"Ah, winter in Vancouver. We haven't seen the sun for three days straight now," she complained. Releasing the bundle clutched to her chest, she emptied her arms, the mail falling to the table top with a thud, shrugged out of her wet coat then returned to the front door and hung it on a wall peg in the hallway. She shivered as a drop of rain rolled off her nape and down her back. "You know, if this rain keeps up, you will need a boat fundraiser to float those homes."

Evelyn sat back and stretched, yawning. "Sorry, what was that?"

"The rain. Don't you wish it was a lovely Christmas snow? Rain is such a bummer at Christmas."

Evelyn yawned again, shivered, then got up and turned on the gas fireplace. Warmth sprung up immediately, the flames casting flickering shadows against the library panelling. "I think it's time for some hot chocolate. Just what we need to chase the chill out of the air." She wandered into the kitchen and picked up the electric kettle, filling it with water, then switched it on. Pulling their two favourite mugs from the cupboard, she set them on the counter. One was in the shape of a Coca Cola Santa, with a jolly bearded mug and a red nose. The other cup also had a red nose, but it graced a cartoon version of Rudolph the Red Nosed Reindeer. She grabbed her tin of Christmas blend hot chocolate (a personal favourite blend of dark cocoa with milk chocolate nibs and peppermint flavoured marshmallows) put two hefty scoops into each mug and then poured the boiling water in. Giving it a quick stir, she carried them back to the table.

Natalie bent over the mound of mail, slashing open the bundle of envelopes with an ancient letter opener, then stacked them neatly in a pile for Evelyn to examine. The mix was similar to what they had been receiving all week, ever since the awards ceremony exposure had pushed Evelyn's SocialBuzz feed to the top of their play charts. They contained a mixture of greeting cards filled with donation cash and cheques, letters from random people asking for money that they had dubbed "Santa Scammers" and the occasional photograph from someone hoping to meet Evelyn. These last two kinds of mail Evelyn tossed in the paper recycling, then sorted the cash into one pile and the cheques into another, after recording the donor's name, address and amount in an online ledger, in order to send them their tax donation receipt. But that task was for the new year. For now they needed to be sure to accurately record the donations that were still flooding in from Evelyn's campaign of a week ago.

Natalie accepted the cup of hot cocoa from Evelyn and cupped her hands around the mug, inhaling deeply to savour the wonderful scent. She took a sip then placed it on the table. Humming a rock version of "Run, Run Rudolph", she gathered up the Christmas cards, then hung them from the strings that now criss-crossed the library ceiling from bookcase to bookcase, like laundry strung between tall buildings.

There were so many, she was having to add more strings every single day. The strings had spilled out into the living room and entrance and would soon be climbing the stairs.

Returning to the library, she saw that Evelyn was bent over a standard sized white envelope, with a formal crest printed on the front. Peering over Evelyn's shoulder, she read the insignia. "Office Of The Mayor, Noelville, Quebec" and a coat of arms of a rearing buck and doe over a frozen pond. "Well, this should be interesting."

Evelyn glanced at her and then slit open the envelope with the letter opener. She pulled the white parchment from the envelope and unfolded the letter. An old fashioned, bronze skeleton key dropped onto the table with a clang as it bounced off the side of the Santa mug. She glanced down at the key and then began to read aloud:

 "Bonjour, Mademoiselle Christmas,

As the Mayor of Noelville, it is my distinct honour to invite you to be the parade marshal of our annual Christmas parade and charity gala, to be held on Christmas Eve, this year.

Your dedication to championing the elimination of homelessness in Canada has inspired the nation, and we would be grateful if you would grace us with your presence for our countdown to Christmas, kicking off

Noelville's advent celebrations. From December 12 to Christmas Eve, is our very own twelve days of Christmas, packed full of events that are sure to inspire you.

While you are here, we hope that you will be willing to assist us with our own Christmas Eve homeless gala fundraiser, inspired by your recent success. It is our way of giving back to our community at this very special time of the year.

We are providing you with a mysterious key, that we promise will unlock secrets of the past. Accommodation with be provided, as will your airfare. A rental car will be waiting for you at the airport on arrival.

Please provide us with your reply as soon as possible so we can make preparations for your stay.

We look forward to celebrating the season with you!

Joyeux Noel,

Marie-Claire Saint, Mayor"

The second sheet of paper was a folded event flyer, like the kind you would staple to hydro poles to advertise local events. Printed on a Christmas background, the flyer contained the twelve days of advent, for the City of Noelville.

12 **Décembre** – 24 Décembre
Le Grande Marche du Noelville Christmas Market
13 Décembre –
Festival Of Lights
14 **Décembre** –
La Fête Des Rois King cake making contest
15 Décembre -
La Pere De Noel Ice Skate
16 Décembre -
Noelville Christmas Candle Making & Tree Lighting Ceremony
17 Décembre -
Toboggan Slide At Maple Mountain
18 Décembre
Maple Candy Cane Pull
19 Décembre -
La Bonnehomme de Neige Snowman Building Contest & Snowball Fight
20 Décembre –
Nutcracker Ballet – Central Outdoor Theatre

21 Décembre -

Gingerbread House Building Contest & Christmas Open House

22 Décembre -

Haunted Christmas Village

23 Décembre

La Parade Des Jouets – Christmas Puppet Parade

24 Décembre –

Midnight Mass At The Grand Cathedral

Natalie picked up the discarded letter and read it aloud. She whistled appreciatively, grinning as she caught Evelyn's eye.

"Wow, a key to the city. Nicely done, Evelyn! And a free vacation thrown in for good measure."

"I can't agree to go, Natalie, and you know it. There is no way."

"No way what? Your schedule is packed with family events? Suitors are knocking on your door everyday, waiting to whisk you away in a horse drawn sleigh? Jolly St. Nick himself has promised you a Christmas Eve tour of the skies behind his team of reindeer? You know very well that the only thing you have planned over the next three weeks is a stack of books, some Christmas cookies and lots of cocoa."

"That's not the point —" protested Evelyn, but she was overrun by her assistant's continuing tirade.

Natalie's fists settle on her hips, the letter crunching in her hand. "Every single year I invite you to come and spend Christmas with my family. We are loud Italians with way too many kids, but there is always room for one more. My six brothers are happily married and producing litter after litter, so they are no threat to you. Every year I am told to bring a second, and every year you refuse." She reached over and plucked the schedule out of Evelyn's hand, then shouldered her out of the way and plopped down in front of Evelyn's open email account. "It's no fun to go alone."

"You should listen to yourself. Where is your significant other? I am sure that's what your parents are harping on about. Not you inviting your boss."

Natalie harrumphed.

"Well, this year, you are going to go someplace very Christmassy to enjoy the holiday. You are accepting this invitation, with grace and charm. If nothing else, you can treat this as a business trip. Since you have gone viral, demand for your services is exploding. This is a good place to start. Christmas in Quebec. What could be more Canadian? I might even join you at some point." She opened up Evelyn's email and began typing. A few moments later she had composed Evelyn's acceptance email, plugged in the mayor's personal email address, and hit the send button. "There, no backing out now. You are going and that is all there is to it."

Evelyn stared at her assistance with bemusement. She really didn't have anything to do this holiday season. She hadn't since her surrogate mother had died. She had been adopted at the age of six by a staff member of the shelter she had been taken to after her birth mother had died of a drug overdose, one of many homeless men and women in the city. She had no siblings, no extended family. Her step mother had been an older lady, more like a grandmother to her, but she had loved her dearly. The years since her cancer diagnoses and eventual death had been lonely ones. Perhaps Natalie was right. She could use a vacation. And she loved snow.

"Alright. You win. What harm can come from attending another gala? Will you be joining me for any of the events?"

At that moment, her email pinged, announcing the arrival of an email. Evelyn looked down and saw that it was the Mayor. "Wow, that was quick!" She clicked on the email to read the reply.

Dear Evelyn,

We are so pleased that you have accepted our invitation and will be joining us for the festivities.

Please watch your email for your reservation detailes and itinerary. We will see you in a week's time!

Bring warm clothes. Quebec storms can be sudden and very intense. All other needs will be provided.

Safe travels,

Marie-Clare Saint

"Ha, well Merry Christmas to you, Ms. Christmas. For someone named after the holiday season, you sure can be a bit of a Scrooge when it comes to sharing time with friends and family. Maybe this trip will open your eyes to new possibilities. It is the season of miracles, after all." Natalie picked up her mug of cocoa and took a big slurp, surfacing from the cup with a melted marshmallow stash. Grinning, she wiped the sticky concoction from her upper lip, then licked her finger. Evelyn grinned at her. It was a standing joke between them that a good hot chocolate should leave you looking like Santa, or it just wasn't hot chocolate.

"I know one thing for certain. If I am going to make that plane in one week, there is a lot of work to get through first, starting with this huge stack of mail. Shall we?" She gestured at the tilting pile of envelopes.

"Absolutely." Natalie picked up her letter opener and attacked the next letter with a flourish worthy of a swordsman. "And then I am going to help you pack. It's my duty as your assistant to make sure you are appropriately glorious for this endeavor. And you will need some practical clothing too."

It was mid afternoon before they finished processing the mail. Evelyn leaned back, stretching her arms above her head to ease the strain in her back. Computers were not her thing and she longed to get back in front of the camera and do what she did best. Perhaps Natalie was right. Christmas gala fundraisers were her thing, and from Thanksgiving in October though mid January there was barely time to be found to herself. She had begun hording the time around Christmas to unwind, cherishing the quiet and peace of her empty house. Even the summer months were full, especially July, as it was becoming an ever more popular month to host Christmas fundraisers. On the west coast the temperate climate made for snowless winters, so events that depended on snow had to be held away from the city, in skiing destinations such as Whistler and Banff.

Quebec was definitely not a place she had ever thought to host a fundraiser. But why not? There were ski hills in Quebec too.

She got to her feet and said with a tired sigh, "I will go fetch my suitcases. Meet me upstairs when you are done."

Evelyn climbed the staircase and taking an immediate right at the top of the stairs, she opened the spare bedroom door. The room was set up as studio of sorts, with mock ups of village and Christmas scenes that played a critical part in her video series. A few steps across the room brought her to the closet and few minutes rummaging through the contents produced her luggage. The Louis Vuitton set had been a Christmas gift before her step mother had died. Red and green plaid screamed Christmas, as did the gold trim and rhinestone studded wheels. She never had a problem spotting her luggage on the conveyor belt in the airport, and the looks she received wheeling it through the airport certainly drew every eye as she passed.

There was an unanswered mystery around the luggage. She had never been able to find out where her step mother had gotten the set. When she'd asked, she had said that she had won it, and thought it the perfect gift for Evelyn. That was the last Christmas they had had together. The sentimental attachment she had to the luggage far outweighed its monetary value.

Evelyn dragged the two pieces out into the hallway, arriving just as Natalie arrived at the landing. Her eyes swept past the luggage and over to Evelyn's bedroom door. "Come on, now for some fun." She took one suitcase in hand and followed Evelyn into her bedroom, setting the suitcase on one side of the bed, as Evelyn opened the second one.

Checking It Twice

The falling rain splattered against the window of his office, carried on a gust of wind that moaned around the structure and whipped the branches of a ragged maple tree several stories below. Even though it was barely 2:30pm in the afternoon, the thick cloud cover cast a gloom over the landscape below. The lowered grey ceiling was thick enough to trick the street lights into winking on, and the Christmas lights in the windows of the surrounding buildings providing the only relief from the monotone landscape.

Nicolas reached up and ran a hand through his dirty blonde hair, pushing it back from his forehead with a careless gesture. It was time for a haircut, but his favourite barber was 5,000 kilometers and a six hour flight away. Perhaps he would be willing to fit him in, despite the lateness of his arrival. His hand picked up his cellphone and he was just about to hit speed dial button to call, when the phone rang in his hand. He glanced down to see his grandmother's number and her smiling face jiggling in his hand.

He accepted the call. As soon as it connected, his grandmother's voice burst into the room.

"I have your flight booked and Yvon has agreed to pick you up at the airport. I asked him to give you a haircut before dropping you off here at the farm. Does that work for you?"

Nicolas chuckled. "You didn't need to do that. I was just about to make the arrangements myself. I do know how to take care of myself, you know."

"Yes, yes, well you are always so busy, so I thought I'd get everything set up. You should be thankful I did! The airlines are nearly full! I got one of the last seats, and let me tell you, they charged me a pretty penny for the pleasure."

"I have no problem finding flights..."

She snorted a very unladylike snort. "Flights? You call those midnight specials flights? More like cargo transport. I am getting too old to be fetching you in the middle of the night. You are booked in on a flight that's arriving at a proper time, 2pm in the afternoon. Enough daylight left to get home before dark. You know how the roads get here, around Christmas. But the reason I called is that I have the last seat reserved for the next 15 minutes. Do you have anyone that you will be bringing home for Christmas this year?" she asked in a hopeful voice.

Nicolas rolled his eyes. Every year she did this, booking two seats in case he was bringing a lady friend with him. Ever hopeful that a flock of grandkids were in the offing.

"I have heard the rumours, you know. Your face is all over social media. You have been spotted at many of the gala events in Vancouver with a certain young actress on your arm. Sophie, isn't that her name?"

"You are perfectly well informed, grand-mere. Omniscient as usual. However, she is only a friend."

"That's because you haven't laid on the charm! She is quite beautiful, but not as beautiful as you, when you focus your smile. Why, I bet she is just dying for you to extend an invitation to Christmas in —"

"I am not inviting her to Christmas dinner," he interrupted, before she could get behind a full head of steam. "Let's stop right there. You know I come home to get away from the lights and media. All I want when I come home is to have a quiet, family Christmas. Besides, you keep my dance card full the whole time I am there, with this event or that. There is no need to overcomplicate things. She will be here when I return."

"Well, if you are sure. But —"

"No buts! No guests! Now email me the details of the flight and I will see you in a few days."

"Ok. Love you. Check your mail. It should be arriving...now."

His phone pinged, announcing that a new email had arrived. On the other end a similar chime sounded.

"Oh, there's the timer for the cookies. Gotta run. Bye!" Her image faded from his phone as she disconnected the call.

Nicolas chuckled. She was impossible.

He clicked open his mail server and brought up her missive. The flight was leaving in 3 days. No wonder it had cost so much. Shaking his head in bemusement, he knew he would never be able to convince her to let him reimburse her for the cost of the flight. He had to admit, he was looking forward to getting home, back to where winter really was winter and not this dreary, dismal, never ending rainfall. He pressed a button on his desk phone, and the intercom button lit up. "Angie, could you come here please." then unclicked the button.

A few minutes later, his assistant Angie appeared in the doorway. Primly dressed in a tailored pinstripe suit, she exuded business professionalism. The image was ruined by the ugly Christmas tree sweater outlined in silver sequins that she wore beneath the jacket. Two Christmas baubles dangled from her ears and an angel halo adorned the crown of her head. The sound of loud Christmas music and laughter followed her into the room. "Yes?"

Ah yes, the annual Christmas office party is in full swing. It was past time that he left. Keeping his inward grimace from showing on his face, he cleared his throat and said, "I will be leaving for the holidays this Friday. Please cancel any appointments in my calendar that require a site visit and have then rescheduled for after January 4th. I will keep the virtual signing appointments. What is left for the rest of this week?"

"You have a noon luncheon with the owner of the Yaletown linen factory building, to discuss the renovation progress of the residential units. I believe before the luncheon, you are meeting the building inspector for the City of Vancouver for the framing and electrical inspection on the phase two construction. Beyond that, your schedule is free, other than on Thursday when you are scheduled to play Santa for the Women and Children's shelter over on 6th St."

"Good, let's keep it that way. I need to get in some Christmas shopping in before I go."

"Anything special planned?" she probed, smiling. "As in a special jewellery item?"

Nicolas groaned, dragging the palms of his strong hands across his face in a sign of frustration. "Not you, too! Did my grand-mere put you up to this?"

"Not at all," she grinned. "But you have all the juniors in the office sighing with frustration, that you haven't noticed them. Seriously, you need to find the one soon, or they will put you up for auction."

Nicolas' hands dropped away from his face, in surprise.

"What drivel is this? You can't be serious. I barely speak to the office staff. They are not my staff, after all. Where in the world would they get the idea that I had any interest in them, that way?"

"It's not what you do, it's what you don't do. You are so mysterious. So aloof and cool." Her eyes travelled over his face and broad shoulders, trim waist and the hint of taut musculature hidden by his tailored suit. The casual sweater beneath hugged his chest. "They notice. You are an attractive man. And single. Probably the most eligible bachelor in the city. You must know how that attracts women."

Nicolas shifted uncomfortably, crossing his arms across his chest, which only served to define the contours of his spectacular upper arms. "Perhaps a bit more work would keep their concentration where it should be, on our clients, and not on me. Besides, I am seeing someone."

"Yes, but you haven't moved beyond this dating phase in over three years. The natives are getting restless."

"My dating life is not for office discussion, is that clear?" Nicolas snapped, good humour evaporating. "And I would appreciate it if you would make that abundantly clear. Now if you are finished, I have work to do."

He turned his back on his assistant and sat down behind his laptop, pulling the machine closer and pointedly ignoring Angie as she left the office, stiff backed and obviously offended. As the door closed behind her, he abandoned all pretense of working and frowned at the closed door.

What was it with women and their pre-occupation for match making? At 30 years of age, he had certainly had relationships, but they had never moved beyond a bit of fun and companionship. As soon as the woman showed signs of wanting to move their companionship into a more permanent relationship, he had ended it. He just wasn't the marrying type. He had no interest in children, no interest in becoming stuck in a dull and boring co-existence with a woman that expected every special event on a calendar to be celebrated with parties and presents. The fake cheer that went with such events had left such a sour taste in his mouth, he would skip Christmas all together if it wasn't for his grand-mere. She was the one bright spot in an otherwise over commercialised time of year. Didn't the mere fact that so many companies relied on the holiday season sales to make or break their profits for the year, demonstrate that it was simply a sales gimmick?

No, despite his unfortunate name, given to him by parents he could barely remember, he was not a fan of Christmas or the Christmas season, with its fake parties, and fake cheer. Little good ever came out of the season. For some reason, the face of the SocialBuzz event organizer floated into his musings, dressed like a Christmas bauble for the event. There was no denying that she had raised an incredible amount of money, but like all charities, she probably took a hefty slice off the top, dribbling small amounts down to the charities she supposedly was fundraising for. A quick audit of her books would show how much deception lay behind her whitened teeth and artificially enhanced body. She was as fake as they came.

Pushing Evelyn Christmas out of his mind, he signed off his laptop and then swung a trench coat over his Armani tailored suit and headed for the door.

The blast of excited chatter and laughter struck him like a gong. He stepped out into a central office transformed into a winter wonderland. Christmas trees had popped up between every desk and imitation snow-covered desktops and the base of the trees. The desks had been pushed back to make room for dancing, and one young lady was demonstrating an Irish jig to great applause. Laughing, she pulled some of her co-workers up to try the steps beside her. The others clapped along, encouraging the trio to higher and higher kicks.

But the minute they spied Nicolas, the dancing stopped cold. Uncertain looks passed between the staff as they made room for him to leave. With a curt nod, he strode through their midst, feeling the eyes of everyone pierce his back with disapproval. Straight and stiff backed, he walked out of the office and into the hallway with a measured step. He pushed open the plate glass door and just as he was about to pass through the doorway, he felt a touch on the back of his head. He looked around quickly to see the dancing trio smiling innocently at him. "Merry Christmas!" they chirped, and pushed a cup of eggnog into his hand. He nodded once again, and then let the door close behind him. Once closed, the noise cut off. The trio waved merrily to him and with a smirk retured to the party.

That had been the longest walk of his life, but he was free of it now. He moved to the bank of elevators and pushed the down button. A few minutes later, the door opened and he smiled politely and entered the elevator, to join two people in the elevator. They smiled back and wished him Merry Christmas. The doors closed and they travelled down to the next stop. Several more floors of greetings and happy holiday smiles and finally the elevator reached the parking garage. Grateful to exit the crowded elevator car, he walked briskly to his BMW parked in his reserved spot. Fishing around in his pocket, he fished out his keys and leaned over to insert his key in the driver's side door lock.

Something caught his eye as he leaned forward, and he gazed closely at his reflection in the glass. There, perched on top of his head like a dove in a pear tree, was a gigantic Christmas bow.

His face instantly flushed with embarrassment as he ripped the bow from his hair. With a snarl, he tossed the bow to the ground and got into his car, ready for this long, cold, dreary day to be over. It was one anniversary he tried to avoid at all costs. But there really was no avoiding it. But he wished he could.

Driving home, all he could think about was the two fingers of whiskey that he would pour, and the solitary toast he would give once more.

In Winter's Grip

The engine of the get revved high for a few moments before fading back a normal sound, but within moments it was followed once again by a rev of the jet engines as they compensated for the heavy wind that buffeted the plane.

Evelyn, seated by the window, fervently wished she had picked any other seat other than the emergency exit. The plane shuddered and seemed to slide sideways as she glimpsed through a break in the snow, they windswept tarmac below. Her hands clutched the arms of her chair in a white knuckled grip to match the drifts alongside the runway. Praying fervently, she mouthed her words, while her eyes reviewed the emergency procedures for opening the doorway.

The engine revved again and then seemed to stall as they burst through the final cloud cover to reveal the snowy airport runway and terminal. Light as a feather, the pilot set the wheels on the tarmac and coasted to a gentle near stop, just in time to make the turn towards the bright lights shining from the terminal lounges.

One by one she loosened the stiff fingers of her death grip, prying them from the armrest. She noticed that the passenger across the aisle from her was doing the same thing. They exchanged a shaky glance and a small, relieved smile.

The low voice of the flight attendant sounded over the intercom system. "Bienvenue, welcome to Quebec City, the official home of La Bonhomme De Neige. The current temperature is a balmy minus five degrees celsius and a light wind. The forecast is calling for a further twenty cm of snow overnight. Please remain seated until the airplane has come to a complete stop and the seatbelt sign has been turned off. It has been our pleasure to serve you on this flight, and we wish you a safe journey and happy holidays."

Evelyn stared outside at the abundance of snow that the plows had pushed off the runway and lay in mounds around the area. It was obvious that they had been working hard to keep the airport open, and by that she meant the runways cleared for flights to come and go. She saw another flight touch down on the runway they had just left and wished them safety.

All this snow! How am I going to find the inn with all this snow? At first it had seemed like a windfall, to have a car at her disposal, but now she was wondering if it wouldn't have been better for her to have arranged a taxi or an uber out to the inn. It had been many years since she had last driven in snow, and she could count on one hand all the times in truth. Snow was rare in Vancouver, although not unheard of.

The plane gave a slight lurch as the pilot set the brake and the passenger walkway began its crawling movement towards the door of the aircraft. The seatbelt light blinked out and with a grateful sigh, she stood up, or rather hunched over her seat and attempted to wriggle into her coat. The plane was full but it was quick to empty as people hurried to gather their belongings and exit the plane. Finally, it was her turn. Stepping out into the aisle, she pulled her suitcase down from the overhead compartment, swung her back pack with her electronics and purse onto her back and followed the line to the front of the plane. Stepping across the threshold onto the walkway, she felt the gust of cold blast her face, as a door opened to an airport assistant bringing a baby buggy to the doorway. She hurried past the man and walked briskly up the tunnel to the warm and inviting airport arrivals lounge of the Jean Lesage International Airport.

Christmas music played a merry tune as she stepped free of the tunnel, and she turned to search for the car rental signs. Spying the one she needed, she moved into the stream of people walking in the same direction. Around her she could hear snatches of conversations, some in French, some in English, and some in other languages. Her high school French kicked in and she soon found herself translating the signs in her head, with a feeling of accomplishment. She headed down to the luggage conveyors and after retrieving a cart, waited for her flight's luggage to be delivered. It was a short wait – soon it was dispensing luggage of every description, but none like her set. She soon spied it rolling down the belt and once she had retrieved all the pieces, she pushed the heavy trolley toward the car reservations desk.

"Evelyn Christmas. A vehicle has been reserved for me I believe?"

The man behind the counter smiled and said "Oui, mademoiselle, we 'ave a jeep reserved for you. Could I have your driver's licence please?" Evelyn passed over the required paperwork and a few moments later was handed a set of keys. "You 'ave emergency assistance if needed. Simply call this number," he circled an area on her voucher, "should require any assistance. Please drive carefully. with this snow, the tow trucks will be very busy."

"Merci," Evelyn said politely, and turned towards the exit doors. It was nearly dark from what she could see, although her watch said it was only 3:30pm. An hour to sunset. An hour until full dark. Yet the thick clouds and the falling snow made it feel more like twilight. She noted the light standards were shining brightly in the parking already. With a grimace, she pulled the fur lined hood of her coat over her head, tugged her gloves on tightly, then headed out through the revolving doors into the snow.

The blast of frigid air hit her in the face, along with the sting of wind driven snow pellets. This was no Christmas snow like in the movies. This was more of an assault, old man winter's way of asserting his authority. Gritting her teeth she pushed the trolley through the slush and into the covered car park, wheels slipping and sliding in every direction except the one she wanted to go. Eventually she got beyond the clinging slush and onto bare cement. Following the signs, she located her jeep and clicked the rear hatch button on her remote. The hatch swung upwards and she deposited her luggage in the back then opened her driver's door and climbed inside, placing her back pack on the empty passenger seat. She started the SUV and then fiddled with the controls until a blast of warm air hit the windshield, clearing the glass.

The app on her phone said the inn was about a thirty minute drive from the airport, but she doubted it would be that quick in this weather. *Well, the trip wasn't going to get any shorter, sitting here thinking about it.* Evelyn reversed out of the parking space and followed the exit signs, winding down the carpark to ground level. Traversing the final turn, she was met with a wall of white. Moving slowly, she left the carpark and began the complicated journey to where she would sleep tonight. The jeep's wipers were hardly clearing the glass, so she increased their speed, hoping against hope that it would be enough to see. Snow soon began to pile up at the edges of the windscreen, and the defrost mode was barely keeping up with the fog that constantly tried to return.

She was not the only vehicle crawling slowly out of the airport grounds. A steady stream of traffic moved at half the pace of the posted speed limit, for which she was grateful. It looked like rush hour had begun early. Yawning widely, she tried to push her tiredness away and focus. She longed for a strong coffee, but even as she thought about it, she knew she wouldn't get one. The thought of taking a hand off the steering wheel for the few moments it would take to lift a cup of coffee to her lips, terrified her. Her knuckles stood out sharply in the lights of passing vehicles as she gripped the wheel. It didn't help either, that the majority of the signs were in French. She had been counting on them being in both languages. Canada was a bilingual country, after all. But as soon as she left the airport ground, English disappeared entirely.

Thankfully she had programmed her map on her phone and it was happily chirping out instructions. "Turn right in 300 meters and proceed along Ed Chauvwau Parkway to Quebec Autoroute 573." She made the turn slowly then sped up a bit as the road had recently seen a plow. Grateful for the cleared road, she sighed with relief and dared to turn on the radio. A French version of "Oh Silent Night" filled the vehicle with its soothing lyrics. The guidance app chirped again, interrupting the song. "In 500 meters, take the onramp to Quebec Autoroute 573 North." Gliding around the onramp, she found herself merging into three lanes of traffic with absolutely no reference as to where one lane began and where one ended. Gulping, she merged into what she hoped was the right-hand lane, following the Quebec plates in front of her. Surely, they were locals and could navigate this highway in their sleep?

The wipers beat a furious rhythm as she squinted through the snow to try to determine where she was at. Jet lag was setting in and she yawned again, staring bleary eyed at the road ahead of her. Finally, the app chirped again. "Continue for 5 kms to Leo Major Route 371." A tense few minutes later and it directed her off the snow packed autoroute and onto Lee Major. After that, she forgot the road names, as they consisted of more numbers. All she knew is that she had left the friendly streetlights of the city suburbs behind and now she really was driving in the dark, as evening fully descended.

The road became a simple two lane and eventually even that nod to civilization disappeared as the snow intensified. Eventually a narrow, one lane covered bridge appeared, crossing over the river to another country lane. The image was so striking in her headlights that for a moment she slowed down, just to stare. Under the covering of the roof, the wooden boards were clearly visible in the headlights – wide, thick planks that looked sturdy enough to carry the weight of a transport truck. However, the height signs made it obvious that they could not. The bridge instantly brought to mind her favourite Christmas movie, "It's A Wonderful Life" and the scene where the main character, played by Jimmy Stewart was praying for a miracle.

The heavy snowfall made her wish for a similar miracle, as she could tell that no vehicles has passed beyond the bridge in a very long time. She pulled onto the bridge and stopped in the middle to consult her app. The map showed that a left turn was to be made after she cleared the bridge, and that the road was a dead-end road. Great. There wasn't a hope this side of Christmas Eve that a plow had been down the road. She squinted at the mileage marker. Four kms to her destination. She could do this. Although it would be a tense drive, night was truly falling. She needed to complete this journey.

Gritting her teeth, she put the rental into four-wheel drive and set off to complete the journey. Thoughts of a hot drink and a warm fire kept her company. The snow had transitioned from the sleet she had seen on landing, to a vigorous snowfall. The wipers kept time to the beating of her heart, as she inched her way along the unfamiliar road in a white out. Squinting, she could just make out trees and the occasional road sign indicating a curve or a hill ahead. There was no one else on the road, so Evelyn centered the jeep in what she hoped was the middle of the twisting roadway. Surely, it was better to ride the center than risk the steep ditches on either side? Besides, if someone was coming her direction, she was sure to see their headlights before they reached her.

Confident in her reasoning, she was not prepared for the snowmobile that crested the horizon at an angle that would promise a head on collision. Evelyn screamed, yanked the wheel and immediately lost control of the Jeep. Spinning out of control, the ditch lurched into view and the next thing she knew, the Jeep had slid off the road and into the ditch with a soft thud and an explosion of fluffy snow.

A Christmas Postcard

E velyn groaned, but not with pain. It was frustration. She was so
close to her destination. It had to be less than a kilometer to the
inn, and of course the idiot on the snowmobile had kept going. She
couldn't see the headlight of the machine anywhere. The lights of the
jeep reflected off the snowbank in which she was buried. Suddenly she
wondered if it was safe to have the car still running, while stuck in the
snow? Was carbon monoxide a real threat? Her heart beat sped up as
she hastily turned off the engine.

Before she could remove the key, the driver's door was yanked open
and a cold gust of snow swirled into the compartment. A helmeted
head loomed over her, "Are you ok?" a rough, masculine voice asked.
"What are you doing out here at this time of the night?"

"I might ask you the same," she said tartly. "I assume you were the
one on the snowmobile. What are you doing driving down the middle
of the road on a snowy night like this? Aren't there trails for that?"

"Not with the first snowfall. The trails take time to groom. Besides,
this is my land and this is a private road. I can drive my sled where ever

the hell I please. Now, are you hurt? If not, then I suggest we take you
up to the manor to warm up until we can get a tow truck out."

"The manor? As in the Manor Inn? I am staying there tonight."

The man snorted. "We don't run an inn. Wait, did you say you
are staying with us? You must be my grand-mere's guest." His eyes
narrowed behind the mask as he studied her face. "I know you," he
growled. "Well come on, you will need to ride behind me." He held
out his gloved hand to help her out of the jeep which was leaning at
a significant angle, making it awkward to exit. Evelyn unbuckled her
seat belt with difficulty, then grabbed her back pack with one hand
and offered her left to the stranger.

He gripped her hand hard then pulled her from the car, walking
Evelyn over to his snowmobile. "Here, take my helmet." he unbuckled
the chin strap then pulled it off of his head. Evelyn gasped. It was the
grumpy man from the SocialBuzz awards ceremony who had been
seated beside her. How could he be here?

"My name is Nicolas Joilie-Saint, but I think you know that. Come
on, let's get out of the storm." He placed the helmet over her head and
then sat down on the skidoo. "Wrap your arms around my waist and
hold on tight."

Evelyn, speechless with shock, settled the backpack on her back and
then straddled the snowmobile and gingerly wrapped her arms around
Nicolas's torso. Nicolas revved the engine and took off into the dark,
speeding down the last few feet of roadway to a set of tall metal gates
that announced the entrance to the manor. He turned into the lane,
which curved slowly around a snowy spruce forest, before revealing
their destination perched on the crest of a hill.

Her first sight of the manor was glorious. Decked out for Christmas, lights twinkled from the eaves and the windows, casting sparkling
lights across the grey stone block that supported the thick timbers of

the entrance to the two-story log manor. A two-story deck wrapped around the building and bright lights shone from the second-floor windows. Everywhere she looked the mature pine and spruce trees were decked out in lights, twinkling in their fresh coating of pristine white snow. It was a postcard scene worthy of a page in a Christmas calendar.

The gears started turning in her head. *This manor would be an absolutely perfect place to host a Christmas Gala fundraiser.* She could think of no better setting. Excitement pierced her as they pulled up to a stop under the portico. Two full-length, stained glass doors with a transom above allowed warm light to spill onto the paving stones. She unwound her arms from around Nicolas and got off the back of the sled, pulling the snowmobile helmet off of her head, just as the front door opened.

An older woman stood in the doorway, dressed in a hand knit sweater and comfortable leggings, and soft shearling boots that could double as slippers. She smiled a greeting and came down the stairs with both hands outstretched to Evelyn. "Ms. Christmas, it is so wonderful to welcome you to my home," the mayor of Noelville said. "Come inside, come inside. Let's get you out of the cold." Turning to Nicolas, she said, "Be a dear and gather her bags, would you? I assume her car is stuck somewhere, as you brought her in this way." Turning her attention back to Evelyn, she took her by the hand and lead her inside.

The blast of warmth that met her as she crossed the threshold carried the Christmassy smells of warm spices. Ginger predominated the scent, followed closely by clove. Evelyn sniffed the air appreciatively as she pulled off her gloves. "I hope you were not injured! Our roads can be tricky during a snow storm and especially an early storm like this one." Marie-Claire's kind eyes studied Evelyn, eyes searching for any sign of injury.

"I am fine," said Evelyn reassuringly. "I wasn't going very fast at the time. I don't think the car is even damaged."

"I am so glad! Come, I have some baking in the oven. You can leave your bag here in the entrance. Nic will bring your things upstairs when he gets back. Come," she said, beckoning with one hand as she turned to lead the way. Evelyn followed her deeper into the manor. The entrance door had doors on either side and a grand staircase that climbed to the second story. The railing was decorated with real pine garland twisted in an artful way to accent the staircase without interfering with its function. Bright poinsettia flowers bloomed in tree stands strategically placed in nooks and crannies. The polished pine floors glowed with a warm polish that spoke of great care. Everywhere she looked were landscape paintings that she was sure were scenes from areas around the manor.

Seeing Evelyn's curious gaze, Marie-Claire gestured the gallery as they passed by. "Those paintings have been added to by every Saint who has lived in the manor. The house has been in our family for over three hundred years, and each generation birthed an artist or two. If you look closely, the year it was painted is worked into the corner with the artist's initials. Every generation is represented except for one." A slight frown flashed across her face, before she forced the smile firmly back in place. "This way, the kitchen is through here."

She pushed open the chef style door that swung both ways on well oiled hinges. Bright light flooded her vision and the smell of gingerbread intensified. A light beeping of a timer requested attention. Marie-Claire hurried over to the double stacked wall oven and opened the lower of the two to check on her baking. She poked it with a finger then closed the door again and reset the timer. "I think it needs about 5 more minutes. Gingerbread needs the perfect bake to be structurally sound to build with, don't you agree?"

Evelyn smiled. "I honestly don't know. I have never made ginger-bread before, and the only gingerbread house I remember making came out of one of those kits. All I really remember is that it tasted horrible." She had been six and the shelter had pulled the gingerbread kit from the back of a cupboard where it had been shoved and forgot-ten about, likely for years.

With a look of outrage, Marie-Claire snatched up Evelyn's hand and dragged her closer to the oven. "Well that will not do, Ms. Christ-mas. You cannot be the world's greatest infuencer and advocate for the homeless, and not know the first thing about building gingerbread houses. I intend to correct this gap in your education right here and now." She snatched up a bright green apron and draped it over her head. "I was just about to start the second batch. You can work along side me and I will teach you."

That is how, ten minutes later, Evelyn found herself with her hair tied back in a plaid ribbon and her sweater sleeves rolled up, standing in front of a Kitchenaid mixer carefully pouring the ingredients for the 'Saint's Secret Gingerbread Recipe' into the steel bowl. The fragrant kitchen was cheery and... homey, that was the word. It felt like a warm hug, standing there doing Christmas baking alongside a woman she had only met moments ago. Yet she felt like she had known her forever, somehow.

"Mayor, did you grow up here?"

"What's this mayor stuff? You will call me Marie-Claire, or Claire for short. And I will call you Eve." That decided, she continued, "And yes, I was born in the house. Nic is my grandson."

"Oh." The obvious question burned on her tongue yet she did not feel that she had the right to ask what she was longing to ask. Somehow it felt important to know. Instead, she said, "And how long have you been mayor of Noelville?"

"This is my third term. For some reason they keep voting me back in. I do enjoy serving the people in this capacity. It is a grand feeling to improve the lives of people who make up our close-knit community. But as is far too often the case these days, we are encountering a surge of homelessness in our community. I was really at a loss as to what to do, to tackle this problem. And then I saw your post on SocialBuzz and I knew that this was the answer I had been praying for. You have proven that there is a way for us all to live together in harmony. But enough of that for now. We can talk more tomorrow." Claire peered over Evelyn's shoulder, checking the contents of the bowl. She switched off the paddle and reached inside the bowl to pinch a piece of the dough. "See how the dough pinches? You try. There you go, pick up a piece between your thumb and forefinger. Can you feel the elasticity? The texture? That's how you know you have it right." She detached the bowl from the mixer and emptied the ball of dough on to the marble countertop. "Most people would roll out their dough at this point, but I believe in resting it." With quick, deft movements, she formed the dough into a ball and then placed a damp cloth over the top. "I will let it sit until morning. Off with your apron. It's time you rested up after your long trip."

At that moment, the door swung open again and Nicolas entered the kitchen. He had taken off his heavy coat. Dressed in a forest green cable knit sweater, the colour complimented his longish hair and skin to perfection. Evelyn found herself staring, before catching herself and looking away, with a faint blush. "Yes, I am feeling quite tired from my trip. If you could show me to where I will be sleeping, I think i'd like to rest up."

"Of course, dear. I have placed a pot of tea and some Christmas cookies in your room as a refreshment. Your suite has its own bathroom, so you should be quite comfortable. Don't worry about what time to get up. We have a relaxed day tomorrow, being Sunday. Off you go. Nic, could you show Eve to the Snowbell suite?"

Nic nodded. Snatching up a cookie from the cooling tray, he gestured to Evelyn. "This way, Ms. Christmas." Eveyln pulled the apron off and placed it on the countertop and with a quick smile of thanks to Claire, followed Nic's broad back out of the kitchen. She studied his back as she followed him, noting his height. He had to be 6'2 or maybe 6'3. He made her feel small and she was not short at 5'10. Leaving the kitchen, he silently led her back to the front entrance and then stooped to pick up her bags. "Your room is the last one on the right. It overlooks the valley."

He proceeded to climb the stairs quickly. Her heavy bags did not seem to bother him in anyway. Evelyn hurried to keep up, climbing the stairs as quickly as he, which left her slightly out of breath on reaching the upper floor. The upper hallway floor was softened by the presence of a hall runner that appeared to have been custom made for the space. The carpet was decorated with hunting scenes, dogs and horses and foxes done up in greens and browns and bright reds. She was so focused on the patterns in the carpet that she did not realize that Nicolas had stopped in front of a door. She ran into his back and with a muffled exclamation she stumbled back from him, barely keeping from landing in a heap on the floor.

"Sorry," she breathed, "I wasn't paying attention."

One eyebrow rose in a parody of Spock. "Do you make this a habit, not paying attention to your surroundings? First the ditch and now you run into me."

A flush stole across her cheeks before she could suppress it. "No, I do not. Now if you don't mind, I'd like to get some rest."

Nicolas smirked, then turned the knob on the door and pushed it open into the room. "After you," he said, stepping back from the opening. Evelyn lifted her chin and marched past him into the room. He placed her bags just inside the doorway, then with a brisk "Sweet dreams," he pulled the door shut behind him. Evelyn sighed and sank back against the closed door, as exhaustion took hold. She only had a moment's respite when her phone beeped.

It was a message from Natalie. "Have you seen this yet? What a jerk! Hope you have arrived safely. Luv, Nat." Evelyn sank into the nearest armchair with a tired sigh. She hadn't even had time to take in her surroundings. With a surge of apprehension, she clicked on a link to SocialBuzz.

Carol Of The Bells

The link was to her very own viral presentation, the one with over four million views now. Fan produced, her presentation was minimized to play in the bottom right corner, while the main video showed a man strolling through the grounds of the abandoned cannery with the once lovely landscaped park, the site of her proposed anti-homelessness, pop-up village location. The man in the video was seen walking alongside what looked to be city planners, inspecting the site and discussing who knew what.

The trio of men and one woman paused beside a dilapidated fountain that sported a statue of a fisherman in hip waders, standing beside his catch. The fountain was dry and leaf strewn, and fallen leaves were stuck in the top of the statue's boots and the rim of his rain hat. The remains of the factory could be seen in the distance, begging to be demolished or transformed in some manner. The site had been chosen by her because of its dilapidated state. No one who sought to make a profit, could afford to retrofit the old structure from the 1920's. But as a shelter from the storms that often wracked Vancouver, the building was extremely viable. Forget about retrofitting the existing building. Utilize it to enclose the pop-up shelters like an indoor mall, and manage the homeless housing needs in that way. It was perfect, and her four million viewers agreed.

The taller man in the video turned and the phone recording the meeting caught the face of Nicolas Jollie-Saint. Zooming in to his face, the audio picked up his words, clearly and distinctly, as he spoke the others with him.

"...despite the bleeding hearts of certain viral sensations in town, this site is best suited to demolition. We have carefully studied all options and the impact of those options on the neighbourhoods surrounding this site, and I can assure you that a bunch of homeless people are hardly going to bring in the tax dollars that the city is looking to recover from this overgrown, derelict and non income producing eyesore. With your permission we can bypass the Christmas lunatics and begin demolition January 2nd..." Nicolas turned away from the secret filmer and continued walking away from the site.

The poster of the video was anonymous. Or possibly a fake account. The name on the account was Vancouver Vigilante with a picture of a Zoro-like figure behind a mask. This was their first and only post. Yet they knew how to hashtag, and the one that was dominating the reposts was her own #Christmassnowqueen, #sharetheroof and #grinchalert.

She closed her phone and gazed blearily around the room. *What was she doing here?* Only now did she begin to take in her surroundings. The suite was huge and did not lack for any creature comfort. The promised tea and cookies sat on a table near the stone fireplace, which occupied a prominent place on the outside wall between a pair of insulated doors that lead to the deck she had seen on arriving. Snow was piling up deeply against the frozen glass panes. The gas fireplace insert cast a warm and intimate glow through the room. She squinted at the mantle on which rested a dozen silver bells with wooden handles, all in different sizes. A framed picture on the wall above the mantle appeared to be a page of sheet music, forever preserved under glass.

On the left was a large, four-poster bed draped in a softly glowing organza. The bed itself was covered in a log cabin quilt done up in pale blue and silver fabrics. Toss pillows decorated the surface. It looked as warm and inviting as you could get. Off to the right an open doorway revealed a bathroom also done up in blues and silver. She quickly used the facilities, splashed some water on her face and returned to the bedroom with only one thought on her mind. Pouring herself a cup of tea, she opened her overnight bag and pulled out her cozy reindeer print pajamas, that she knew had been packed by Natalie. Stripping off her travel-stained clothing, she pulled on the pjs with a shiver, then took up the cup of tea and her phone charger over to the bedside table and then climbed into bed.

It was every bit as cozy as she had anticipated. She took another sip of the apple spice tea, then snuggled down into the covers. Her eyes fluttered closed and her last thought was of her grumpy faced grinch of a host, and how was she ever going to convince him to leave the cannery alone?

Evelyn woke the next morning to brilliant sunshine streaming through the frosted window panes. Intense blue skies, the kind that you can only find in the crisp cold of a winter day, crowded the view from her four-poster bed. But it wasn't the gorgeous skies that had woken her. No, it was the delicious smell of holiday coffee, buttery croissants and the sweet tang of orange marmalade that set her stomach to rumbling. She sat up, pushing the heavy fall of hair off her face then stretched. She couldn't remember the last time she had slept so well and so deeply. Rubbing the last vestiges of sleep from her eyes, she gazed around the room, mouth dropping open as she really took in the decor for the first time.

Shades of blue to match the sky outside were interspersed with winter white and silver. Everywhere silver sparkled, from the door handles to the light fixtures, to the silvery toss pillows that decorated the powder blue couch and ottoman. The bells that she had noticed last evening sparkled in the sunshine streaming into the room. Silver birch trees decorated the feature wall behind the bed, matching the area rug in shades of grey that warmed the floor.

But it was the bells that truly dominated the room. Curious, she slipped out of bed, and snatching up a croissant, she wandered over to study the sheet music that had intrigued her last night. The score was old, and hand written by the musician that had composed the piece. She didn't know much about musical composition, but the title at the top of the score was enough to let her know what musical piece she was looking at. "The Carol of the Bells". *Well, that explained the bells, and the name of the room too.*

Evelyn munched on the tasty pastry, studying the composition. Stuffing the last bite in her mouth, she picked up one of the bells and shook it. A clear chime rang as the metal ball inside struck the side of the bell. Curious, she picked up the next one in line and shook it. It gave a deeper but equally clear tone. With a smile, she filed the information away. These were musical instruments, and a wonderful idea was forming in her head. Bells were a tried and true Christmas tradition. Nothing tugged at the heart strings (and by extension the purse strings) as the sound of a bell at Christmas.

At that moment a knock sounded at her door, and Marie-Claire's voice carried to her ears. "Good morning! If you are up, you can join us for breakfast in about an hour. Come on down when you are ready, Eve." Muffled footsteps receded down the hallway.

Suddenly eager to get on with her day, she hurried over to her suitcase and pulled out the first outfit that presented itself, a buttery soft mohair sweater in her favourite shade of pink and a pair of boot cut blue jeans. Grabbing socks and underwear, she hurried into the shower. Moments later, she was clipping her Christmas lightbulb earrings into her ears and slid a couple silver bracelets onto her wrist, the slid her feet into a pair of penny loafers and left the room.

She followed the smell of cooking and ended back in the kitchen she had vacated last night. It was empty except for Marie-Clare, who was stirring a pot on the stove. Seeing her enter, she cast Evelyn a smile over her shoulder and gestured to a high-top chair on the other side of the island. "Have a seat and pour yourself a cup of coffee. There is cream and sugar on the tray. Nic will join us shortly. He had some errands to run this morning. But I expect him back any time now. Eggs?"

At Evelyn's nod, she slid two perfectly cooked sunny side up eggs onto a plate and added a potato pancake and a roasted half of a tomato and a piece of toast. Evelyn smiled her thanks and took the plate. "Do you always cook like this?"

"Oh no, dear. My usual breakfast is a bagel with cream cheese on the way to the office, but it's the holidays. And I do love to cook." She pushed over a jar which contained a colourful condiment. "Homemade chutney, all from my garden this past summer. It's a spicy one, I forewarn you."

Evelyn added a spoonful to the top of her eggs and dug in. Ravenous, she ate faster than she intended, swiping the slice of toast through the remnants of her plate with a satisfied sigh. "I can't believe I ate all of that. I guess I was hungry!"

"The fresh air does that to you. You will get plenty of that this Christmas. So many of our activities are outdoor, and we love to participate in them all. Besides, the mayor is expected to attend each and every event. I'd like you to accompany me. It will give me a chance to introduce you to the town, let them get to know you before the big event."

"I think that is an excellent plan. I was wondering, do you have a location set for the gala? I couldn't help but admire the manor when I arrived yesterday. It seems to be the perfect backdrop for a Christmas gala. All those romantic winter log cabin vibes. Have you ever hosted a party here?"

"Oh, not in a very long time. We used to have an annual Christmas ball here at the manor. It was the crowning event of the Christmas season," said Marie-Claire with a wistful smile.

"Why did you stop?" asked Evelyn, curiosity getting the better of her.

"It's none of your business," said Nicolas bluntly as he walked into the kitchen, shrugging off his parka. "Are you always this nosy of a house guest?" His eyes flashed with an annoyed expression.

"Nicolas Jollie-Saint. Don't be rude. Evelyn is my guest. And yours. It was a perfectly normal question to ask."

"Well, it is one I do not wish to discuss, so I would appreciate it, Ms. Christmas, if you could rein in your curiosity about our family and focus on the task you were invited here to perform." Nicolas sat down in front of the remaining plate of food and picked up his fork, quirking an eyebrow at Evelyn in a manner that she was now beginning to recognize as his signature sarcasm.

She stared at him, nonplussed. "Are you always this obnoxious?" she asked with equal bluntness. "You have been nothing but unpleasant to me since the moment you set eyes on me, at the SocialBuzz banquet. Have I offended you in some way?" She sat back, crossing her arms across her chest in a defensive manner. His eyes followed her movements, moving up to study her face.

"I don't like Christmas. I don't like the season. I don't like those that do. I don't like the fake cheer, the greedy charities, the desperate shop keepers. I don't like how it makes me feel."

"Bah Humbug," retorted Evelyn, turning away from the sour faced bachelor. "Marie-Claire, I will be overjoyed to help you with your preparations here, and for the gala. Christmas is my name, after all." She beamed a smile at the mayor, then picked up her plate and fork and carried them to the kitchen sink to rinse them before placing them in the dishwasher.

When she turned back around, Nicolas and his plate of food were vanishing out of the swinging door, and she caught a frowning look on Marie-Claire's face. "I must apologize for my grandson. He is not normally like this, but this time of year is hard for him. No, I won't go into it. Suffice it to say his Christmases have not always been joyous. But enough of that," she said, clapping her hands together. "First on the agenda is the opening of the Christmas Market. There is a red ribbon cutting at noon and then we will be assisting with the stringing of the lights throughout the promenade. There is a whole crew of volunteers of course, but many hands make light work."

"Now go grab your coat and gloves and meet me in the lobby in ten minutes. Nicolas is going to give us a ride into town."

Moments later, Evelyn found herself seated in the back seat of Nicolas' BMW, watching the sun sparkle off of the fields of freshly fallen snow. She'd been surprised to find her car parked in the driveway when she exited the manor. Nicolas handed her the keys and as his fingers brushed hers, she felt a frisson of awareness shoot up her fingers. She dropped her eyes and murmured a hasty "Thank you" then hurried outside.

Noelville

arie-Claire kept up a constant chatter as they made the short journey into the village.

"As mayor of Noelville, it is my honour and my job to promote the village and especially at this time of year. Its very name harkens to our long-lived Christmas traditions, that have been foundational in the lives of our residents. Naturally we embrace all faiths holiday traditions, as you will see once we reach the village proper. The months of October through mid January feature festival after festival. But the culmination of the year is our countdown to Christmas from December 12 to the big day. Ah, here we are. Nic please park in front of Nana's bakery. You can let us out there."

Nicolas eased his way through the heavy traffic, both vehicular and pedestrian. There were just as many people walking on the streets as there were cars. "Do they close down the street to vehicle eventually?" asked Evelyn, wondering why no one was getting hit as they randomly crossed in front of the BMW.

"Oh yes. You will see. From noon today, the only way to get around is by foot, toboggan or horse drawn carriage. We take the village back in time. There are the larger carriages, drawn by our draft horses, and also the petit covered carriages drawn by one horse. It has become quite the competition here in town, to see who can decorate their horses and wagons the best. And the bells! There is nothing like sleighbells to put you in the Christmas spirit! So much better than car horns, with their rude sound." Marie-Claire pointed out her window. "See there? That is the main stable. It has stood there for over two hundred years. During the summer months, it is our local farmer's market location. But at Christmas it reverts to its original usage, as a place to park your wagons and stroll. My best advice there is to stick to the boardwalks unless you have some very high heeled boots," she laughed.

"Of course, not everyone has a horse and carriage, so most people park at the fairgrounds. There are a steady stream of carriages bringing people down to the downtown core here. You will see. We ask for a donation to the local food bank as the cost, and of course some carrots for the horses. We encourage our visitors to dress in period pieces to add to the flavour of the festivities. We do not call this 'Victorian dress' as they do in the rest of the country. We are French, so we refer to our French fashion flair, and call it Renaissance dress or '*robe de la Renaissance.'* "

"Oh no! I did not know. We didn't pack any of that kind of role-playing clothing. I have a Christmas sweater or two, but nothing that would work for this theme," said Evelyn.

Nicolas flashed her a grin in the rearview mirror. Evelyn had the sense that he was laughing for both of them, having heard his grand-mere's build up to Christmas in Noelville, his entire life. *What kind of period dress is lurking in his closet? Something decidedly grinchy, she decided with a smirk of her own. Or possibly something befitting Scrooge.*

"A recent addition to the traditional strolling minstrels and carolers has been street entertainment. This was voted on a few years ago by the youth of Noelville. They wanted to incorporate some of the local talent into the festivities, so now we have magicians dressed as Pere de

Noel, and jugglers dressed as elves. People flock to the market just to walk and take in the joy of the season," Marie-Claire finished with a satisfied sigh. "There, Nicolas, let us off by the mailbox."

Nicolas pulled smoothly over to the curb and Evelyn and Marie-Claire exited the sedan. Marie-Claire leaned back inside the car. "As soon as you are finished delivering that batch of baking to the Women's Shelter and the No Child Hungry initiative at the cathedral, come back and meet us for lunch at the diner." Nicolas nodded, the door slammed and he eased back out into traffic.

Turning to the buildings surrounding them, she took Evelyn by the elbow. "The shops up and down the street here are gearing up for the season. Many have decorated early, it is true, but all wait for this evening to light up the street. That's when all the displays come alive. Let me introduce you to some of the local shop owners."

For the next few hours, Evelyn wandered from store to store as the mayor made her rounds of her constituents. By the time lunch rolled around, she was parched and famished and slid into the diner booth with a grateful sigh. She couldn't remember the names of anyone except for the lovely owner of the flower shop and her incredible Christmas floral arrangements. Crystal was her name, and her shop sparkled with a similar energy.

A smiling waitress greeted them then reeled off a list of holiday specials, placed a glass of water in front of both of them and left them with menus to peruse while she went to take another order. The door opened to a jingle of bells and Nicolas walked in, brushing snow from his coat. Evelyn glanced outside. The sun of the morning had disappeared behind fresh clouds and a light snow was falling once again. Marie-Claire waved at her grandson, catching his eye. As he moved in their direction, her cell phone rang. "Allo," she said, then began speaking in rapid French, in the Quebecois dialect, so fast that

Evelyn could not keep up with the conversation, which was one sided in any event. She noticed that Nicolas turned to listen in, fiddling with his gloves as he waited for her to finish her call.

She disconnected and then gave Evelyn an apologetic smile. "I'm so sorry, but an emergency has come up and I have to go to City Hall to sort it out. I will have to bow out for the rest of the day, but Nicolas has nothing on his agenda. I am sure he will be happy to continue the tour and show you our town." She stood up then patted his cheek. "You have a good time, you hear?" and then picking up her handbag, she left the diner.

Nicolas slid into the booth across from Evelyn. She glanced at him and then picked up her menu, busying herself with translating the words, to give her something to do rather than stare into his beautiful, stormy grey eyes. She winced when she realized what her thoughts had been. Beautiful eyes or not, there was simply no reason for her to be thinking of him in this way. Her mind drifted back to their first disastrous meeting, and the words blurted out of her mouth before she could stop them.

"Why do you hate me so much?"

Great, Evelyn. Nice conversation starter.

"Hate you? Whatever gave you that impression?" he said, eyebrow quirking in that Spock-like mannerism.

"Oh, the cold shoulder at the SocialBuzz event. The loathing stare in the lobby when I first arrived. The annoyed expression when you saw it was me in the snowbank. And this —" She pulled out her phone to show him the clip in which she had been tagged, and the damning statement. "Well?" she said, finding her courage. "What do you have to say for yourself?" She placed her phone on the formica countertop and sat back, folding her arms under her chest. "I'm waiting."

The eyebrows twitched between quirk, frown and back to quirk, climbing even higher at her defiant, self-righteous air. "Well, what? You have completely misread everything. And that video? That was pure malice. We were on private property and that recording was illegal if nothing else. Who sent that to you? They were tresspassing and eavesdropping on confidential conversations. That's illegal. Obviously, they have their own agenda."

"Maybe they do, but you do realize that the cannery building is the same site we have proposed to the City of Vancouver, to house my homeless initiative? The funding we have raised is going towards establishing a community there, and the city planners are all on board. You could ruin everything! So many people are relying on me, on us, to bring this to life. So many lives to be saved. We are bringing dignity and hope of a positive future to these people who have been ignored by society." Evelyn ran out of breath, and the waitress, seeing a lull in their conversation, shuffled over to the table, pausing to take in Evelyn's flushed countenance, and Nicolas' perplexed expression.

"I'm sorry, am I interrupting? I thought you might be ready to place your order."

"Thank god," breathed Nicolas. "Yes, we need to place our order. What do you recommend?"

"The tourtiere here is our specialty. it comes with a green salad, pickled beets, and homemade green ketchup. We make a festive special by adding in a creme brule for dessert. If you are interested in wine, we have a lovely local merlot that is great with it."

Nicolas took one look at Evelyn's closed expression and said, "We will have two, please. And bring a bottle of wine." The waitress nodded and left to submit their order.

"Wine? At noon?"

"You know what they say, when in Quebec do as the Quebecois do." A real grin split his face, and Evelyn struggled to not gape. When his face relaxed, it took on a boyish innocence, eyes coming alive with merriment, and lips curving into a pleasing shape. Dimples appeared at the corner of his mouth, carving deep cavities into his stubbly cheeks. Evelyn had to resist the urge to reach over and pinch them.

"Should we begin again?" Nicolas got to his feet, took up her hand and bowed over it, placing a light kiss on the back of her hand. "My name is Nicolas Jollie-Saint, and I am the grandson of Marie-Clarie Saint, and son of Madeline Jollie and Jean Pierre Saint. I am at your service." He bowed again formally over her hand then returned it to her and sat down. "I am also a real estate broker and contractor who specializes in the conversion of derelict or decommissioned commercial real estate that has either been abandoned or taken over by the province due to back taxes owing. I help communities repurpose these buildings and bring them back to life to take up an important part in the tax structure of the community. And I did not know that you had or have an interest in the cannery site. That is a mistake I plan to rectify."

"Wow, that is quite the resume. How exactly do you plan to 'rectify' your mistake? I assume that means you are planning to research me and figure out a way to get me out of the way."

Nicolas' smile widened. "Planning to research you? You bet, best to know the competition, especially someone like you who can gather a virtual lynch mob in seconds, or so it seems."

"Lynch mob! How dare you?" She glared indignantly at her lunch companion.

The waitress arrived placing a plate of food before each of them, then went to retrieve the bottle of wine and two glasses. "Who will be testing the wine?" she asked brightly, missing the tension in the air.

"Evelyn will. I am sure she has a very refined palette." The waitress turned to Evelyn and poured a measure of wine into her glass, then paused, waiting expectantly. Evelyn schooled her expression, pulling back the glare, and smiled at the waitress.

"My father was a vintner,' she lied, the words dripping sweetly from her tongue. In actual fact, she had taken a six-month, half credit course in college. Hardly the stuff of expertise. But...she swirled the wine in the glass as she had been taught, letting the air mix into the swirling red amber to heighten the flavours, then sniffed it, checking for sour notes that would indicate it was spoiled. Next, she tipped the glass to let the wine coat the curved surface and then straightened it, letting it roll down the side and develop 'legs'. Satisfied, she took a sip. letting the wine roll over her tongue. "Mmmm, I taste a hint of raspberry and citrus," she said, nodding to the waitress. "It is fine, you can pour." She placed her wine back on the table top and watched as the waitress poured an exact measure. *Pretty fancy for a diner*, she thought, *but then again, this is little France. They take wine with breakfast, no doubt.*

Nicolas sat back, watching her with interest. He nodded to the waitress, dismissing her, then picked up his glass. "I offer a toast. To forgetting bygones and embracing the future. A fresh start." He held it out to her.

Evelyn tilted her head, studying the man. *Could they have gotten off on the wrong foot? Well, she was not one to hold grudges.* "To new beginnings." She touched her glass to his, then took a second sip and focused on her plate, suddenly ravenous. "This looks amazing. I am so hungry!" and forgetting Nicolas, she dug into her lunch, ignoring his cutely crinkled smile and laughing eyes. Food was all she wanted in those next ten minutes and she ate with a gusto. When her plate was empty, she sat back with a sigh. "That was great! So delicious!"

Nicolas grinned as he scooped up the last bite of tourtiere from his plate and then pushed it aside. "I agree. It has always been a favourite of mine this time of year. This diner," his gaze swept the faded furnishings and decorations, uncaring of age or modernization, but spotlessly clean for all of that. "It is one of those places that ground you. It's always been here, at least for my lifetime. I come every year... an annual tradition, I guess. I am glad you liked it."

Evelyn emptied her wine glass, surprised to see it and the bottle empty. "Wow, I am surprised we finished that. I was sure we'd be leaving half of the bottle behind."

"Not when a good meal is present."

"Well, where to now?" asked Evelyn, giving Nicolas the first truly genuine smile she had ever given him. Nicolas stared at her lips, transfixed. "Hello?"

He started. "Well... as you are new to Noelville, and we are here to see the market light up, I suggest we start with the lights for the carriages. Come on, they are just around the corner." Gesturing to the waitress, he summoned the bill and paid it, then stood. "Come on, we only have an hour or two till dusk."

Evelyn stood and put on her coat and gloves, then followed Nicolas out of the diner into the snow.

One Carriage Leads To Another

Nicolas pulled open the heavy wooden door and stepped inside the dimly lit barn. The structure was hidden behind a large stone building that had once been the town smithy and metal working shop. Now it housed city hall, with a modern, two-story glass atrium built street side to welcome the public. But at the very back of the grounds the original stables still stood, housing the town's lawn equipment and a dozen white carriages.

The dusty lights of the barn were not the brightest, but the addition of piles of Christmas lights, plugged in for testing lit up the shadows and gave the interior a festive feel. Teams of volunteers were going over the carriages, checking the wooden wheels for cracks or breaks, and tightening the nuts. Springs under the seats were oiled (one particularly enthusiastic teen was vigorously bouncing up and down on a squeaky seat, drawing frowns from the adults and roars of laughter from the other teens as everyone responded in kind to the provocative sound. Eventually he got off the seat and greased the underside where the spring met up with the seat, and tested it again, snickering. This time it was quiet.

Evelyn smiled at the antics and then said to Nicolas, "We are here to decorate the carriages, correct?"

"Yes, starting with the first in line. It has been prepped already and is ready to go. Let's grab a basket of the verified lights and get started." Evelyn followed him over to where an older man stood, scribbling on a piece of paper attached to a clipboard.

"Bonjour, Monsieur Perrault, we are here to help with the decorating of the carriages. This is Evelyn Christmas."

The man swung around to face Nicolas, grinning from ear to ear, and throwing his arms wide to scoop them both up. "Nicolas! 'ow good to see you, and your lovely girlfriend!" He gave them a generous squeeze and then released them.

Nicolas and Evelyn exchanged glances, then looked away. Evelyn blushed. "Sorry, she is not my girlfriend," Nicolas said, just as Evelyn piped up, "No, no, you have it wrong. Nicolas is not my boyfriend."

"What? Well, you two should fix that. You two look great together! Come, let's get you set up with some decorations." He led them over to the lead carriage, gesturing to a couple of boxes along the way, that they picked up and carried to the first carriage. It shone with a pearly gloss of a freshly washed paint. It was obvious to Evelyn that the carriages were well cared for. She could hardly believe they were over 100 years old. Even the leather looked supple and soft. "You remember how this goes, Nicolas? Make sure that nothing interferes with the horse tack and movement. Keep the decorations to the carriage itself and leave the prepping of the horses to their owners."

"No problem. We will have this one done up in no time." The overseer nodded and them moved away checking off something on his list before speaking to the next person waiting in line.

Nicolas put his box down and then opened it up to reveal garland greenery. "You have the freedom to decorate the carriages any way you want. But the people must be able to get in and out easily and the horses must not be spooked or bothered by the decorations. They will have silver bells attached to their tracings and also worked into the braiding of their manes and tails. So, it's not about the sound as much as it is about touch or sight. I tend to do minimal decoration on the front."

"I think the focus should be on the back. There we can really put together something stunning," Evelyn said. "This is a open carriage. The covered ones have even more possibilities.

For the next hour they worked side by side, draping garland and stringing lights which eventually plugged into a portable battery unit set in the front dash of the coach beside he driver. Evelyn happily added touches here and there while Christmas carols played from speakers set up around the barn. Humming softly along to the Carol of the Bells, she remembered the picture above the fireplace with the sheet music and the collection of silver bells. "Nicolas, the bells on the fireplace mantle in my room. Are they used during the holidays? They look to be real bells."

Nicolas visibly stiffened at the question. His head came up and a frown straightened his mouth. All cheer vanished instantly from his expression. *That's strange,* thought Evelyn, *did I touch on a sensitive subject?* Nicolas met her eyes, then looked away. *Oh yes, there is some history behind them that he doesn't want to share.* Curious to see what he would do, she waited for him to speak.

"The bells were once part of our family traditions, but they are no longer. They belong in the past." His closed-off expression discouraged any further questions or inquiries on the subject and reluctantly, Evelyn let the matter drop. He glanced at his phone, then said "We have just enough time to finish this second carriage and then we must be getting back to the manor. I have a meeting to attend."

Oh yes, we are totally closed off now. He is back to his former self, aloof and distant.

They worked in silence for another few minutes and then it was time to pack up and leave. With the supplies returned to where they found them, they left the building and walked to Nicolas' car in silence. Guilt nagged at Evelyn and when she could take it no longer, she blurted out, "Look, I am sorry. I didn't mean to pry. I can see that this has upset you. Whatever this is, you don't need to tell me anyth—" She stepped back as Nicolas abruptly stopped and spun around to face her.

"You have no right asking about anything you may see, or overhear while staying in my home, do you understand? You are a *guest*. Nothing more."

Shocked, Evelyn stepped back. "I'm sorry," she gasped. "I didn't mean to pry. They were just so lovely, I was curious about their history."

Nicolas stared into her eyes. As she stared back, the look of agony faded away. He hunched his shoulders, then shrugged to loosen them. He took a deep breath, then let it out slowly, deflating like a pricked balloon. A blush of embarrassment stole up his neck. Shaking his head, he said, "No, the apology should be mine. I over reacted. You weren't to know that it is a sensitive subject. Please forgive me." He reached out and opened the car door for her to enter. Evelyn gave him an uncertain smile, then seated herself in the passenger seat. He closed the door with a snap and then went around to the driver's side and climbed in.

A few moments later, they were driving slowly back to the manor, windshield wipers doing a decent job of keeping the windscreen clear. She gazed out at the decorating going on all around her. It didn't seem to matter what the weather was doing. People were out and about anyways, decorating the fronts of their homes, and stringing lights in trees. She had to admit, the snow did add so much to the feeling of the season. Now, if only her grumpy companion could unbend and acquire some Christmas spirit, it would be truly magical.

Seeing her curiosity about their surroundings, Nicolas began to point out local landmarks and historical structures, telling her the history of Noelville and how the town came to be, through its heritage. "Most of the residents are descended one way or another from the first French explorers, Samuel de Champlain to be specific. Quebec City is a Unesco World Heritage site, did you know that? Look it up on your phone."

Evelyn opened her phone and soon found the piece that Nicolas was referencing.

"Historic District of Old Québec"

Québec was founded by the French explorer Champlain in the early 17th century. It is the only North American city to have preserved its ramparts, together with the numerous bastions, gates and defensive works which still surround Old Québec. The Upper Town, built on the cliff, has remained the religious and administrative centre, with its churches, convents and other monuments like the Dauphine Redoubt, the Citadel and Château Frontenac. Together with the Lower Town and its ancient districts, it forms an

urban ensemble which is one of the best examples of
a fortified colonial city.[1]

"Oh wow! I didn't realize this area was so old! Do you think we
could go visit the old city? I'd like to get a feel for the culture and the
people."

"I am sure we can fit it in. I think some Christmas shopping
might be in order. Noelville was an offshoot of that original coloniza-
tion. While Old Quebec City preserves the old-world religious roots,
Noelville has a more modern focus, having absorbed some of the
English traditions and the traditions that have sprung up away from
the strict focus of the Catholic church. Multiculturalism has created
a opportunity to blend the holiday traditions from many cultures,
mixing them into something truly Canadian. Traditions are meant to
be created and adapted to meet the needs of each new generation. Or
at least that is what I believe."

Evelyn stared at Nicolas, offering him a tentative smile. She thought
this was the most words she had ever heard him speak. "Do you know
where grand-mere intends to host the gala? Is there a spot that is
traditionally used for this event?"

Nicolas glanced at her, his expression neutral. "The past few years,
it has been held in a community hall. But she has not been happy
about it. She wants a more festive setting, someplace that screams
Christmas. Unfortunately, those kinds of venues book up even before
the current season is done, and so they are almost never available. And
she cannot go outside of her municipality's borders. It wouldn't be
right. As mayor she needs to show support for the local people. But if

1. https://whc.unesco.org/en/list/300/

she had her way," he said as he turned between the gates of the manor, "she would make the event in to a Christmas Spectacular. I suppose that is why you are here." He glanced at her briefly before focusing back on the driveway.

"Yes, I suppose it is. I hope to sit down with your grand-mere very soon so we can start planning. It is a very short time till this event and I need to see this hall she has rented, so we can get some initial promotional shots arranged. It takes time for a campaign to take off. Kinda like a avalanche. You need that initial trigger, then it will gather strength and grow as it rolls down hill. It's time to light the spark. After all, its only twelve days until Christmas."

The car rolled to stop and Evelyn got out, pulling her coat tight around her body as a gust of wind swirled around the corner, pushing an eddy of snow through the portico. She shivered and moved closer to the door. She reached out to put her hand on the door handle, the door swung open. An older gentleman stood there, stepping aside for her to enter. Nicolas followed her up the steps and into the house and nodded greeting to the man. "Thank you, Georges. Has my grand-mere returned yet?"

"Yes, she is in the library. Would you like me to bring tea?" He held out his hands and realizing that he was asking for her coat, she shrugged out of the garment and passed it over to him. Nicholas did the same.

"Thank you, that would be appreciated." Taking Evelyn by the elbow, he steered her to the left wing of the manor.

"You have a butler?" she whispered, not wishing to be rude.

"Yes, it was his day off yesterday. Come, the library is through these doors."

The double doors to the library were constructed of oak panels, with a honey stain and brass levers. Swinging them open, Nicolas left them a jar and led Evelyn into the cozy room. Bookshelves in polished oak lined the walls and a real fireplace crackled with heat. Marie-Claire sat behind a writing desk, typing away on a keyboard, a cup of cooling tea at her elbow. Seeing the pair of them, she took off her reading glasses and smiled warmly. "There you are! I was hoping you would return before it got dark. We have planning to do!"

Evelyn sank into a barrel shaped chair padded with thick leather across from the desk. Nicolas took the second chair and moments later Georges returned with a tray laden with a tea pot, cream pitcher and sugar bowl, and a plate of Christmas cookies. He placed them on a side table from where they could serve themselves, bowed and left the room, pulling the doors closed behind him.

Evelyn got up and poured tea for everyone, then brought over the plate of cookies and placed them on the desk, then sat back down.

"So, tell me what you have planned so far. I need to know the details so that I can prepare my campaigns. If you could bring me up to speed, I will take notes," said Evelyn.

Marie-Claire passed a tablet to Evelyn, open to a screen with several tabs already established. "I have prepared a summary of our plans so far but none of them are set in stone as of yet. We managed to secure the church hall in the basement for the gala this year, at a very reasonable price. But it can only hold so many people and so attendance will be limited. We have received a couple of quotes for hors d'oeuvres, however neither supplier can guarantee delivery due to the demand this time of year. The ladies of the church have volunteered to decorate using the church's decorations. I haven't had a chance to inspect them to see what they have. Perhaps you can go there tomorrow to check out the site and see what else might be needed? Nic, could you take her where she needs to go? You can check out the party supply store also."

Nic nodded. "Yes, I can take her around and show her the venue and any other place she needs to go. I don't have anything on my agenda tomorrow. But if you will excuse me now, I do have a business call to make." He got up and returned his cup to the tray, then left the library. Evelyn watched him go. When the door closed, she turned back around to find Marie-Claire watching her with a smile.

"Now as far as a guest list, you will see that pdf on the tablet screen. Invitations are set to go out. We are just waiting to firm up a couple more details and then they will be off to the printers. They advise a two day turn around window, which basically means they need to go in now. However, with you here, maybe they are just tradition and not really necessary at all? I've told you where we are at, and now I'd like to hear your ideas." Picking up her cup of cooling tea, Marie-Claire took a sip and waited.

The Perfect Setting

"Well...how honest do you want me to be? You brought me here to create a Christmas Extravaganza that will fund your homeless initiatives. Why don't you tell me about some of those first? What are you trying to accomplish?" said Evelyn.

Marie-Claire put her cup of tea back down on the desk, then got to her feet and walked over to the fireplace, holding her hands out to warm them. She sighed, her face sobering. "Over the past few years, we have seen a combination of factory closings combined with soaring housing prices. People began losing their jobs and couldn't find replacement ones in the community that could cover the cost of their bills. One by one, people began losing their homes. Families were split by divorce and many moved away. But some had no place to go. No family to lean on to get through a rough time. We were unprepared for such a large influx of people seeking basic shelter, but with no jobs to rent a place, they soon found themselves sleeping on the street. The local agencies have been overwhelmed. There are two people homeless for every shelter bed available, and they are always full. To be fair, they are offered on a first come, first served basis, and many have stopped showing up, as they have been turned away too many times."

"This is Quebec. Our winters are not like Vancouver. They are harsh and cold. You can easily freeze to death here, and every winter we lose people to hypothermia. It is a crisis that is being repeated in cities all across our great land. It is shameful that in a country so blessed with wealth, we have not figured out a way to care the poor."

"Then one day I came across your feed on SocialBuzz and I thought to myself, here is a young advocate who has her stuff together. Not only are you passionate about your causes, you are brilliant in bringing people together. You have a talent for unifying people into a cohesive unit then finding ways for them to help and support each other, and at the same time solve some of the desperate need that is out there. Food, clothing and shelter. These basic things should be a right for every Canadian citizen.

"So I reached out, to you." She turned away from the fireplace, and Evelyn could see the anguish in her lined face. "As mayor, this homeless situation here deeply affects me. I do not want to see the people of this community suffer any longer. Christmas is a time for hope, for peace...for miracles. I am hoping together we can create a similar one to what you have done in Vancouver. We are only a small community here, but i am sure I could call on the mayors of surrounding communities including Quebec City and garner their support, for the right set of circumstances. But I need your help creating the perfect campaign to make this gala event the envy of the country."

Evelyn nodded. "I understand. But, after looking over this plan that you have created, I do not see a way to make this a viral event. A church basement? That has dungeon written all over it," she said bluntly. "We need a space that inspires people, not depress them. We need to bring the magic of the season to the campaign. I need to ask you, does it need to be an indoor event? Could we stage something outside, like in a park pavilion, or a baseball stadium... or a skating rink? Somewhere that a lot of people can gather, mingle and take in the festivities we create?"

Marie-Claire stared at her, a tragic expression on her face. Evelyn could see a tear forming in the corners of her eyes as they began to glisten. *Oh no, I have done it again! What is it with me and this family, that I keep stepping on their toes and hearts?* "Marie-Clarie? What is it? Have I said something wrong again?" Evelyn got to her feet and hurried over to the older woman, taking her wrinkled hands in her own. She pressed her fingers, conveying warmth and sincerity. "I'm so sorry, I seem to be upsetting you and Nicolas at the strangest times and I don't know why. I apologize if I have once again opened old wounds. I sincerely did not intend to hurt either of you."

Marie-Claire shook her head. "It's not your fault, dear. We are suffering from the ghosts of Christmases past. It is something we—Nicolas and I — battle with every year, regardless of how much time has passed. You couldn't have any idea." Marie-Claire released her hands and then reached for a tissue to dry her eyes. "I suppose you will need to know, so that you do not accidently stumble on the truth elsewhere. Come sit beside me." She moved over to a comfortable chesterfield and sat down, patting the cushion beside her. "Sit and I will fill you in."

Evelyn moved over to the sofa and sat down, waiting expectantly. A thrill of anxiety chased down her spine. She wasn't sure she wanted to hear what Marie-Claire was about to say. But she remained silent and waited for her to continue.

"On Christmas Eve, twenty-two years ago, tragedy struck our family. My son and daughter-in-law were killed when a drunk driver, who was leaving the Christmas Gala that year, crossed the center line and struck the vehicle driven by my son head on. Both my son Pierre and his wife Madelaine were killed on impact. Only Nicolas survived. Madelaine was six months pregnant at the time. In that one instant our lives changed forever. The drunk driver also died on impact. We later found out that this was the third accident he had been in that evening. He was the CEO of the local factory that employed half the town. The ensuing lawsuits bankrupted the firm and it closed a few months later. We found out that the bank had called the operating loan for the firm and speculation rose later on that the man may have been on a suicide mission that evening, that only ended when he struck my son's car head on."

Evelyn's gasp of horror was muffled by the hands she pressed to her lips. Tears of her own sprang up and rolled down her cheeks. "Oh my god," she cried, and soon thereafter Marie-Claire was crying too, then both woman were hugging, offering comfort that flowed back and forth like a river. They sobbed into each other's shoulders for a few moments before recovering sufficiently to sit back. Once she felt reasonably in control, Marie-Claire continued her story.

"So many lives were changed that day and over the course of the next year. I took over Nicolas's care and raised him, put him through university. He and I are all we have left of our family. I guess you could say we are both orphans. He left Noelville to pursue his career in Vancouver, so eager to get away and never return to Noelville. I hear he is wildly successful in his chosen career. I keep hoping he will bring a nice girl home, get married, and settle down again in Noelville. But never a word comes from his lips and everything I hear is via the tabloids and social media, who report that he has a new girlfriend every other month. One starlite or another, the relationships are invariably shallow and uncommitted. I suspect that is more on his side than theirs." She shrugged. "Once a year he returns to be the anchor of the Christmas parade, where he is the Jollie Saint Nicolas for a day. He even has his own special sleigh, did you know? I will have him show it to you tomorrow. If it wasn't for the parade, and a special barber here in town that he likes, I wonder if he would come home at all. But there you have it."

"The bells in my room. I asked him about them today and he just about bit my head off. What is their significance?"

"Oh. Yes, that would upset him. They were his mother, Madeline's. She was a classically trained musician, and the bells were her specialty. The score that is framed and hanging above the fireplace, that was her composition, her reinvention of the Carol of the Bells. Nicolas never enters that room, you know." Evelyn winced again.

"So are there any other things I should know so that I don't upset him any further?"

Marie-Claire smiled gently at her, pushing back a strand of hair to look into her eyes. "Such a lovely colour and so soft, both your hair and your eyes. There are a couple of other things but I think it might be best if Nicolas told you about them himself. Honestly, I can't really explain them, as they are his own personal demons."

"Ok. I will tread carefully with my questions. Where is his sleigh? I'd love to see it. Is it being stored in town with the carriages?"

"No, its here on the grounds of the manor. I will have him take you out to it tomorrow and you can take a look at it. Perhaps it will give you some ideas."

"Yes, that sounds great. I will bring my camera. As much as the phone cameras are great, nothing beats my old Nikon. The phone will be great for capturing some video of course. You know, my first thought on arriving was that this manor would be a wonderful place to host the gala. Have you ever thought of throwing the event here?"

Marie-Claire sighed. "And just like that, you step on the next sore spot. I don't know how you do it."

"Well, its obvious, isn't it? Everything that is good about this town and its people comes back to the pair of you. I wonder if you realize how much your family's suffering has become a symbol of the ghosts of Christmas past, that haunts you all. It's time to join everyone in celebrating Christmas present. It's time to heal the rift to the past. Only by doing so, can you look forward to Christmas future. I think that is really why I am here. Tell me, is the factory still standing?"

At that moment, Nicolas strode back into the library, just catching the last part of the conversation. He paused in front of the two women, who looked up at him with identical expressions of interest. "Why do I get the feeling I have been the subject of an intense conversation here?" He mock-frowned down at them. "Georges advises that dinner is prepared and that you are to come to the dining room immediately 'or his delicate soufflé will be ruined.' "

"Well, we mustn't keep the dear man waiting." Marie-Claire stood, signalling the end of the conversation, then led the way out of the library and into the dining room, which was set for three. Marie-Clare took the solo spot on one side of the table, leaving Nicolas and Evelyn to sit side by side as dinner was served. A creamy carrot soup was followed by roast duck with peas and mashed potatoes, and then followed up with a raspberry soufflé for dessert. As they ate and drank, Nicolas skillfully turned the conversation away from family ghosts and tragedies and onto other subjects of interest to them all.

"Were you aware that the homeless shelter is looking for volunteers to go out into the community and speak to the people who are most desperately in need of shelter? They are trying to gather numbers on how many are being left out in the cold, so that they know what kind of funding to request in the new year." Nicolas looked at Evelyn, who smiled back at him. "Naturally, I thought of Evelyn, so I put her name forward as one of the volunteers."

"I think that is a fabulous idea!" said Marie-Claire. "Nicolas, I need you to show Evelyn your Santa sleigh tomorrow morning, and then you can both head over to the shelter and get started. This will actually be great research for our fundraiser too, and what better way to become passionate about a cause, than to place yourself right in the middle of it."

"Yes, I think I should accompany her. The homeless aren't dangerous, but still, it is best to stick together in pairs. Safety in numbers. I'd also dress simply, so as to not stand out too much."

"I agree. I will wear jeans and sensible hiking boots and my short jacket. I am looking forward to speaking with them. I have done this before in Vancouver. I think we should bring coffee too. Do you think the local coffee shop could set us up with cups and one of those large pour cardboard coffee containers? And some doughnuts?"

"That's an excellent idea. I will have Georges place an order right now. For how many people should I say?"

"Let's say 100 people. If there are left overs, I am sure it won't be for long."

Marie-Claire got up from the table and went into the kitchen to find Georges.

"What time can you be ready in the morning? It's a half hour walk to where the sleigh is stored."

"Really? That's curious. Why so far way?" By the darkening of Nicolas' expression, she knew she had done it again. "Never mind," she said hastily and changed the subject. "Do you have your own horses or reindeer to pull it?" She smiled brightly, refusing to give in to his sour expression. Once again, she found him staring at her lips and licked them unconsciously. His eyes widened and realizing what he was doing, he turned away abruptly.

"No reindeer. We have a matched team of white horses that are boarded at a neighbouring farm. They are too much work for grand-mere now."

"Ah, of course. Well, I think I will retire for the evening. It has been a long day." The yawn that escaped her lips was not fake. She really was tired. Plus, she needed to do some work of her own, as her viral campaign couldn't run itself. "I need to check in with my assistant back in Vancouver. I have business to address." She pushed back her chair and got to her feet. "Have a pleasant evening, Nicolas."

"Nic. You can call me Nic."

"Nic. So be it. Goodnight," she said softly and left the room.

Coffee For One Hundred

The next morning found Nicolas waiting in the foyer with a travel mug and a basket of freshly baked croissants with jam in the other hand. He held them out as he watched Evelyn descended the last of the stairs. "Georges advises that we need to pick up the coffee and doughnuts in 30 minutes, at the bakery. That was the only time they could guarantee due to the Christmas rush. They worked all night to fill out order. He made you breakfast to go."

Evelyn took the basket and gave it a sniff. Delicious pastry smells wafted up from the surface and her stomach gave a growl. Smiling, Nicolas opened the front door and they stepped out into a beautifully clear day, with the morning sun sparkling off the pristine snow. Evelyn took a deep breath of the cold, refreshing air and gave Nicolas a return smile of pleasure. "What a beautiful morning! This is going to be a fantastic day," she said brightly, as she waited for Nicolas to open the passenger door. It as a bit awkward getting into the BMW with her coffee in hand, but she soon found a cup holder and placed it securely in the tray, then settled herself with her pastry basket on her lap. Once

Nicolas was seated and the engine started, she said, "Have you eaten already?"

"Yes, I was up at 6:00 am. I usually have coffee and a quick bite such as this and then return emails for about an hour. They tend to arrive overnight, with the time difference."

Evelyn nodded. "I am the same way. But my assistant is taking great care of the campaign. She has an accounting background, and worked for the CRA in taxation for several years, so record keeping is her jam. She is great at that aspect. She makes sure that we can pass any audit, with flying colours."

Nicolas quirked his eyebrow with that endearing tweak that she was beginning to recognize as his signal when his curiosity was peaked. "I'm impressed. Having an assistant that is that well trained and re-sourceful can certainly set you up for corporate success. So many char-itable agencies fail when the CEO gets sticky fingers. Or the organiza-tion swells with personnel so their overhead eats up all the donations. How many people are on the payroll of your charity?" asked Nicolas.

"Only two. Myself and Natalie. And we operate on a contingency fee structure, based on how the campaign does. The amount we are paid is a percentage of the overall campaign after expenses. That way our success is tied directly to the success of the charity we are spon-soring."

He looked at Evelyn, surprise evident in the crinkling of the corner of his cool grey eyes. "That's impressive, and a model that I fully endorse. Tell me, how did you become a SocialBuzz influencer? It's an unusual career choice."

Evelyn picked up her cup of coffee and took a careful sip. It was a hot and delicious mocha, rich and sweet at the same time. "I fell into it, truth be told." She looked over at Nicolas, wondering how he would react to her own personal demons. But she had nothing to hide. It was her own personal tragedy that made her such a great advocate for the under privileged. "I don't know how much you have heard about me, or know about me, but my last name wasn't always Christmas. Evelyn Christmas was the name given to me when I was discovered as a new born infant, lying beside my dead mother, after she died giving birth to me in a Vancouver park. She was a druggie and died of an overdose she had taken to kill the pain of child birth. It is a miracle I was even born, let alone survived one of the coldest Christmas Eve's on record. December 24th really is my birthday, but that's as far as anyone knows of my family history. No one was ever able to trace the identity of my mother."

"I am sorry to hear that," murmured Nicolas sincerely. He continued to stare straight ahead, solemn faced.

"The social worker who found me named me Evelyn and mistakenly filled in the last name portion with the date I was found, and that became my legal last name. Later on, she adopted me and I grew up with her. She died about ten years ago, and I have been alone ever since. I inherited her home in Vancouver. She had never been married and left me everything. But the nature of my birth has always haunted me, and so the issue of homelessness has always been a prime motivator for me. Solving this issue is important, and very, very personal," she said quietly. "It's not about money."

Nicolas digested her words for a few moments, then looked over at her and gave her the first genuine smile she had ever seen on his face. "Thank you for sharing this with me." He reached over and took her left hand and gave it a strong, masculine squeeze. "You are incredibly brave, to put yourself out there in this fashion, before all the cameras and bright lights. You are forcing the spotlight of the country on to this national crisis, with no thought to your own discomfort." He let go of her hand.

They drove in a companionable silence for several minutes. Peering around, Evelyn said, "Is it my imagination, or do we make a giant horseshoe, travelling from your place to the city center?"

"No, you have it right. The town is located on the other side of the river, so we have to travel to the bridge and then back track."

"Was it always this way? It seems awfully inconvenient, for such a prominent location."

Nicolas glanced over at her and smiled again. "There is a short cut. Maybe I will show you later."

"Sounds like a date!" She grinned at him, then suddenly blushed. "A date as in an engagement. No wait, as in an appointment. Geez..." she peeked at him from under her lashes. "I am usually better with words than this!"

Nicolas grinned back. "A date it is. Now finish your breakfast. We are nearly there."

They had entered the edge of town and Evelyn noticed they were skirting around the downtown core where the main Noelville Christmas activities were being set up, and instead took a side road that took them through an industrial portion of the town. Just as they were getting to the far end of Noelville, Evelyn spied a two-story brick building built tight against the river that flowed through town. The windows were still intact, and naked vines clung to the aged brickwork. The grass had been cut, but with the efficiency of a ground crew that was maintaining the grass due to bylaw and not with the careful attendance of a prideful owner. She stared at it curiously, then glanced at Nicolas. She was almost afraid to ask, but powered on anyways.

"What is this building?" she asked quietly.

Nicolas pulled to a stop at a stop sign facing the old structure, then flipped on his signal to turn right. He glanced at the building and then dismissed it. "That is the old, town sugar factory. Yes, we had one similar to the one you are interested in, in Vancouver. This one closed about thirty years ago. It processed all different kinds of sugar."

He turned right and then drove back towards the downtown core. Evelyn peered over her shoulder at the building. Such potential. "Is there a way that I could get a look inside of it?"

He looked at her, shook his head, then said with a smirk and a smile "Yes, I happen to know the mayor. The town owns the building."

"Oh! That's perfect!" said Evelyn happily.

They arrived at the coffee shop and together they went inside to pick up the coffee and the doughnuts, putting them in the back of the BMW, then continued on to their destination. The homeless shelter was located in an old concrete block building that was hospital like, with whitewashed walls and tiled floors. Doors led off the main hallway and as they passed by them, they saw rows and rows of bunkbeds set up. Currently they were empty. Role call was at 7:00 am and those who were housed that evening had been roused, offered warm showers and a meal, and then moved on for the day, to allow the volunteers to clean and prepare for the evening's batch of guests.

Nicolas led Evelyn to the main office, identified by a hanging sign outside of the doorway. They entered to find a man their age typing away at a keyboard. He looked up as they entered. "Hi, Sam, Good to see you hard at it already." Sam rose to his feet and shook Nicolas' hand. "This is Evelyn. She is keen to meet the locals. We brought breakfast. Where do you suggest we set up?"

Sam walked over to a map on the wall. "I'd suggest you park in this area of green. Most of the homeless are sleeping close to the seasonal toilets, which we have kept open for now. We will need to close them down soon, as the plumbing there isn't insulated and the pipes will freeze. We have some space heaters running for now, but we are running out of time this year. Here are a stack of surveys and some pencils," he walked over to a box he had prepared and picked it up, handing it to Nicolas. "If you can get them to complete the survey that would be great. We really hope you can reach most of the people who refuse to come to the shelter. We would like to know what we can do to help them best." He turned to Evelyn. "I hear that's your area of expertise. I look forward to hearing your insights."

"Right on. We will return these by mid afternoon. Looks like a nice day for visiting the park." They waved goodbye and headed back out to the car, settling the new box beside the coffee urn for support.

A short drive later found Evelyn in the midst of a riverside park, with tall trees and a bandshell built into a hillside. Ratty tents and makeshift shelters built of whatever scraps could be found, filled the bowl and rose a fair way up into the benches. They picked up the coffee, doughnuts and box of surveys and walked over to the pop-up village. Faces popped out of tents, and people got up from benches where they had been stretched out, soaking in the warming rays of the sun. They were a ragtag bunch, dirty and disheveled, yet they greeted them as if they were expected guests. A tall man walked towards them and took the box of surveys off the top of the stack of doughnuts, lightening Evelyn's load.

"That coffee smells great," he said, leading them over to a wooden picnic table that had been carried over from who knew where, but was serving as their outdoor dining spot. An old metal barrel filled with scraps of burning wood provided a warming station and also doubled as a cooking surface, with a grill placed above it. Something was burning on the top of it. Evelyn thought it might be a slice of pizza that the owner was trying to warm up.

Placing the boxes of doughnuts on the table, she flipped open the lid and then set the up the coffee station. A line up sprang up out of nowhere, men and women, teenagers and older people, all eagerly digging into the food and coffee. Evelyn noticed that the maple glazed doughnuts disappeared first. She started working her way through the crowd, greeting each of them like a long-lost friend and handing out surveys and pencils. She jumped up on an old crate that was being used for a chair and clapped her hands to gather their attention.

"We ask that you complete the surveys that I just handed out to you. We are gathering information on what your needs are. How can Noelville best help you? As you can see on the form, there are questions around housing, employment, education and health. At the end of the survey we also ask you to rate, one through ten, your top priorities. What would enable you to make a transition back into regular society? What is your biggest barrier? Your responses will be held in confidence. This is for our internal planning only, and will not be shared outside of this group. Your privacy is being respected and protected."

"I know you all know who I am," chimed in Nicolas, hands shoved deep in the pockets of his jacket. "We have a long history together in this town. I know many of you personally." He gazed around at the faces, who peered back at him with a mixture of anger, and curiosity. "I know I have not been here for you. I also have come to accept that, and wish to do better. I promise that I will be personally overseeing this effort, because none of you deserve to be living this way. Please. Fill out the survey and let us work on ways to help you all."

Evelyn watched the faces of the onlookers. A couple threw the surveys on the ground and stomped on them, then walked away. But most filled out the forms. Once they had gathered the responses, they thanked them, and left.

Once back in the car, Evelyn began flipping through them and organizing them based on the final answers given, ranking their priorities.

Unsurprisingly, at least to Evelyn, the number one response was overwhelmingly 'employment'. "Can we keep these surveys for a day or two, to analyze them?" she asked.

"I think that is the idea, seeing as you are spearheading the gala fundraiser," said Nicolas.

"Good. I want to study all this. There is a fundraiser keynote in this stack of gold and I want to dig it out." She buried her nose in the responses, completely forgetting her companion, much to his amusement.

"Ok you can get out now."

"What?" Evelyn raised her head from reading a particularly poignant response, to see that they were sitting in the driveway of the manor. "Oh! Sorry, I didn't realize we had arrived." Blushing slightly, she unfastened her seat belt and gathered up the responses, hugging them to her chest.

Nicolas laughed. "Come on, put those away in your room. We still have a sleigh to inspect, remember?"

"Oh yes! I almost forgot!" She jumped out of the car and ran up the steps, depositing the papers on the desk in the room. She paused for a moment to use the facilities and then checking her hair in the mirror, left the room.

By the time she had returned downstairs, Georges stood there with a frown on his face. "But you have not eaten a proper meal. At least take these sandwiches with you. It is a good hike back to the sleigh."

"I will take them, but I have a faster mode of transportation in mind, other than our feet. Ah, there you are Evelyn. Come, we are taking my snowmobile." Taking her by the hand, he led her outside to where his snowmobile idled, waiting for passengers. Securing the lunch box on the back of the sled, he handed Evelyn a helmet that fit her much better. "Climb on!"

This time she was prepared for the spurt of speed as he revved the throttle and took off down the lane. Laughing out loud, she clutched him around the middle and hugged him tight. *Strange, but it doesn't feel awkward at all,* she thought. She pressed her face into his back, shielding it from the sting of the cold breeze, while still trying to see where they were going. Nicolas guided the sled down the road to where a cleared laneway appeared. Nothing had disturbed the pristine snowfall, and the sled powered into the drifts like a thoroughbred, grinding through the snow with ease. The lane was wide enough for a single vehicle, or two snowmobiles travelling side by side, or a single horse drawn sleigh, she thought with a smile. It twisted through the forest like a snake, each curve showing a new vista. Evelyn smiled with pleasure. "This is spectacular! What beautiful scenery!" she shouted at his back. He nodded and kept driving.

Eventually they spilled out into a clearing in which a large barn was built. Post and beam construction, the sturdy structure was two stories tall and painted red, with a green steel roof. A set of wide double doors were perched at the top of an earthen ramp, obviously meant to be slid wide open to allow larger items to pass through into the structure. curiosity overwhelmed Evelyn as she released her hold on Nicolas and got off the snowmobile. She unbuckled the chin strap and pulled off the snowmobile helmet, placing it on the seat and shaking out her fall of long hair. Eyes glistening with excitement, she squeezed Nicolas' upper arm.

"This is an amazing barn. So huge! What do you use it for? It can't be just for storage? That would be such a shame! Why i bet you its large enough to hold two hundred people. Maybe three hundred! Can we go look inside?"

The telltale twitch of Nicolas' eyebrow brought a fit of giggles to her throat. Throwing caution to the wind, she grabbed his hand and dragged him up the slope to the main barn doors, and then stood there bouncing on the toes of her boots in anticipation. "Come on, Spock. Open it up! I want to see the sled. Hurry!"

Nicolas laughed, then said, "Stay here." Moving off to the side, he fished a key out of his pocket and inserted it into the lock of the man door. He disappeared inside and a few minutes later, while Evelyn bounced up and down, grinning from ear to ear, the barn doors slid apart. Evelyn took several steps and then entered the interior into which the late afternoon sunlight flooded, illuminating the most gigantic, glistening sleigh she had ever seen. Built for a family of elves, or just an extended family, there were four rows of benches and a huge compartment at the back for Santa's bag. The front of the sleigh curved in a delicate wave, and sparkled with embedded silver filigree. The pattern was repeated on the sides of the sleigh, splashing their way to the back where the motif suggested a plume of snow jettisoning out the back of the sleigh.

"WOW," breathed Evelyn. "This is your sleigh? Of course it is. Santa would have the sleigh to slay them all," she giggled, drunkenly. She hadn't had a drop to drink, but was intoxicated all the same, with the beauty of the season, and the applications that were possible for this sleigh. "Your family must have loved Christmas growing up. This is magnificent! Did you ride in it with your family? What wonderful memories you must have! Nic, this is so great...." She ran down, then realized she was walking around the sleigh all by herself.

Peaking around the side of the sleigh, she sought out Nicolas. It was as she feared. He was standing ramrod straight in the entrance of the barn, staring at the sleigh and stricken with emotions that he fought to control. His jaw flexed, muscles clenching as he ground his teeth, fighting back the wave of emotion. "Oh no, no, no, no! I am not going to cause you grief again." She rushed over to Nicolas and touched his arm. feeling the tension there. "Let me in. I can help."

Nicolas took a deep breath, held it for a moment, then exhaled slowly. He filled his lungs and repeated the process, eyes squeezed tightly shut. Evelyn joined him in the breathing exercise, doing nothing but breathing in tandem with his rhythm. She felt the quiver of tension under the hand that still clutched his arm, lessen. Like a fine thoroughbred, he was learning to deal with the tension.

In...and out. Breathe. In...and out. Breathe.

Santa Fills A Vacancy

N icolas kept his eyes closed as he breathed, fighting through the demons that still plagued his psyche. These breathing exercises he had performed since he was a child, first taught to him by the grief counsellor who had been assigned to him after his parent's death. He had never shared this process with anyone. Until now. Yet the light touch of Evelyn's hand was grounding. He focused on the warm there, drawing comfort from her presence. That was something else he had never done. Allowed himself to unbend enough to accept solace from another human being.

His eyes opened and he captured her concerned gaze in one. Rosy lips slightly parted, she continued the breathing rhythm and he instinctively followed. Her face was open, honest and carried none of the conceit and hidden agenda that he was used to seeing on the faces of the celebrities he normally dated. They were easy to predict, easy to control, easy to keep at arm's length. But this woman... some how she was slipping past his defences, like a prized winger who could slide around the defence, and rag the puck like it was attached to the end of the hockey stick with a rubber band. This woman, without even trying, could find every crack in his armour and slip inside.

He shook his head, and the spell vanished. Cold washed over him as his focus shifted to their surroundings. Instinctively, he glanced back at her, gauging her reaction. There was no pity in her gaze, just a clear understanding of grief and the burden of carrying it. She patted his arm a couple of times, and then released him. "That's better. Slowing our breathing helps bring down the hormones that trigger our panic response. A yoga instructor I once had, believed that we could heal any ailment our body had, simply by breathing. I'm not sure i'd go that far, but I do know it can create changes in our stress levels which does affect other parts of our body. Meditation and breathing really does center us. I am glad to see you know this." She smiled brightly up at him, her grin infectious. "Now, are you going to show me the features of this lovely sleigh or do I have to inspect it myself?" and she marched away to lower the step and then climbed aboard.

Grinning slightly, and totally bemused, he followed. Taking a deep breath, he said, "Yes, this sleigh has been in my family for generations. As you guessed, it is large enough to carry Santa, Mrs. Claus and a whole host of elves, which in times past were the children in our family. It has always been a special honour to play the role of Father Christmas in Noelville, and the privilege always fell to the eldest son, once they reached the age of forty. In my family's case," his face darkened slightly, but he held it together, "my grandfather continued to play the role up until his death, due to the tragedy that happened when I was young. You see, my family—" he paused at her light touch on his hand.

"I know. You do not have to tell me. Your grandmother let me know about your parent's tragic deaths."

He nodded, grateful that he didn't have to tell the story. A weight lifted from his chest, one he didn't even realize he had been carrying.

Somehow the burden of having to share this news with her, had been causing endless agony. He realized suddenly, that he had been worried about how she would react. Knowing that he cared that much about her opinion of such personal tragedy, shocked him. He'd never cared about it before, with any of the other women he had shared his life. He gazed at Evelyn, eyes searching her lovely face. What was it about her that made him cringe to tell her his deepest, darkest secrets. Why did he care so much, what her opinion of him was?

He cleared his throat. "Well. Yes. The sleigh." He cleared his throat. "Since my grandfather's death, I have taken over the family tradition, and have come back every Christmas to play Father Christmas. But there has been no Mrs. Claus and certainly no elves. Honestly, I feel very ridiculous up there, seated like a king on a throne. It's embarrassing, honestly. Here, let me help you up and you can see how huge this sleigh really is." He climbed into the sleigh and then held out his hand to help her up the couple of steps needed to reach the main body of the sleigh. Standing beside him, he noticed that she was just the right height to tuck under his arm. He resisted the impulse, and instead moved back to give her room.

Evelyn spun on the spot, arms outstretched. "Oh, this is glorious! I've seen the Toronto, Vancouver and New York City Christmas parades and their floats don't hold a candle to this beautiful piece. Can you imagine what this would look like in a promotional video? The whole purpose in me being here is to help fundraise for the homeless initiative here, and this sleigh is just the stage we need. I know that traditionally only your family is on the sleigh, but what we look at this more figuratively? Widen the definition of family? We could invite some of the homeless volunteers to become Santa's elves, his adopted family. I mean, does Santa actually have children? I don't think so. He adopts the elves, who very well may have been homeless before he built the North Pole with his workshop at the center. Think about it. Santa is the gold standard for community. For love and inclusion."

Nicolas started at the animation that lit up Evelyn's face. Her enthusiasm was catching, and addictive. He couldn't get enough. He started until she stopped spinning, and her arms dropped. Uncertainty flashed across her face. "Oh no, did I say something wrong again?"

Nicolas' twitched his eyebrow, holding back his laughter, hiding it behind his regular shield of sarcasm. "Why would you think that?"

"I think you know I am really good at putting my foot in it. By now, you must cringe whenever I open my mouth."

Nicolas couldn't hold back the laughter any longer. He let his stern expression drop and laughed out loud. "I will grant you permission to use the sleigh and by extension me, in your SocialBuzz feeds." Her eyes lit up and her mouth opened, but he pressed a finger to her lips, silencing her. He ignored the tingle that raced down his finger and hand at the contact. "On one condition. That you will sit beside me as my Mrs. Claus and endure the parade at my side. That way you can have the spotlight and it will be off of me for a change." He removed his finger, regretfully. "Deal?"

"Oh yes! Yes, yes! I completely agree. This is going to be fantastic!" She spun in a circle one more time taking everything in. "Your horses must be huge! This is a big carriage. When can I see them? We need to start some promotional footage as soon as possible! There is no time to waste. Christmas is coming, as they say!" She beamed happily at him, eyes sparkling.

Nicolas chuckled. "Not until tomorrow. It's almost dark now. But I promise I will have the horses brought over and we can get them hooked up and take this buggy out for slide. There should be enough snow now. Now let's eat those sandwiches and you can tell me about your thoughts for this promotion." Nicolas hopped down and retrieved the basket of sandwiches and a thermos of hot chocolate from the snowmobile and then climbed back up into the sleigh. They sat and ate and he watched Evelyn outline her plan for the first promotional shoot, nodding when she paused but otherwise not interrupting her vision.

He had to admit. It was a good plan and if anything could put Noelville's homelessness plight on the Christmas map, it was this.

Swallowing her last bite of ham sandwich, she chased it down with a swig of hot chocolate, then swiped her hand across her mouth to remove the last vestiges of hot chocolate. She missed a smear at the corner of her mouth and Nicolas smiled, then reached out with his napkin and dabbed the spot clean. The action brought their heads close together and he breathed in deeply. She smelled of clean sweat and a light perfume that reminded him of freesia. He stared into her eyes, and she stared right back, gazes locked.

Suddenly a loud crack sounded, as a tree limb heavy with snow broke and fell away from a tree outside. The sound was enough to startle them back to the present and with a sheepish grin, they looked away from each other.

"Come, we must be getting back. There is much planning to do, and those surveys are waiting for us." Nicolas stood and then helped her out of the sleigh. Evelyn paused at the top of the ramp and looked around, while Nicolas went down to the snowmobile and started the machine.

Evelyn allowed her gaze to wander around the environs, picking out likely filming spots. Through a gap in the trees, she spied a rooftop made of cedar shakes, but the rest of the building was hidden b the forest of spruce that filled the valley.

She pulled on her gloves, blew a kiss to the sleigh then pulled the barn doors closed, locking them with a click. Spinning on the spot, she took a running leap and then slid down the slope to the waiting snowmobile. She donned her helmet and took her now familiar place on the sled and wrapped her arms around Nicolas's waist. As he revved the engine and took off down the lane, she brazenly rested her head on his back and sighed.

The ride was over too fast in Evelyn's opinion. She reluctantly let go of Nicolas and climbed off the machine, then picked up the empty basket and carried it to the front door. Georges greeted her as she opened the door and stepped through, offering to take her coat. She shrugged out of it with a murmured "Thanks!" and then stretched, a yawn escaping. Food and a surfeit of fresh air had her yawning tiredly. She wasn't used to such brisk weather, and the cold was making its presence known.

"What time is it?"

"It is a little after 5:00 pm. Dinner will be served in a hour," said George, accepting Nicolas' coat as he shrugged out of the heavy jacket.

"I am thinking I might skip dinner tonight. We just finished this delicious lunch an hour ago."

"Yes, I quite agree. Georges, we will take a light repast in the library, please. Tea and biscuit. We have some planning to do." Georges nodded and left for the kitchens while Evelyn went upstairs to retrieve the surveys and her phone and tablet, then joined him in the library.

The tea had arrived. Evelyn put down her armful and welcomed a cup of the cinnamon spiced blend then sank down into the soft couch with gratitude. She took a warming sip, sighing with pleasure, then put the cup aside and opened her phone. There were six text messages from Natalie, telling her to check her email. She put the phone down and signed onto her tablet, then into her email. Natalie had sent an update on their own viral campaign which now showed donations in excess of $5,000,000 dollars.

She let out a low whistle and smiled at Nicholas. "We just went over $5,000,000 in pledges. And Natalie advises the first shipment of homeless pop-up shelters have arrived at the docks and are being offloaded as we speak. They are being stored for now, pending the outcome of our application for use of the old cannery building." She looked at Nicolas, evaluating his expression. "It feels strange to be discussing this with you, sitting here in your home. Hopefully when we get back to Vancouver, we can work out some kind of compromise that straddles both of our needs and perspectives. It seems obvious by the pledges, which way the supporters are leaning. There could be a lot of good will generated by aligning your firm's interests with ours."

"A week ago, I would have told you to go fly your proverbial kite, but now...let's just say that I am not against looking at other avenues and uses for the old structure. Perhaps there is something we can do together that will benefit both."

Evelyn grinned happily. "Look at you go. I do believe your heart has grown a size or two."

Nicolas smirked, then let out a low laugh. "Don't count on it. Now, what else is going on? Should we sift through these surveys?"

Evelyn picked up the sheaf of pages and handed them to him. "I already made some quick notes and observations. You take a read through while I reply to these emails and get them out of the way."

Silence descended while they each went about their tasks. It was a companiable silence filled with clicking and rustling of papers. She hit send on the last reply then opened a word document and titled it 'Noelville inaugural Homeless Gala' and waited.

Nicolas looked up from his perusal of the surveys. "Your comments have captured the essence of these surveys very succinctly. Where did you learn to summarize in this fashion? You have picked out the top three needs, as voiced by those seeking help, in just minutes. Call me impressed."

"It's just a knack I have. It is part of what makes me a great fundraiser and event planner. I know how to get a crowd excited about an event and that usually translates into the opening of hearts, which is soon followed by the opening of wallets."

"Well, I agree with your summation. Number one on their list is "Education", followed by "Shelter" and third "Job Experience". I think you have hit it on the head."

Evelyn typed the three categories into her document and underlined them. "These are going to be tall orders to fill, even for Santa." She stared at the words for a few moments, thinking. Then her head came up, and she said, "Can we look at that factory tomorrow? I'd like to see inside it. What was it used for, before? I know you said sugar, but what does that mean?"

Nicolas put down the surveys and eyed her once again. Evelyn could sense that he was struggling once again to keep his face straight.

"It seems that you will have all of our secrets whether we want to give them or not. It is too late in the day for more of such talk. I will speak to my grandmother and get the keys for the old building. Yes, I will take you and when I do, that is when I will tell you the story of the old building. It is pretty much frozen in time. Little has changed inside since the day it closed. Now, I have other work to attend to. I wish you a pleasant evening, Evelyn." Nicolas got to his feet and with a final, brief smile, left the library.

Evelyn watched him go. *So many mysteries in this old manor. But slowly I am getting the answers I need.* A picture was forming that was exciting and unnerving. She felt she was on the verge of unlocking Nicolas Jollie-Saint. The question was, what would come with that unveiling?

The Mysterious Village

E velyn sat up in bed, stretching her arms over her head. Dawn was just peeking over the horizon out her window, highlighting the underside of a cloud bank that promised more snow. Struck by a sudden desire and strange urgency to get on with her day, she swung her feet to the floor and padded into the bathroom for a shower.

Moments later, dressed in a heavy wool sweater stitched with Nordique snow flakes, and a warm pair of pants, she brushed out her hair and secured it with a stretch hairband, then headed downstairs for breakfast. Georges was just setting up a series of trays over warmers when she entered the dining room.

"Good morning, mademoiselle. Both Nicolas and Marie-Claire offer their apologies, but they have already left for the town, in response to an urgent matter that arose overnight with the fire hydrants in town. I believe one or two may have frozen. They said to make yourself at home and they will be back as soon as they can."

"Thank you, Georges. I will eat some breakfast and then I think I will go for a walk and take some preliminary footage for the campaign."

He nodded. "Be sure to dress warmly. There is a northern chill to the air today. A scarf would not be amiss." He gave her a slight nod and then left her to eat in peace.

Somehow Evelyn was not surprised to find herself on her own this morning. She could hardly expect them to shuttle her around everywhere. Besides if she really wanted to go into town, her vehicle sat in the driveway, where it had sat since her fateful arrival. No, what she wanted to do today was something that had to be done on foot. Mind you, she could still take the jeep for part of the journey, and it could act as a warming center if she got cold.

Plan formed, she tucked into her eggs and Canadian bacon, gulped down a cup of coffee and orange juice, then went into the kitchen to find a travel mug. Topping it up with hot coffee, she found herself behind the wheel of her jeep and wheeling down the driveway just after 9:00 am. The trip back to the laneway was short, their trail undisturbed from their previous journey along this route. She pulled up a little way away from the barn, then grabbed her camera and started snapping photos of the barn and surroundings, taking pictures from all angles. The valley was breathtaking, with the pure crust of undisturbed snow and tall jack pines lining the edges of the forest. It almost looked like a toboggan run. She wondered if it had been used for this purpose in the past.

With her cellphone buttoned up inside a secure pocket, she headed in the direction of the roof she had seen from the barn yesterday. She skirted along the edge of the pines and spruce forest, which thinned and then disappeared entirely, to be taken over by the naked trunks of trees that she thought might be maples. After a short search she was rewarded with a cleared trail that was marked with white dots on the trunks of the maple trees, clearly identifiable by the plastic tubing that was strung like a thick spiderweb through the forest of trees. The further she walked along the path, the more tapped trees she saw stretching as far as her eye could see. The network of lines was a masterclass in organization, as whoever had tapped these trees had to know where to bring all that sap when it began to run in late March to early April.

Her walk was tough going. The thin crust over the snow broke under the weight of her foot and her boot sank down into the snow, making walking difficult. It took her about 15 minutes of breaking through the crust to finally reach the clearing she thought must be at the end of the path.

What she found took her breath away. Instead of the humble hut she had expected to find in the clearing, she found a multitude of structures clustered around a central green covered in snow. Each building appeared to have a different purpose. The largest by far was the one that carried thick pipping into the structure. A large chimney dominated the roofline and the structure looked like it could easily old 30 or 40 people. Build of handhewn lumber that she suspected came from the very ground on which she stood, the structure sported a second story balcony and a gingerbread-like soffit. A multitude of windows were visible on three sides, allowing natural light inside, when they weren't shuttered as they were now. Closed tight, she couldn't even get a peek inside, but she thought she knew what this building was. An authentic maple sugar shack, built with the sole purposes of distilling maple sap into that most luxurious of ingredients, maple sugar. More precious than oil, a barrel of maple syrup sold for twenty times more than a barrel of crude.

Evelyn peered around again, noting the rest of the buildings. She wasn't sure what their purpose was, but a wonderful idea was blooming in her mind. She had stumbled upon her very own Christmas Village! And not a thing needed to be built. It was all here! All they had to do was decorate and stage it. What could be more iconic than a Christmas Village in the middle of a maple forest? Grabbing her camera, she began taking pictures of every building from every angle, so that she could study them later and make a plan for their use. She also grabbed her phone and shot multiple videos of the clearing and then she turned the camera around and videoed herself against the village. "Natalie, look what I just discovered. And actual Christmas Village! Think what we can do with this! I might need you to fly out. This is too much for me alone to handle. Toodles!" and then she hit send.

The wind picked up, blowing eddies of snow through the clearing like miniature dust devils. She shivered. It felt like snow was coming. Wrapping her scarf tighter around her face, she secured her phone once more and then walked across to the other side of the village where she could see the path continued. She wanted to know where that path led, before giving up for the day ahead of the incoming snow fall.

Ten minutes later, she found herself coming ouf of the forest once again, but what she found before her stunned her.

She was looking across the river at the very park where they had met with the homeless, and directly in front of her, the closed-up factory hugged the waterfront. She could see an overrun garden out back and then a bridge that was gated off at both ends. The bridge crossed the ice-covered river, and landed precisely at her feet. This could not be co-incidence. There was a story linking these structures and the park. She pulled out her phone and took a few more videos, then turned back around and hurried back to her car. By the time she got there, the snow was falling in earnest, and she was happy that she had thought to bring the jeep.

Driving back was quick and she parked the jeep haphazardly then hurried inside and up to her room. She had research to do and time was wasting away.

Several hours later, she sat back with a tired sigh and stretched her arms above her head. She had spent hours researching the history of Noelville, something that was long overdue. She couldn't believe she hadn't done it before. The internet was a gold mine of information. Using only a few essential keywords, you could find out anything. Well, almost anything. She now understood why the factory had closed and who had been responsible, and who all those homeless and displaced people were. It had bugged her as to why such a small town would have so many displaced people. But when the major employer shut down under suspicions of fraud and manipulating the books, it was no wonder that the people had lost faith in the powerful families that had made up the backbone of the community.

One of those families had been this one, and with the double tragedy of losing so many key people in such a small community, well it would set the town back on its heels and scrambling to survive. That so many had stayed was a testament to their love of the town and an underlying sense of home.

But what to do? She could see a plan, a marvelous plan that could heal old hurts, mend old wounds and catapult the community forward, essentially wiping out the past 25 years of misery. But there were two key people she had to convince. And both lived under this roof. Maybe three, if Georges had anything to say about it. And somehow, she thought the old retainer did.

Eveyln steepled her fingers then pressed them to her lips, not exactly praying, but seeking guidance from the universal powers that surrounded them in this area of the country so steeped in history.

She had sent off an urgent summons to Natalie, asking her assistant to grab the first flight out, regardless of the cost. She needed her here, to pull off this event. She couldn't do it alone. And true to her word, she had indeed grabbed the first flight east. It was a red eye special that would land at 6:30 am. Evelyn had already arranged an uber for her, and that should put her at the door just in time for breakfast.

At that moment she heard the door open and Georges' dulcet tones greeting Nicolas. She sprang up and almost ran for the door, pausing only a moment to check her hair, and then bounced down the stairs with excitement, face flushed and eyes sparkling with excitement.

Nicolas looked up and stared, mouth slightly ajar.

Georges looked from one to the other and smiled. "Ah there you are, Mademoiselle. Dinner is served. If you will wash, Nicolas, I will begin service. Your grand-mere is seated and awaiting your arrival." Nicolas nodded then headed upstairs while Evelyn followed Georges into the dining room. Marie-Claire looked up and smiled at her excited, bubbly entrance.

"Ah there you are! You look positively radiant! What has you so excited? I take it you found something to do with yourself? Tell me about your day."

Evelyn sat down and nodded to the bottle of wine proffered by Georges. He poured her a measure of wine, topped up Marie-Claire's glass then stepped politely aside to await Nicolas. "My day was wonderful! I went exploring and took some preliminary photos and video out by the barn, for the campaign you know. And then I went exploring and I found the charming little—"

At that moment the door to the dining room opened and Nicolas reappeared, having exchanged his sweater for a casual, button down shirt. The first two buttons were undone, allowing a curly glimpse of light brown hair. Nicolas seated himself and then gestured to Georges, who stepped forward and poured the wine, then left it cooling in a wine bucket full of ice and left to bring the meal. Evelyn tore her eyes away from Nicolas, completely distracted and forgetting her train of thought for a moment.

"Now that Nicolas has arrived, please continue what you were saying," said Marie-Claire, taking sip of her wine as Georges laid the salad course before them. A light, smoked salmon mousse was delicately wrapped in butter lettuce and served with a lemon and dill aoli dipping sauce. She swirled a piece through the sauce and popped it into her mouth.

Evelyn, who was famished after all her exercise and fresh air, took a moment to eat her salad and then continued, "I came across this charming little village of buildings, hidden in a maple tree forest. It looked like the trees were being tapped for maple syrup. Is that correct?"

Out of the corner of her eye she saw Nicolas stiffen, but it was Marie-Claire who continued. "Yes, that is the closest maple acreage under production. There are one hundred acres around the manor here that we keep tapped."

"How many acres are there in total, of sugar maple forest?" asked Evelyn, with a fascinated expression.

"The manor currently has one thousand acres of mature maple forest," she said, nonchalantly.

Evelyn choked on her sip of wine. Coughing, she cleared her throat and took a sip of water. "A thousand acres?"

"Oh yes, this is the original homestead of Noelville. Way back when, Samuel de Champlain himself handed the deed to our ancestor. It's been in the family ever since. Despite my grandson's feelings on the matter, it will never be sold. Some traditions need to be maintained, and a Saint as owner of this land should never change."

"It's barbaric and feudal, grand-mere," interjected Nicolas. His stare was all for Evelyn though, as he said the words. "If this land was split up, think how many families it could benefit."

Evelyn stared from one to the other, Deep familial currents were swirling around her and she wasn't sure which side of the debate she fell on. Happy to shut up for once, she listened. Hard.

"Not enough to make a difference. Besides, I have already told you my feelings on the matter. The estate could and should be brought back to its former glory and prominence in the community. Evelyn has found the old Christmas village, the one you and your father—"

"Enough!" snapped Nicolas, showing anger for the first time. Evelyn watched, wide eyed, taking it all in. "I will not reactivate the sugar shack, and that is that."

Marie-Claire sniffed angrily, then gestured for the next course. Georges cleared their plates and then then served a delicately carved loin of lamb with minted peas and chutney, a thoroughly English dish if ever there was one. It was delicious and Emily dug in, eating hungrily while she listened to what appeared to be an old and ongoing family argument.

"I have said it over and over. The sugar shack is the answer to all the estate woes. You refuse to see it because you are not invested in the estate anymore. With your fancy Vancouver job and all those silly starlites you are dating, you have forgotten your upbringing. The answer here is in the soil, in our family roots. Open your eyes and see!" Marie-Claire glared over her dinner at the last of her lineage. Evelyn could see the pleading look hidden beneath the surface anger. "You are the last of our line. It is your duty."

"Duty," spat Nicolas. He made it sound like a swear word. "My duty ended when my parents and unborn sibling died. My duty ended when their legacy collapsed due to corruption and theft. My duty," he spat again, "is to myself. I have no heirs, nor do I intend to have any. Let the past be forgotten at last.

His intense, stormy blue-grey eyes turned to fix on Evelyn. "Some things are better left buried under snow. The village is one of them."

A Change Of Heart

E velyn looked from grandmother to grandson, sharing a perplexed frown between the two of them. This time she was going to intentionally step on their toes. Both of them. She picked up her spoon and started tapping it on the side of her wine glass, shutting them both up and drawing their attention. Even Georges, standing silently in the wings, looked over.

"Listen to yourselves," she scolded. "How long have you two been arguing over this?" She saw Georges roll his eyes and shift his feet. *That long, huh?* she thought. "I am amazed and a little ashamed at the pair of you."

Marie-Claire looked chagrined, her face falling with embarrassment. Nicolas looked like he was chewing on nails, waiting for his words to burst out of his mouth. Evelyn held up a finger to him, like she used to do to the children she'd met during that one term of early childhood education in college. "You will hold your tongue until I have said my piece. That is how polite discourse happens." Nicolas glared at her but remained silent. Barely.

Once she was certain she had their attention and neither would interrupt, she continued, "I have been here less than a week and even I can see that you love each other dearly. But the past is dividing you, when it should be uniting you. Marie-Claire, you cannot expect Nicolas to do things the same way that your son and daughter in law had planned to do things. I do not know the full story yet and," she swung around and poked a finger in Nicolas's chest, "you are going to tell me everything," she warned. Swinging back to the mayor she said, "Marie-Claire, you invited me to come here and help with the homeless situation in Noelville, and I intend to do exactly that. But to do so, I need free rein to plan this event, so that it has the best chance of going viral. SocialBuzz is a platform that builds on several smaller campaigns until the collective package goes viral. That means that I will need to be able to take what film I need, to post what I see, to explain the problem and the solution in ways that capture the attention of the rest of Canada and the world. I cannot be tied down by past expectations. Do you understand?" Marie-Claire nodded. "Good. First thing in the morning, I want to visit the factory that closed."

She swung back to Nicolas and captured his stormy eyes with her own clear, honest gaze. "And you. You will tell me everything. No more secrets. No more hiding. No more stepping unsuspected emotional land mines for me. No more ghosts rattling around in the closets to be discovered. If i am going to do up a campaign that paints everyone in the best possible light, I cannot have ugly secrets waiting to be shoved in my face. I have spent the better part of today researching this town and its inhabitants. I know what is available online. Now, I want to know the inside story. All of it, Nicolas. Starting with why you mothballed the sugar shacks and ending up with the reason the factory is in the hands of the town."

Nicolas frowned and frowned at her, his face dark as a thunder-cloud. Seeing his unrelenting, stubborn expression, she reached out and placed a gentle hand on his arm. "Think of it as therapy. Have you ever told anyone your feelings? Have you ever gotten this off your chest? I promise, I will not share this with anyone outside of those of us who are in this room, right now. Give yourself permission to grieve. Trust me."

Nicolas put his fork down on his forgotten plate of food and searched her face, the anger in his own face slowly leaching away. The stormy colour faded and a soft blue hue flooded his eyes, as he considered her words. She could feel the tension leaving his arm. "Alright. I will tell you everything. Don't expect it to change my opinion of things, but my grand-mere did bring you here to do a job, and you do not deserve to be blind-sided."

Georges let out an audible sigh and quietly collected their plates, then placed a slice of pie in front of each of them, poured tea, and quietly left the family to their discussion. Marie-Claire relaxed visibly, stirring cream and sugar into her tea. Evelyn waited patiently, her focus entirely on Nicolas.

"Where do you want to start?" he asked tentatively.

"With the mysterious maple shacks. They look purpose built— as though they were designed to become something. They remind me of a quaint village, honestly. Especially the way that they are built so close to the river and the bridge to the park. Why didn't you tell me about the bridge and where it went, when we were in the park?"

"Why? Because it's all part of the tragedy that has defined my life. Yes, the village was built for a special purpose. You see, my family was so in love with the holiday season, that they decided to expand the original maple sugar shack and build an entire Christmas village for myself shortly after I was born. The idea started out as play houses, but as my father started to build, it morphed into actual, full-sized buildings."

"It was in that original sugar shack that the first maple candy was produced by my mother. She loved to pull taffy and what could possibly be better than real maple syrup taffy? But she went far beyond that and started designing a whole line of maple confectionary. She had a real knack for it. Initially she created her concoctions only for friends and family, but as word got out and the sweet treats shared with others, requests began to pour in for her to create special order batches. Soon, the number of orders became too much for her and her tiny kitchen. She outgrew the maple shack and asked my father about expanding into the factory across the way. It had been sitting empty for several years, when my father bought it."

Nicolas got up from the table and started pacing around the room. "I was just a child then. Most of what I remember is sitting on a stool in the shack while the big cauldrons bubbled away, reducing the raw sap down into what you think of as syrup. It is a long process to boil off that much water, and so the shack was always running. It's a warm, cozy memory for me."

Marie-Claire offered a tender smile to her grandson. "Your mother spent hours and hours out in the sugar shack. You were with her from the moment you could walk, while she developed her recipes. Your father decided that other buildings were needed and that's when he decided to build a destination, a Christmas village if you will. And why not? With the history of the family and the traditions that were already in place, it was a natural extension of your mother's efforts. So, in total he built the five outbuildings. In order of construction, he built the Sugar Shack, the North Pole Post Office, The Sugar Plum Bakery, the Sleigh Barn —yes that sleigh barn—and Santa's Workshop. At first they were just empty buildings, like a western town, but when people in Noelville started asking if they could book events and birthday parties and such there, well then he started working on the various interiors. It took him years. In the meantime, he purchased the old factory building and set up a sugar factory there, that processed not only maple sugars, but also corn, cane and beet sugars. And in one corner was your mother's candy shop. The sugar factory grew rapidly and within a couple of years, it employed half the town, or so it seemed." She paused, thinking about the past, lost in thought.

"And that's when the accident happened," she continued. "It was mid December, only days before Nicolas' next birthday. They were travelling home from the company Christmas party at the factory, when they were struck by the drunk driver, who turned out to be one of their own. Funny things had been happening in the rapid growth of the company. Shortfalls started happening and suppliers were not being paid, collection notices started arriving. And the hired CEO at the time was later found to have been skimming the profits of the company in conjunction with a girlfriend in the accounting department. When your father found out, he called the police. The scandal for the company sent shock waves through Noelville. No one knows to this day if the accident was an accident, or intentional. The CEO had been arrested earlier that day and released on bail. He was not at the party."

"And that is when my life changed. I begged them to come home early so we could spend time at the village, decorating for Christmas. I was only a child. I am the reason they died. If I hadn't had a temper tantrum, trying to get them to come back early, maybe they would still be alive today," said Nicolas in a bitter voice. "Now all I have are pictures and vague memories, and my own self loathing. Without them here, the village project was abandoned. There was no one to complete. I was only a child. And by the time I was old enough, I had no interest in visiting the ghosts of my parents. I moved on. My one concession was to take over the role of Saint Nicolas when I reached 18 years of age. To this day, the only building I have visited is the Sleigh Barn."

Evelyn's mouth dropped open in surprise. "You have never been back to village? You have never gone inside of any of those buildings?"

Nicolas shook his head. "No. I had no desire to go. Georges has gone inside though. He is caretaker and butler so he takes care of all the outbuildings as well."

"And the factory? What happened to it?"

"The company went into foreclosure. The building went empty and eventually the town took it over for back taxes owed. As far as I know, nothing has changed there either. I think they tried to sell it but no one was interested in a former sugar factory," said Nicolas.

"That's right, the town took it over. When would you like to go see it, Evelyn?" asked Marie-Claire.

Evelyn gazed at both of them, measuring their expressions. She had an idea, but she wondered if it was too soon to suggest it? "I'd like to see the village first. Could we do that in the morning? And then stop by the factory after lunch? I have an idea, but I don't want to share anything more until I've seen their state of repair. I am going to think on it overnight."

Nicolas offered a small smile. "You are really something else. None of this horrid business bothers you, does it?"

"Why should it? Other than feeling normal sympathy for a sad situation, it is all in the past. Your parents would not want you to close yourself off from the wonders of living. I think you have been too long trapped in the darkness of the past. It's time to step into the light. It's time I performed a small miracle!" Evelyn beamed at both of them.

"Well we are going to need help, I can see that already," said Marie-Claire.

"Help! Oh my! I almost forgot to tell you. I have my assistant flying out from Vancouver on the red eye special. She will arrive about 7am. I told her to come here, is that all right? I need her help with the campaign."

"Certainly. I will have Georges make up a room for her. And Evelyn, you have carte-blanche to do whatever you feel is needed to make this campaign of yours a success. Do not think that you need to get permission from me in advance to start posting to SocialBuzz. I trust you to carry out this campaign with dignity, honour and professionalism." Marie-Claire gave Evelyn a warm smile then got up and left the dining room to find Georges.

"You think you will need your assistant? You have that much confidence that you can pull off a fundraiser that will require extra hands?"

"Without a doubt," said Evelyn. "I've done it before. I will need all kinds of help to make this the success I envision. You, kind sir," she tweaked his nose with the tip of her finger, "will have to trust me. I know exactly where to go to find the help I need." She sat back in her chair with a satisfied smile, as though all things were settled and all that was left was the event.

Nicolas shook his head slowly, cracking a smile. "Well then, Mrs. Claus. What kind of Santa would I be to stand in your way. Charity begins at home, they say." He smirked, his lips twitching, but it was a gentle teasing. "What is next?"

Evelyn got to her feet. "I am going upstairs to do more planning. You have a free evening. But I warn you that tomorrow will be super busy." Evelyn got up and made her way out of the dining room and to the foot of the stairs. "Would you mind asking Georges to bring me some tea in a bit? Something soothing."

Nicolas nodded, still smiling. *When he smiles like that, he looks like a different person. Years younger…*with a start, she realized she was staring at him. Flustered, she dropped eye contact and fled up the stairs, Nicolas' gentle laughter pursued her until she pushed the door of her room closed behind her cutting off the sound.

Evelyn stood before the fireplace, watching the dancing flames. The glint of orange reflected off the bells, so lovingly lined up in a row. Picking up the smallest one, she gave it a shake and a high pitched, clear ringing tone filled the room. She looked down at the little bell in awe. She had no idea how such a small bell could create such a full sound. Curious, she picked up the next, and the next, until she had tested them all.

Oh yes, these bells were going to feature in her plans. She just had to plan the right event to display them to their fullest.

She left the room to go to the bathroom and splash some cold water on her face. She was dead tired but she wasn't willing to go to bed quite yet. Not until she had jotted down every point she had been musing about over the last week. She needed to be ready for when Natalie arrived tomorrow morning.

She heard the door open and called out "Just place the tea on the table please, and thank you Georges." She finished drying her face then left the bathroom. The room was empty but a tray with a pot of tea sat beside the desk. She walked over and saw that a second plate held two decorated sugar cookies. Santa and Mrs. Claus. Smiling she picked up Santa and took a big bite. Glancing back down she saw a folded piece of paper under Mrs. Claus. Reaching down she plucked it from the plate and opened it.

"There is a Chinese proverb that states "If you want happiness for a lifetime, help somebody else." Thank you for all your efforts on our behalf."

The note was unsigned.

Natalie's Arrival

The ringing of the doorbell at 6:00 am woke Evelyn from a dead sleep. She sat straight up in bed, rubbing sleep from her eyes. That must be Natalie! she thought and sprang out of bed, pulling a red house robe over her Rudolph patterned pajama top and bottoms. She rushed over to her door and yanked it open, colliding with someone in the hallway. Nicolas, looking sleepy eyed with tousled hair and a day's growth of beard, stood before her, t-shirt stretched tight against his chest as he grabbed her by the arms to keep her from falling.

"Watch out! You just about bowled me over." He released her left arm and rubbed his chest where her elbow had landed particularly hard.

Evelyn stared up at him, wide eyed. Where his hands had gripped her, her skin burned with awareness. "Natalie," she gasped. "She's here early." She had a hard time dragging her eyes away from Nicolas. He looked absolutely adorable. *Adorable? Really, Evelyn? Is your brain on vacation? What are you, six?*

Nicolas broke eye contact first by looked over the railing down to the foyer below. Sure enough, Natalie stood in a puddle of melting snow, handing her soaked coat over to Georges, who stood before her, impeccably dressed as always.

"Well, it looks like your assistant has arrived earlier than expected. I am going to make myself scarce while you chat over breakfast. I am sure you have lots to discuss. I am going to go get dressed." He released her arm, gave her one last look, up and down then said "Nice pajamas, by the way." Grinning he returned to his quarters, while Evelyn ran lightly down the stairs to hug Natalie.

"You are here a full hour early! How did that happen?"

"We had a great tail wind apparently. I was glad to land once I saw what the weather was like outside. I almost got stuck three times! And I missed the gates and had to back up in the dark." She shuddered, dramatically. "Toto, I don't think we are in Kansas anymore. But it's good to see you!" She pulled Evelyn into a hug, which was returned enthusiastically.

"Mademoiselle, we have prepared a room for you. If you will follow me, I will see you to it and then retrieve your luggage."

"Oh, that's ok," said Natalie, "I can go get it, it's just outside."

"Nonsense. This way please," and Georges started up the stairs. Evelyn leaned over and whispered in Natalie's ear, "That is Georges. He's the butler and he rules the roost here. I'd follow him if I were you."

Looking startled, Natalie nodded, slipped off her boots and then followed Georges up the curving staircase and to a room beside Evelyn's, where he held open the door. "This is the Gingerbread room."

Natalie stepped inside and her eyes widened. Everything in the room was in the soft brown butter and nutmeg and ginger tones that suggested gingerbread. Against the back drop of the polished whole log walls, the room was cozy and very comfortable, like a pair of old slippers. Georges disappeared and then reappeared moments later with Natalie's luggage. "Breakfast will be served in thirty minutes.

Mademoiselle Evelyn knows the way." He pulled the door closed, leaving them alone.

Somehow, he had managed to get a pot of tea in place in the room, which Natalie exclaimed over, pouring two cups and handing one to Evelyn. "I'm so cold!" she said in between grateful sips. She sank down into an overstuffed chair by the fireplace, in which flames danced merrily on gas logs. "This place is amazing! How has your trip been so far? Tell me everything!"

Evelyn spent the next half an hour bringing her assistant up to date on the goings on at the manor. Natalie gasped in the appropriate places and sat listening to the tellings, enthralled. When Evelyn stopped talking to sip her now cold tea, Natalie said, "Oh my gosh, this family has been through so much. We HAVE to rock this fundraiser for them. Their hearts are in the right place, you know. Even Mr. Grinch there deserves that much help. Where you two hugging each other when I arrived?" Natalie tilted her head, studying Evelyn. "I mean, I could feel the waves of attraction from all the way downstairs. When did this happen?"

"What? NO! There is nothing happening. You have that all wrong." Evelyn blushed.

"Do I? I don't think so. The attraction between you two is almost palpable. I knew there was something up at the SocialBuzz party, but I had no idea he was connected to this mayor. What are the chances of that? I say it's Karma. You were fated to meet." Natalie grinned, white teeth flashing in the firelight. "It's about time, you know. I knew that red dress was a man killer outfit."

"Stop it, will you? I am not here for romance. I am here as a guest, and so are you. We have a job to do."

"So? It doesn't mean you can't have some fun too. Speaking of which, what are we doing today? Do I have time to take a nap?"

"No, you don't so I hope you slept on the plane." She glanced up at the mantle clock and saw that it was almost 6:30am. "If you want to freshen up, I'd do it now. We have to head down to breakfast."

"Where no doubt, Mr. Hunky is waiting for you."

Evelyn picked up her slipper and threw it at Natalie, who ducked out of the way. "I am going to dress. I will be right back." Chuckling, Evelyn put her slipper back on and headed next door for a quick change.

Moments later they were seated to a typical French breakfast of baked goods both sweet and savory, and a platter of cheese, and coffee.

Marie-Claire was not to be seen this morning, having an early appointment in town. But Nicolas made an appearance slightly before eight and re-introduced himself to Natalie. "Evelyn tells me that you are an 'assistant extraordinaire'. It will be interesting to see what skill set you bring to the event planning." At her curious expression, he said, "She has already told me about your professional background with taxation. I want to know what other skills you have, that make you so qualified for this endeavor, or for your own campaign, for that matter." Nicolas quirked his eyebrow and Evelyn snickered.

Natalie looked from one to the other, studying their reactions. They were like two cheshire cats at the same bowl of cream but studiously ignoring each other, lest the other one realize they are there, also. "Didn't you say we had a busy schedule today? Some village to go check out?"

"That's right. I'm glad to see you dressed warmly," said Nicolas.

"Let's go in my jeep. All of my camera gear, is already in there," said Evelyn.

They hurried to finish breakfast and then with a flask of hot chocolate provided to each of them by Georges, they headed out to the jeep and drove the short distance to the Sleigh Barn. Now that she knew its history, she was even more excited to explore it. Natalie looked around with keen interest, taking in the beauty of the quiet Quebec forest and the peacefulness of the snow-covered hillsides. Once Evelyn had parked the jeep, she jumped out of the back seat and scooped up a handful of snow in her gloved hands, testing its compactability. When it stuck together to form a perfect snowball, she squealed with excitement and promptly threw it at Evelyn. The ball hit her dead center of her back with a smack and then dropped back to the ground.

Whirling around, Evelyn scooped up her own missile and promptly threw it at Natalie. This one struck her in the face and she squealed again. Suddenly a second snowball lobbed itself over the jeep and struck Evelyn in the side of the head. Evelyn ducked down behind the jeep and ran to the front, crouching in front to rapidly create a pile of snowballs. She could hear the others doing the same. The silence of the frosty morning was broken only by the sound of excited breathing and suppressed giggles. Peaking over the hood, she started to throw her snowballs at anything that moved. Natalie and Nicolas returned the favour and snowballs flew in all directions.

With a satisfying splat, her snowball struck Nicolas in the chin and the fallout slipped down the front of his coat. "Oh man, that is cold. Cheap shot there, Evelyn," he called as he scooped out the melting slush from his clothing. Laughing hysterically, Evelyn stepped out from the shelter of the front of the jeep and pelted Nicolas with snowballs, just as Natalie did the same from the back of the jeep. Nicolas staggered around as though shot and then collapsed onto the snow, laughing.

Evelyn walked over to him, her fuel spent, then offered him a hand up. Nicolas rolled over, reached for her hand and abruptly yanked her arm, pulling her down into the snow. She landed face first beside him with a startled "Oh crap!" then lifted her snow-covered face from the snow bank. She held up a hand and called "Truce! I call a truce!"

Natalie, who was the only one with any snowballs left, giggled once again and let them drop. "You two look ridiculous, but in a good way," she said, grinning down at them. "Would you like a hand up?" she held out her hand to Nicolas, who smiled sweetly at her, then yanked her head first into a neighbouring snow bank. "Ahhhh!" she screamed as she pushed herself up on her elbows.

"Truce accepted," smirked Nicolas, while Evelyn spasmed with fits of giggles beside him.

Evelyn got to her feet, brushing snow off her jeans and hiccupping. Nicolos also got to his feet and this time reached down and pulled Natalie up to her feet. "Come on you two. You wanted to see this village. Well, there is lots to see, starting with the barn."

He walked back up the ramp they had traversed the day before and once again unlocked the doors, pulling them open wide so that the sunshine flooded the interior. Evelyn walked inside, this time wandering deeper into the old barn. Her eye had been caught by what looked like wall of upright boards, stacked against the far wall. "What are these?" she said aloud, but before anyone else could answer, she reached the objects of her curiosity.

Stacked against the wall were over two dozen wooden toboggans. "Oh my gosh, I have never seen so many toboggans in one place, outside of a sporting goods store. These are the old-fashioned ones! I remember these from when I was a kid!" She ran her hand down the side of the toboggans as she walked. They came in multiple sizes, from two seaters to six seaters. Each one had the telltale curved front to tuck in your boots and tough cord long enough to pull the toboggan behind an adult. Excitement bloomed inside her as possibilities spun in her mind. "We can use these. That's what that big hill out back is for, isn't it? It's a toboggan run."

Nicolas smiled as her face lit up. "Yes, it's a toboggan run. It also doubles as a bunny ski hill for beginner skiers. There is no lift though. You have to walk all the way back up to the top."

"That doesn't matter. It's the family fun aspect that will attract the locals. Natalie, let's count the number of toboggans that are here, and note their condition."

Evelyn and Nicolas pulled out the toboggans one by one and Natalie took notes on her tablet, noting the colour, size and any repairs required. Once they were done inspecting and cataloging the toboggans, they ended up with 31 serviceable sleds, and 6 that required some kind of repair. Only three were not able to be repaired, at least for this season.

"Well! That is certainly better than I expected!" said Evelyn.

"What are you planning to do with all of these?" ask Nicolas, tilting his head bird-like as he stared at her, a quizzical expression curving his lips.

"I will tell you that once I see the rest of the village. Come on, Natalie, you can explore the sleigh later on." Natalie had climbed up into the sleigh and was taking video on her tablet, of the two of them examining the toboggans and discussing their condition. She took a panorama shot and saved it, then climbed back down.

"That's one big sleigh! I'd love to know the story behind it," said Natalie.

"Later," hissed Evelyn, in an aside meant only for Natalie's ears.

They followed Nicolas out of the barn and then down the trail that led to the maple sugar shack and the other buildings that surrounded it. Now that Evelyn knew about the bridge, she realized that the path was large enough to handle the sleigh. She was betting the bridge was large enough also. No need to transport the sleigh to festivities when you could just cross a bridge. She tucked this thought away for now, as the trail opened up into the clearing. Seeing it again for the second time, she grinned ear to ear. It was perfect. She had her very own North Pole to play with.

It was a fundraiser's dream come true. Now it was time to see how much work would be needed to bring her vision to life.

Santa's Elves

Nicolas pulled an old-fashioned metal ring full of jangling skeleton keys from his pocket and started sorting through them. Evelyn stared at the monstrous keys and smiled.

"I see your parents had a sense of history. Did they want to make the buildings more authentic?" Evelyn asked.

"No, they were just cheap and didn't want to buy new locks, so they reused these old ones we had rattling around in the basement. Just as well they did. A little oil and these old things will last for another hundred years."

Finding the one he was looking for, he stepped up to the door of the maple sugar shack and slid the key into the lock. He had to work it a bit before the old lock would turn, but with a squeal it did turn, unlocking the door. He pushed it open, then fumbled around on the left for a moment and came up with a kerosene lantern. Pulling a lighter from his pocket, he held the flame to the wick. Lamp light flooded the room, which was a lot larger inside than she had been anticipating.

The interior was one large room, with open rafters and walls made out of pine boards, with the same pine boards used for the floor. Strange tools hung from wooden pegs. In the middle of the room, a large stainless steel boiler stood with a large exhaust hood that rose up and exited through the roof, and an equally large tub below to hold the maple sap. A stainless steel firebox that reminded Evelyn of a steam engine's coal burning oven, heated the underside of the appliance, boiling away the water of the sap until only a sticky, sweet syrup remained.

Evelyn moved around the shack. It smelled like maple syrup even after all these years of being closed up. At the back of the shack a pantry had been built against the outside wall. Empty jars stood like toy soldiers waiting for the next batch of syrup to be made. Large ladles and spoons hung from rings and other canning devices were stacked on lower shelves. She moved over to a set of drawers and pulled open the top one. Inside lay a spiral binder and a faded sticker that said "Recettes" in a woman's handwriting. Eyes widening, she carefully pulled the aged binder from the drawer and placed it on the table top.

"Nicolas, could you come here? I think I found your mother's recipe book." Nicolas looked up from where he was crouched down in front of the fire box, peering inside, then stood and walked over to Evelyn's side. He gazed over her shoulder, his warm breath tickling the nape of her neck, warming her. She was instantly aware of his height and the breadth of his shoulders as he towered over her.

"Yes, that is my mother's handwriting." He reached out to open the book at the same time as Evelyn, and their hands tangled for a moment. Evelyn pulled hers back and allowed him to open the book, peeking at him out of the corner of her eye. Each page had what looked to be a recipe hand written on the page, plus a faded picture of the completed product. There were multiple kinds of candy, cookies and pies, cakes and brownies, a maple coated Halloween apple and even a recipe for what looked to be a maple spirit of some kind. She squinted down at the recipe. She thought it was a maple flavoured hard apple cider.

"I think we just hit the jackpot. If these are your mother's original recipes, we could make this the center piece of the campaign."

Nicolas frowned down at her. "In what way?"

"Well... we could make these recipes and auction off gift baskets. Or we could have a bake sale and invite the locals, something like that."

"I don't know," said Nicolas. "That sounds like an incredible amount of work. It is such a small price point compared to your housing initiative in Vancouver, where supporters were sponsoring entire shelters for the homeless. That was a very elegant campaign, by the way. I was watching it, I have to admit."

"Thank you," said Evelyn, acknowledging the compliment. "Let me think on this some more. Can we check out the other buildings?"

Collecting Natalie, who was peering up the exhaust chimney of the maple boiler, they headed back outside and on to the three buildings which stood across the clearing from the maple shack. They were intentionally clustered to look almost like a western town facade, except these ones reflected more of a gingerbread house feel, with delicate carvings decorating the soffit and carved shutters for the windows. Nicolas paused in front of them, looking from one to the other. His face reflected an array of emotions as he looked them. "I have not set foot inside these three buildings, since the day they died. Everything remains as it was the day my father locked up the door, never to return," he said softly. "My grand-mere has checked on them, of course, but even she didn't have the heart to really do anything with them."

Nicolas lifted a finger and pointed from right to left. "That's the North Pole post office. In the middle is Santa's Toy Shoppe and on the right is the Sugar Plum bakery. Which one do you want to look at first?"

It was Natalie that spoke first. "The bakery. I have an idea and I want to see what equipment is in there."

Nicolas led the way over to the bakery and opened the door. He lit a second lantern and hung it from a peg. Natalie walked inside and looked around. "Is there power to these buildings?" as she noticed the ovens on the back wall, and a couple of stand up coolers.

"We have never run power out here as it was not being used in a fashion that made any sense to incur the expense. However, each building is wired to a panel with a propane powered generator outside. It is possible to bring in cannisters for propane or even install a tank if needed. At this time, this village is all off grid."

"Well I was thinking about solar panels, actually," said Natalie. "The technology has come so far that it is really isn't that expense anymore, to put an installation together. But good to know we can get full power here, via the propane set up."

"The off grid set up is perfect!" beamed Evelyn. "When you are working with the homeless, the less support they need in the form of bills, the better it is for everyone. That's why I was so drawn to the pods with the built in solar panels, for the Vancouver campaign." She wandered around the small shop, noting the pans and bakeware available, the candy molds and presses. An idea flared to life. "This is perfect!" She swung around and announced, "We are going into the candy business, using your mother's recipes. It's time the Sugar Plum bakery went live. Come on, I want to see the other two buildings." She literally ran for the door, pulling it open and heading over to Santa's workshop where she stood at the door, bouncing with excitement.

Nicolas shook his head, laughing at her antics. Unlocking the next door, he said, "After you, Mrs. Claus." Evelyn flashed him a cheeky smile and headed inside. This building was filled with work benches and older sewing machines, and a lot of tools. Half finished toys littered the benches and several prototypes sat on tables to the side. The walls were covered in toy design sketches, faded but still legible.

Grinning ear to ear, she made a quick tour of the building then headed outside to the post office, where a similar tour occurred. The post office had wooden niches on the back wall, for letters and a huge metal mailbox painted in candy cane stripes and a flag on top that said "North Pole". It looked like a converted Canada Post mailbox, the kind that no longer existed, with the curved top to shed snow. Evelyn ran her hand over the top of it.

"Natalie, fetch the hot chocolate from the jeep please. We are going to plan this event right here and now. And you are going to be filming. Did I see some Santa mugs on the shelf over there?" Evelyn had spied a small kitchen at the back of the post office where colourful mugs were lined up on a shelf. She grabbed three of them, wiped them out and carried them back to the post office counter. Nicolas knelt in front of an old pot belly stove, loading it with wood and some old newspaper, then lit the stove. Immediately the chill left the room. He then took a taper and lit the rest of the kerosene lamps, mostly hanging from the ceiling. The gloom disappeared and a pleasant wood smoke smell filled the post office.

Natalie re-entered the post office, and grinning appreciatively at the cozy setting, poured hot chocolate into their mugs. "Ok, out with it, Eve. I know that grin. You have a campaign spinning in your head. I will begin taking notes.

Evelyn took a huge sip of hot chocolate from the deep mug, and came up with a hot chocolate moustache. She wiped it off with the back of her hand. Nicolas reached over to wipe a spot she missed off of her top lip. "You missed a spot."

"Oh, thank you." Her cheeks went rosy. She hoped he put the sudden glow down the warming cabin after the cold of outside.

"Ok, here is what I have in mind. The way I see it, we need to tug on the heartstrings of not just this community but also similar towns and cities that are facing similar issues of unemployment and homelessness. As prices increase nationwide, so does the pressures to find affordable housing. Nicolas, didn't you say that a lot of the homeless in Noelville were former employees of the factory? That they lost their jobs when the scandal hit?"

Nicolas frowned, not wanting to be reminded of this failure. "Yes, but that was a long time ago. Most of those people have either moved on or died. Not everyone was a part of the factory's demise."

"But some are. Do you know if there are enough former employees there that would know how the sugar factory worked?"

"I am sure there are some."

"So, here is what I am thinking. We have a lot of people who are living rough and trying to stay alive. We also have the factory buildings sitting there empty, right on the banks of the river. I can see it from here. We also have a bunch of people who currently have no jobs. I don't see them as anything more than a workforce waiting to be put to work. And here, we have a Christmas village waiting to be brought to life. We have you and me, Mr. and Mrs. Claus. What's missing?"

Natalie grinned, eating it up. "Elves. We have no elves."

"Exactly! We are in desperate need of elves, and there they are!" Evelyn got up and pointed across the river. "All of our elves are right there, waiting to be called in to work. So, let's do it! Let's make this Christmas village a destination for this holiday season, and let's show the world that just because someone is homeless doesn't mean they have no value. Let's show what kind of Christmas miracle can happen when we all work together."

"Ok, I get that. Let's suppose that they are willing to come work in the village and do whatever it is you are thinking of having them do. How do we pay them? We are talking hundreds of people here." said Nicolas.

"We pay them with housing and a warm belly. We open up the factory and convert some of the rooms into dorms, where they can sleep and reopen a kitchen or the staff lunch room, something like that. I will have a better idea once we tour it tomorrow —it's going to be tomorrow because we need to fully plan the village operations today — but it's just down the street to the actual homeless shelter. I am sure we can make arrangements to have food brought in from their kitchens. This is a totally different campaign from what we did in Vancouver, but this fits Noelville's history and circumstances."

"Ok, let's pretend that everything you have outlined here is a go. What is the goal of this campaign? What happens after the Christmas season is done? This is one small capsule of time in a year. What is the plan for the other eleven months?" asked Nicolas.

"Your mother's recipes. We are going to reopen the factory and instead of a sugar factory, we perfect your mother's candy recipes, starting with everything maple. The sugar shack will need a serious upgrade in time, but that is better suited to a modern factory set up anyways. You have all the trees here on your estate, just waiting to be tapped. They just need to be set up to be harvested. That is a narrow window between now and the beginning of March, right? So, the homeless who are not interested in working in the candy making side of the factory, can help farm the trees and work with the maple syrup collection in the spring and its later refinement."

Nicolas looked at her, in amazement. "You thought up of all of this, just since we got here?"

"No, it's been rolling around inside my head for a while. But I needed to see the village first, to know if the plan made any sense at all. It's a big plan, and ambitious, but I really think this could work. And I think the response we will get will blow your mind."

"This is a huge undertaking. I think we need to divide up and gather some teams around us. Do you have any friends we could call on, Nicolas?" said Natalie, looking from Nicolas to Evelyn.

"One or two. The first person that comes to mind works for the city, as a facilities manager. He was a high school buddy of mine. Alvin Coal m. He could help with the factory reopening and conversion."

"Then I need you to introduce me to this guy," said Natalie, "because we need to get this rolling, fast. You two should continue to focus on the Christmas village theme. Does this guy have access to decorations? Something we could borrow, or even rent for the event? There is a gala at the end, after all, and I think that the factory would be a great place to stage that dinner dance. It would allow people to come and view the facilities before hand. Have a cocktail evening in advance, to show off the venue."

Nicolas pulled his cell phone from his pocket and dialed a number. "Hi Alvin? Nicolas Jollie-Saint here. Yes, long time no talk. Yes, I am back in town for the holidays. Listen, I am helping my grand-mere with the fundraiser and I need access to our old factory on Riverside. Could you meet me there at 10:00am tomorrow morning? Yes, we will need the lights turned on. Great. See you then." He disconnected the call. "We are all set up."

"I think we should inventory these buildings and start making lists of items we will need including cleaning supplies. I also want to take home your mother's recipe book so I can study it overnight," said Evelyn. "let's also note any repairs that are needed to any of the buildings."

"I can handle any repair that is needed," said Nicolas. "It is within my skill set as a building contractor and real estate agent."

"Great! That will help so much!"

They spent the rest of the day inventorying the structures, examining what was available to be utilized and what they would need to purchase or have donated in order to make the village come alive.

"We have a whole storage closet full of outdoor decorations over at the house. Tinsel and garlands, string lights, even a couple of six-foot outdoor Nutcrackers. I am sure won't need much other than some replacement bulbs for a few strands of lights. I will see if Alvin can spare some of his summertime crew to come help with set up."

"Perfect," said Evelyn with a yawn. Her stomach rumbled, announcing it was time to wrap up their day. "I am famished," she said as her stomach protested again. "The light is fading, so I think we should call this day a wrap."

Nicolas shut down the lights and locked the doors to all the buildings, and then then made their way back to the manor, the recipe book carefully cradled in Evelyn's arms. The book fascinated her, and she was eager to study it with Natalie and pick out various recipes to use in the upcoming festivities. They had a lot of planning to do, beginning with some teaser filming starting tomorrow. With a 10:00 am appointment at the factory, they would need to be up early to catch the first filming light. All in all, it had been a long but satisfying day.

The Factory Tour

A ray of sunshine poked Natalie in the eye, waking her fully. Realizing that it was a perfectly clear and cold day outside, she bounced out of bed and hurried to get ready. She loved the spontaneity of filming days. Somewhere, deep inside of her, was a film maker dying to escape and make her imprint on the world. Evelyn was good at taking short selfie videos to post, but for something as important as this, she needed to not be distracted by the tech. This was Natalie's specialty and where she shined. She was eager to get started.

Ten minutes later she was knocking on the next door and not waiting for a reply, she opened the door and called out to Evelyn. But the bedroom was empty. Pulling the door closed, she followed the smell of breakfast and found Evelyn already seated at the breakfast table with Marie-Claire. The two looked up as Natalie entered the room, smiling. "I was just about to wake you," said Evelyn. "Dawn's early light is here and we need to take advantage of this beautiful day. The forecast is for more snow tomorrow."

Natalie took an empty seat and accepted the platter of scrambled eggs and bacon from Evelyn, piling her plate high. She was famished. She knew she would burn off the calories of this breakfast and more today. "Yes, we need to get filming. I'd like to start with some shots out front of the manor. I was thinking a monologue about the charity and its goals, and some basic history about the village." She reached inside her pocket and handed Evelyn some hand written notes, written on the back of some Christmas wrapping paper. "Sorry, this is all the paper I could find in the room."

Evelyn grinned and took the wrapping paper. "You could have just emailed me the word document. My tablet works fine."

"Yes, but they are so hard to read in bright sunshine. This is better, trust me."

Evelyn looked over at the woman beside her and smiled. A coiled notebook lay open between them. It was Madeline's recipe book. They had been pouring over the possibilities and as it turned out, Marie-Claire had provided a lot of insight into the top selections. Not every recipe had been tested, but the ones that had been perfected Marie-Claire was able to point out. They had narrowed the list to ten.

"Well, here is our list," said Evelyn, pushing her tablet over to Natalie. "These are the ones we should make. No need to check the list twice, as Marie-Claire thinks we can whip up a batch of each in her kitchen tomorrow, while it is storming. So today, its filming and leg work on the factory, and tomorrow, we bake!"

At that moment Nicolas walked in. He shrugged out of his coat and hung it on the back of a chair and sat down across from Evelyn. His cheeks were a rosy match to his nose. "It is cold and crisp outside. Make sure you dress warmly for your filming this morning. You have," he checked his watch "about 90 minutes to do your filming and then we must leave. I cleared the driveway and the walkway." He picked up the plate of eggs and emptied the balance onto his own plate then grabbed several slices of toast and dug in.

"Noted," said Evelyn, giving him a quirky eyebrowed response, which he totally missed because he was concentrating on his fork. Natalie caught it though and giggled, and Marie-Claire also smiled.

"Right. Natalie, we should get going." Georges appeared as if by magic, with two thermoses of cafe au lait, which she accepted with a whispered *Merci*. Evelyn rose and left the dining room, gathering up Natalie as she did so.

A few moments later they were outside and choosing the best locations for filming. Natalie's favourite device was a small palmcorder with a big mic and night filming mode. A swivel screen let her see the shot as it would appear in the feed, and the quality was amazing. It was super light weight, battery operated and wifi capable. Natalie pointed to Evelyn to get inside her jeep and them pretend that she had just arrived at the manor. Evelyn got inside the car and backed it up onto the road, then at Natalie's signal, drove slowly through the gates and up under the portico, with Natalie filming the entire time. She climbed out of the jeep and looked around with interest.

Turning a bright smile towards the camera, Evelyn called out "Joyeux Noel to all the followers of my SocialBuzz channel and affiliates! It is the season of miracles, and we are on the move and live streaming, to bring a Christmas miracle to the village of Noelville, Quebec. This village has a long and proud history that dates back to the 1600's when the first explorers of this great country stepped foot onto its frozen soils, and met the indigenous peoples living here. Without those first contacts with the native peoples, these early explorers would have perished through their first harsh Canadian winter. It is through their compassion and cooperation that we exist today. So as always, we wish to begin with a land acknowledgement, honouring the ancestral home of the Huron-Wendat. In fact, the name Quebec comes from the Algonquin word "Kébec" which in their language means "where the river narrows".

"Indeed, the river narrows just a few feet from where I am standing now, outside the beautiful manor house of one of Noelville's founding families. The Jollie-Saint homestead is the home to the mayor and she has graciously invited us to stay at her home while we bring the plight of Noelville's homeless into the spotlight."

Natalie followed Evelyn as she walked to the front door and rang the doorbell. Marie-Claire answered the door, smiling warmly. She stepped out onto the front porch, joining Evelyn. "This is Marie-Clare Saint, Mayor of Noelville and our host for the weeks leading up to Christmas. Marie-Claire, could you let my followers know why you reached out to me? Surely you have sponsored successful fundraisers in the past, for your community."

Marie-Claire turned to Natalie and addressed the watchers of the live feed. "I want to thank Evelyn for making the trip and offering to help us with our fundraising efforts. After her viral campaign in Vancouver, we couldn't think of a better person to help us address this sensitive and critical problem in our community. Being blessed to live here, to live in Quebec and in Canada as a whole, it should go without question that we all have a home. But too often, people find themselves on hard times, and whether through their own mistakes or outside forces, or even a combination of both, no person should be homeless. We, here in Noelville, have an intimate and personal reason for addressing this problem at this time. With Evelyn's help, we intend to eliminate homelessness in this town."

Evelyn took her hand and held it for a moment. "We are happy to give our help." Evelyn let her hand drop and smiled brightly at the camera. "Look at what a gorgeous day it is here, today! And to start off the fun of this fundraiser, we are sharing with you the beauty of this rural countryside. It is the perfect Christmas post card. Come with me." Evelyn turned away from the house and walked a short distance around the side of the manor where the hill fell away to reveal a snow-covered vista. At the base of the hillside, was the Sleigh Barn, gleaming red in the bright sunshine, and easily seen against the white backdrop of snow. The snow sparkled with thousands of embedded fairy lights, or so it felt. It was actually the crystal construction of the snow that gave that impression, but the effect was magical.

Evelyn paused for a moment, pointing down into the valley. "See that red barn? That barn holds a secret of the season. That barn will feature heavily in our campaign. I am going to open up the comments section and I want to hear what you all think is hiding in that barn. Use our trending hash tags and give us your best guess! #homelessgiving #sharetheroof #Christmasviralcharities, #Christmaseve #Christmaswithevelyn, #chirstmassnowqueen, and two new hashtags special for this event, #maplecandyChristmas #Christmasinnoelville.

"One random fan will be chosen to receive a special Christmas hamper from our Noelville elves, who you will meet later! They are all busy at the moment, as Santa's elves are this time of year. Of course, our donation pledge window will open at 9:00 am tomorrow. We will bring you the countdown tomorrow, direct from our Christmas kitchen here at the manor. So if you are in search of a great new recipe, join us tomorrow and we will let you in on the secret of some of Noelville's best loved recipes."

At that moment, Nicolas exited the back of the manor and walked past Evelyn and Natalie, smiling from ear to ear. He watched the girls as he passed by, pulling on a pair of gloves as he carried a set of Christmas lights over to an antique tractor and began stringing lights over its frame. He looked up and smiled again, then returned to the house.

"Evelyn, did you have more to say?" Natalie prompted, as the camera still rolled.

Evelyn gave a start and realized she had gone silent and was openly staring at Nicolas the entire time he was working on decorating the tractor. "Oh, yes," she said, blushing slightly. "That is Nicolas Jollie-Saint, who will figure prominently in this year's campaign. He has a very special connection to Noelville and to the mysterious building below! But that reveal is for another day. Right now, we are off to a special location that will hopefully become the backbone of this homeless initiative. More to come, so stay tuned! This is Evelyn Christmas wishing you holiday cheer on the countdown to Christmas, Quebec-Style!"

The camera light winked out and Evelyn walked over to Natalie. "How do you think that went?" asked Evelyn, the stain of her blush still present and obvious.

"Perfect, except that you froze when Nicolas walked out. We will see how everyone reacts to that gaff. I live streamed it, so no chance of an edit."

"Ugh. I was hoping you had a delay on it. Oh well, it will be fine," Evelyn shrugged. "I think it's time to head to the factory, come on."

This time they took Nicolas' BMW which purred along the drifted roads, not caring if they were snow-covered or not. A few minutes later they pulled up in front of the old factory. Nicolas shut the engine off and they got out and approached a tall man with dark, windswept hair and a trimmed beard and wearing a red toque. He stopped shovelling as they arrived, leaning the shovel against the railing of the stairs that led up to the front doors. They mounted the cleared steps then Alvin reached out and took Nicolas' outstretched hand and pulled him into a vigorous bear hug. "Nic! It's about time you called! When did you get back? I have been waiting for you to give me a buzz. We need to set up a Christmas pub crawl." His eyes turned to the ladies and focused especially on Natalie. "And who are your lovely companions?"

"This is Evelyn. And this is Natalie. They are here to help with the mayor's homeless fundraiser. They want to tour the old factory and see if they can work it into their plans."

"Welcome ladies! Let me be your guide. My father worked here, you know." He turned and led them up the last couple of steps and into the building.

The main foyer was three stories tall, with a wide central hallway, wide enough for ten people to walk side by side and not touch. A grand staircase climbed up either side to a second story hallway of similar width, which was repeated for the third floor. Natalie could see that doors periodically came off the hallway. Light spilled into the space at a crossing about half way down the building.

"This is 'Le Grand Vestibule' or the main public entrance to the factory. The rooms on this floor were for the public, with production occurring on the second and third floors. Service elevators at the rear of the building brought raw product up and finished product down. You would think that the main production facilities would be on this level, but they had planned for an entire storefront to be built here, before the factory's demise. Come let me show you around. Feel free to ask any questions that come to mind."

"Is the factory still for sale?" asked Evelyn.

"Yes, but the price set basically covers the back taxes, which are substantial. Noelville has been trying to lure a business to town for a decade now, but we've never found the right buyer. Came close a couple of times. Usually, financing was the reason it didn't fly." He paused in front of the first door and opened it wide, turning on the light. "I will to open the other doors and you can check them out."

The rooms were long rectangles and each room had its own bathroom at the rear on the outside wall. It put Natalie in mind of a kindergarten classroom, except the fixtures were adult sized. There were no shower facilities, however the bathrooms had enough room to build a couple of stalls, easily. There were a total of twenty on this side of the first floor and in the middle of the building another staircase that wound up three stories. The wings on either side of the central courtyard were set up like a cafeteria, with long service counters and room for tables for eating. It put Natalie in mind of a food court in a mall.

"What were those original rooms for?" asked Evelyn.

"The factory owners hoped to attract small business entrepreneurs who would prominently feature the sugar products that the factory was producing. They never got to that phase however, before the factory closed," said Alvin.

On the far side of the 'food court' as Natalie was calling in inside her head, there were less doors. The first that they entered was a huge space. It was completely empty. Hardwood floors ran from doorway all the way to the far wall, in which was set eight tall windows, almost floor to ceiling height. The ceiling was finished with tin tiles reminiscent of the 1920's and bare wires with pigtails hung from the ceiling. "This was once a ballroom," said Natalie, guessing at its purpose.

"You are correct. The original chandeliers were taken down and packed away for safe keeping. They are located in the basement. Here," Alvin said, walking over to a faded picture that still hung on the wall. "You can see the room just after it was finished. The local newspaper took this photo." He pointed to the photo and the crowded around it. There were four massive chandeliers that hung from the tall ceilings, more than enough to add ambiance to a room this size.

"Those are gorgeous!" said Evelyn with an excited gleam.

Recognizing her expression, Nicolas said, "Let me guess. You are thinking this would be a perfect place for the gala."

Evelyn swung around, deep dimples forming in the corner of her mouth. "You bet! This is absolutely perfect and its available!" She swung back around to Alvin and said, "Does the manager of facilities have access to tables? Tall ones would be great! Chairs are optional but even an eclectic mix could be placed around the walls of the room for people who need to sit. Otherwise, I see this party as a mix and mingle venue, with waiters floating through the crowd and drink stations at either end of the room. We could even have some raffles set up, for fundraising of course.

Natalie nodded her head. "Yes, I can see it all now. This would be perfect!" In unison they turned on Alvin with focused intent. Alvin took an involuntary step back at their combined focus.

Nicolas chuckled, then patted Alvin's arm. "You will get used to it. The mayor has said that these two have carte-blanche to bring alive their vision. You can take their requests as commands."

Laughing, Evelyn spun on the spot, taking it all in.

"Can we see the rest of the building?" asked Nicole.

"Right this way," said Alvin.

The rest of the tour took another three hours and included the basement which revealed a treasure trove of items including vintage Christmas decor. By the time Alvin locked the doors, the sun was low on the horizon and they were all famished. But the women were buzzing with excitement as a solid plan had formed and Alvin was sent packing with a long email waiting for him of what they needed, to prepare for the campaign.

It was with grateful sighs that they all climbed back into the BMW and headed back to the manor.

Decorations For Two

The next morning dawned to the sound of sleet pinging off the window. The sound woke Evelyn and she sat up, surprised to see that it was already light outside. Knowing that she had a lot to accomplish and that the calendar was counting down, she sprang out of bed and rushed into the shower, then dressed in a cozy grey sweater and leggings patterned with snowflakes and candy canes. She tied her long hair back with a red ribbon and headed downstairs.

Georges was bustling around in the foyer, with a hand cart loaded with boxes. As she came downstairs, the top one tilted suddenly and began to fall. Evelyn jumped the last step and threw a steadying hand against the side of the errant box. "Whew, that was a close one!" she exclaimed, peering around the stack at Georges. "What do you have inside these boxes?"

"Oh, bonjour mademoiselle! Merci. Your assistance is appreciated." He released the handles of the cart. "These boxes are more Christmas decorations. Nicolas requested that I bring them up from the basement. There are quite a few."

"Why don't I help you?"

"You do not need to dirty yourself with this work. Breakfast is waiting for you in the dining room. It will get cold."

"Nonsense. It will only take a few moments for me to give you a hand." Evelyn stood up straight then swept her hand to one side. "Lead the way, good sir."

Georges gave her a grateful smile, then tugged the cart from beneath the stack of boxes and led the way to the stairs that led to the basement level. Several trips later, the boxes had been delivered to the foyer. As the last box was unloaded from the cart, Natalie appeared, walking down the stairs.

"What are all these? It reminds me of the scene in "The Santa Clause" when Scott Calvin receives his naughty and nice lists." She smirked. "I bet Nicolas would love that."

Evelyn laughed. "I bet he would. But it's nothing so dramatic. These are extra decorations. I think we can find some great things here to use at both the Christmas village and at the factory."

Natalie whistled. "These are a lot of boxes. It will take a full day to sort and go through things."

"Exactly. Which is why you are off of baking duty. Divide and conquer. While you are sorting and planning here, I will help Marie-Claire in Mrs. Claus' test kitchen."

Natalie nodded, grinning. "I think that's an excellent idea. But first, breakfast."

They wolfed down a plate of blueberry pancakes and maple syrup. Just as they were finishing up, Marie-Claire entered the room. She was rosy cheeked and sporting an apron sporting an elf costume, so that she looked like she was wearing one herself. "There you two are. Nicolas wanted me to let you know that he has work to do this morning and so he will be shut away in his office until after 11:00 am, but then he will be free to help you bring the decorations over to the

Christmas Village and the factory. Once you have them sorted, he will take care of the transportation."

"Natalie will be doing the sorting. I am helping you with the baking," said Evelyn.

"Well come on in when you are finished eating. I have the first batch of sugar cookies prepped and ready to go into the oven." Marie-Claire bustled out of the room, and the girls took one last sip of coffee then parted to concentrate on their designated tasks.

Evelyn was blasted with warmth as she pushed open the double swinging door. The scent of warm spices filled the air. Cinnamon, cloves and nutmeg mixed with the smell of cooking berries, and dominating over it all was the smell of maple. She sniffed appreciatively, then joined Marie-Claire at her side, peering down at the open recipe. Marie-Claire tapped the page and said, "This was one of Madeline's favourites. She thought maple and blueberries were a match made in heaven. Of course she gathered it all from the acreage here. 'Maple Blueberry Fudge' topped the page along with a long list of instructions. "I'd like you to tackle this recipe while I finish off her sugar cookies.

On the table top were three silicone baking sheets filled with cookies shaped like Santa, reindeer, and Christmas bells. The wall oven beeped announcing the correct temperature and Marie-Claire opened the oven and slid the trays inside. Setting the timer, she turned back to Evelyn, to see here standing there in bewilderment.

"What's wrong, dear?"

"I have never made fudge in my life. Isn't it fussy?" She squinted down at the recipe with trepidation.

"It's not that hard. You need to pay attention to your temperatures, that's all. Baking and candy making is a science. As long as you follow the formula, you will get the proper results. Tell you what, we can make this first batch together, so you are comfortable with the process."

Evelyn picked up the measuring cup and filled it with the correct amount of sugar then poured into a waiting saucepan. Together, they boiled and mixed and measured and within thirty minutes the first batch of fudge was cooling on the counter. "Now once this reaches room temperature, we will put it in the spare fridge to completely set. That wasn't so hard, was it? Now you try the next batch alone."

Working side by side, they soon filled the large island with multiple trays of baked goods, waiting for decoration. Evelyn had switched the blueberries for raspberries at one point a chocolate base rather than maple, so that two flavours were available. The next recipe was for hand spun candy canes. Shaking her head, she said aloud, "I don't think I have the skill to do this. You will have to show me again."

Marie-Claire looked up from the Santa hat that she was outlining with frosting. "Give me a hand with flooding the last of these sugar cookies and we can work on that together, once we finish these."

Evelyn picked up the bag of white icing and began piping snowflakes down the front of Santa's jacket and along the top of his boots. Marie-Claire looked over at the younger woman and said in what was meant to be a casual tone, "You and Nicolas seem to be getting along much better."

Evelyn looked up from her work and gave the older woman a small smile. "We certainly got off on the wrong foot. Did he tell you he came to the SocialBuzz awards ceremony and was seated right beside me."

Marie-Claire returned the smile with one of her own and her eyes twinkled. "Oh yes, he told me all about the pompous young woman who won the awards ceremony and how he walked out before he spoke to you because he couldn't stand the idea of hiring an air head for a corporate gig, regardless of the "number of followers" she had.

Marie-Claire sketched air quotes with her fingers, then laughed. "Well naturally, that got me curious. Anyone with the ability to get under his skin that quickly, and female also, well that was someone I needed to check out. He never lets people get to him, and especially not women."

Evelyn gazed wide eyed at her. "So that's why you hired me? Because Nicolas had a bad reaction to me?"

Marie-Claire mock frowned at her. "Of couse not. The reason I hired you was because you were obviously the best person for the job. Your credentials ae impeccable. The reason you are staying here is because of Nicolas' reaction." She winked at Evelyn. "I thought it would be interesting to see how you two reacted to each other if forced into each other's company and actually got to know each other. And it doesn't hurt that you are a beautiful young woman."

Evelyn digested this with a bit of sour stomach. There was no question that she was attracted to the grumpy bachelor, but did he feel the same? She didn't know. Was there a way to find out? She stared at the cookie in front of her, not seeing anything. A blob of icing dripped from the end and fell with a plop right on top of Rudolph's head.

"Are you all right dear?" said Marie-Claire.

Evelyn jerked back the present with a start. "Oh, I'm sorry," and started trying to wipe off the blob.

"I think you should go check on Natalie. It's nearly 11:00 am. She might need some input on the decoration sorting. Come back after they leave and you can help me clean up. I will finish off here."

Evelyn nodded, then pulled the apron off over her head and placed it on a hook. "Good idea. I will be back shortly." She hurried out of the kitchen, suddenly eager to be away from the cookies and confusion over Nicolas.

In the foyer she found Natalie happily chatting with Nicolas about the sorting. Natalie looked up as she heard her friend enter. "There you are, Evelyn. I have finished dividing everything up and Nicolas is going to have Alvin come out and pick up the ones that are destined for the factory. I was thinking I might hitch a a ride with him and stay overnight in town. I want to do some Christmas shopping tonight. So no need to worry about me. I will go over to the factory in the morning and begin doing some set up. Alvin has a team of ten people coming to assist with cleaning and setting up the main hall."

"That's an excellent idea," said Evelyn, "I'm glad that Alvin was able to come through so quickly with some help."

"That leaves you and me to take this bunch of boxes over," said Nicolas, gesturing to a stack of about twenty boxes to the right of the door. "If you can spare some time later, we can do some unpacking. As soon as Alvin arrives, I will help him load up the truck and then start taking this lot over to the village." He looked outside and frowned. "The weather is worsening. Hopefully he gets here soon."

At that moment they heard a horn, and opened the door to see a cargo van with the Village of Noelville logo on the side of the sliding doors. Alvin got out of the car and walked around to the back, opening both sets of doors wide.

"I will leave you to load up and go finish off in the kitchen." She gave Natalie a quick squeeze. "Have fun!" she teased, then returned to the kitchen, in time to see Marie-Claire reloading the icing bags for the final tray of decorating.

Looking up she said, "I've got the decorating of these. If you want to clean up, we can wrap this up in about 30 minutes." Evelyn loaded the dishwasher and washed the larger pots, then wiped down the countertops. It took less time than she figured and once everything was back in order again, she excused herself and returned to the foyer. It was empty and felt strangely forlorn without the bustle and busy work of sorting the boxes. She took three steps towards the library, wondering if Nicolas was inside, when the front door opened to a blast of wind driven snow. Nicolas entered, stamping his feet and spying Evelyn said, "The storm is worsening. Pack an overnight bag. We can stay in the village and get some work done, rather than trying to return here."

Evelyn paused. "Really? Where is there to sleep?" The thought of sharing a room with Nicolas made her shiver and her heart race.

He grinned, as though reading her thoughts. "The Sugar Plum bakery has two lofts and I took the liberty of blowing up some inflatable mattresses we kept there for emergencies. I have the woodstove going. We will be perfectly fine. Now go and pack an overnight bag, while I have Georges prepare some food."

Evelyn smiled back and ran up the stairs, suddenly eager to get out of the manor. By the time she had returned with an overnight bag in hand, Nicolas was ready, a large picnic style hamper in each hand. Seeing her surprise at the food hampers, he rolled his eyes. "Georges seems to think we might get snowed in and need extra provisions. I humour him. I learned long ago that it's useless to argue. He will see you fed whether you want food or not. Come, the car is warm."

Evelyn opened the door then followed him out into the storm.

Sugar Plum Noel

The trip to the little Christmas village was slower than she had anticipated. The snow was at least a foot deep in spots and even though he had switched to his four-wheel drive truck, the snow was greasy, which made it hazardous to drive down the narrow lane to the barn. The fact that it was a steep descent didn't help matters. But they made it safely following Nicolas' former tracks and eventually they were backing up to the door of the little bakery. Bright lights shone through the window panes and she could see the flickering light cast by the burning logs in the woodstove.

It looked cozy and inviting. Even a little romantic. She smiled and got out of the truck, grabbing one of the baskets and her overnight gear and then following Nicolas into the bakery.

They had only spent a few minutes in this cabin the other day, and now with all the lanterns lit, it felt a lot bigger than she'd initially thought. The woodstove was located in the corner of the room, with a comfortable couch and a couple of wing chairs positioned to keep its occupants facing the warmth. A hand braided rug in reds and greens decorated the floor.

To the right of the stove, a hand made ladder leaned against the upper story where she could see the loft area. The heat from the woodstove would rise and keep the upper area toasty warm even on a snowy night like tonight. Down below was the bakery kitchen with another woodstove for cooking (this one was also lit and providing warmth) complete with cast iron cookware and kettle. An old-fashioned cooler stood at the back of the room, the kind that accepted a block of ice to cool the interior. There was no lack of ice at the moment and when she opened the door, it was pleasantly cool inside, perfect for cold storage. So far, they were not lacking in the least. Electricity was available if they needed it but Evelyn thought it was perfect just the way it was.

The boxes of decorations were piled in the center of the room, waiting their attention. Evelyn looked outside and guessed they had about two hours before dark, judging by the quality of the light.

She looked around then asked the obvious question. "Do we need to gather any more firewood before dark?"

Nicolas shook his head. "No, there is wood stacked out the back, and there is a storage bin with access from inside. We just have to lift the bin and pull out what we need, See?" He walked over to what she had thought was a storage container and lifted the lid. Inside were neatly stacked, split firewood. He put the lid back down and arranged the cushions which doubled as seating for a small eating area.

"Ingenious. This is really wonderful, you know. Your parents thought of everything."

"Pretty much. This was their pride and joy. They wanted an authentic Christmas village that ran on love and Christmas miracles. No pollution from civilization. A totally off grid experience." He picked up a hamper and started unloading it. "Are you hungry? There are sandwiches in here and a plate of devilled eggs, a charcuterie board with cheeses and sliced meats, and a pickle tray with sweet and savory options. Oh, and also a couple bottles of wine and glasses." He put the items on the table top along with a wine opener.

"I'd love a glass of wine and the charcuterie is calling to me," said Evelyn. "It's been years since I have had devilled eggs. Yum!"

Nicolas chuckled. He uncorked the wine and poured two glasses, then handed one to Evelyn. "A toast. To a successful campaign and an end to homelessness everywhere."

"To success." They clinked glasses and Evelyn took a sip. The wine was cool and fruity and delicious. She popped a devilled egg into her mouth then wandered over the first box of decorations and opened it. Inside were Christmas lights in various shapes and sizes, for outdoor use. They would look great once strung up outside. A project for tomorrow. She put the box aside and moved on to the second one.

Over the course of the next two hours, they gathered a game plan for the following day, sorting the contents into which building they would look best. In the last four boxes were Christmas trees, one for each building. She chose the white frosted tree to put up in the bakery, and the purple and pink ornaments, pure white lights and the bird feathers. "It looks like we can put up this tree this evening," She smiled happily. "I love Christmas trees. They bring the holidays to life, for me."

"Well, if we are going to 'deck the halls' and 'rock around the Christmas tree' we might as well have some music." Nicolas walked over to what Evelyn had at first taken to be a tall storage container of some sort, but antique. Nicolas lifted the lid and there sat an old-fashioned Victrola, complete with a wind-up handle. Evelyn's jaw dropped and she moved over to stand beside it. "I have only ever seen one of these in the black and white movies. Does it work?" Fascinated, she ran a hand over the polished wood surface, then touched the huge horn that acted as a speaker.

For an answer, Nicolas opened a cleverly concealed door at the bottom and selected an album, then placed the record on the turn table. He cranked the handle, setting the turn table spinning and then placed the needle on the edge. A slight click was heard as the needle made contact, and then the rich, dulcet tones of Frank Sinatra filled the air. "I'm dreaming of a white Christmas..." floated into the air.

"Oh, this is perfect! Come on!" She grabbed Nicolas' hand and dragged him over to the parts of the tree and began assembling the parts until the tree stood ready for decorating. They worked in a companionable silence for a while, humming away to the various songs, which turned out to be a collection of Christmas songs that were popular in that era. When the record came to an end Nicolas flipped it over to side B and refilled their wine glasses.

"Thank you," said Evelyn, accepting her refreshed glass. "I have been thinking about the other buildings. I think the sugar shack should have a real tree. It won't be maple, obviously, but I think it needs a real tree, given its purpose. What do you think?"

"It won't take long to cut one down and bring it in. We can leave that one to last," said Nicolas.

She nodded. "Yes, we have a full day already for sure. I want to do some more filming tomorrow, too—a couple of quick live streams showing us decorating, but not a picture of the entire village, you know what I mean? Some short, teaser shots that will give our followers something to buzz about, and get them talking about the campaign and sharing it with their friends. Do you have any suggestions on what to film? Or what you would like to see highlighted?"

"Me? No, I avoid the spotlight as much as I can. I have never liked it. I will leave that social media stuff to you."

"That's strange coming from someone who dresses up in a red suit and plays Santa Claus every year. You, shy of the camera?"

"That's different. Because I am dressed up, I can pretend no one knows it is me. And it's not my real life. That, I like to keep private."

"Hmmmm. Well, I can see how that is working out for you," she grinned teasingly. She picked up the last bulb and placed it on the tree. "I'm famished. Let's grab that charcuterie board and bring it over to the coffee table and relax a bit." She glanced outside, surprised to see that it was already dark. An involuntary yawn escaped her lips. "This day has flown by. I'm ready to relax."

She picked up the tray and carried it over, setting it down then sinking into the couch with a grateful sigh. The sound of a cork popping announced that Nicolas had opened the second bottle of wine, and he carried fresh glasses over to the table and sat down beside Evelyn. They ate and drank in companionable silence for a while and then Nicolas got up and refilled the woodstove, topping up the logs. Once he was finished, he grabbed a blanket from the blanket stand and brought it over to Evelyn, who accepted it gratefully.

Settling back against the sofa, she sighed contentedly and said "So tell me, how does the most eligible bachelor in Vancouver end up not on the married list as of yet? I would have thought someone would have snagged you a while ago. According to the gossips, you have a least three young beauties vying for your affections. And two of them have been on that reality show, "The—"

Nicolas cut her off with a finger to her lips. Where they touched, her lips burned, instantly silencing her. "I don't want to talk about those girls. They are frivolous and attention seeking, and way too much work. Not my type at all."

"But you date them? Why bother if they are not your type?"

"Because it keeps the others away, ones that would really try to dig their claws into me." He waved a hand at the cabin around them. "I am the sole heir to this property and it is not the only holding we have. If I am honest, I do not need to work. Much like you, I work to try to better my community and my city."

"Oh, I need to work," grumbled Evelyn under her breath.

"You know what I mean. I do not want to date a woman who is attracted to me for my wealth. I want them to see me as I am, and not as a bank account. So, the fancy socialites are a kind of shield. I use them and they use me. It works."

"Including the one that was on your arm at the SocialBuzz awards? Sabine Perdue? She seemed very intent on keeping your attention on her. My guess is she would like something more."

"Do I hear a hint of jealousy in your tone?" mocked Nicolas.

"Jealous? Of what?" shot back Evelyn, then ruined the effect with a crocodile sized yawn. "Is there any tea available? I think I've had enough wine for one evening."

"I believe Georges sent some along. I will go make you a cup."

"Thank you," she said with another huge yawn.

Nicolas got up and busied himself with putting water in the iron kettle and setting it on top of the cookstove, then took the opportunity to load more wood into it. While the water was warming, he wandered back over to the Vitrola, gave it another few cranks and then changed the album to an early rendition of the Nutcracker. As the mellow tones of the ballet filled the air, he returned to the kettle and fixed two cups of tea, then carried them back to the couch.

Evelyn had slid sideways on the couch and was dead to the world, gently snoring. Her long fall of hair partly hid her face and she hugged the blanket to her chest. Smiling slightly, he removed her shoes and then gathered another blanket and placed it over her, then picked up the second cup of tea, climbed the ladder to the loft, and went to bed.

Grinched

E velyn blinked. Then blinked again. Disoriented, she sat up. Recognition flooded her mind along with the delicious smell of eggs and bacon. She stretched, pushing the covers off and slipped her feet into her boots, then stood up and followed the wonderful aroma that had woken her.

Nicolas looked up from where he was stirring scrambled eggs in a cast iron pan. Beside it, bacon sizzled and popped, and judging by its colour, it was ready. Nicolas took in her appearance and smiled. "Sleep well? I thought the smell of bacon might wake you better than me leaning over you and shaking your shoulder."

Evelyn smoothed her hair. *I must look like a wreck*, she thought. She yawned again.

Seeming to read her thoughts, Nicolas said, "You look great, don't worry. There is coffee in the percolator over there," he gestured with his head. "Help yourself while I finish off these eggs."

"Thank you. This is very kind." Evelyn grabbed a clean mug and filled her cup, adding a teaspoon of sugar and some cream from the ice box. "Would you like a refill?"

"That would be great." He pulled the pan of eggs from the hot plate and divided them between two plates, added bacon and butter toast and then carried them over to the coffee table and set them down. Evelyn followed with the cups of coffee and then went back for utensils.

"How long have you been awake?" she asked, digging into the eggs. They were surprisingly good.

"Oh, about an hour or so. Long enough to restock the woodstoves and make some breakfast. And take a quick shower." At her look of surprise, he chuckled. "There is a heat on demand hot water tank that supplies the sink and also a shower spigot in the bathroom. Yes, you can have a hot shower. As long as there is propane."

"Oh good!" Evelyn smiled. "I am one of those who does not fully wake until they have showered." Picking up the last piece of bacon in her right hand, she stood up and gathered her overnight bag. "I will go take that shower now, so we can get started."

Fifteen minutes later, she was back, dressed warmly in a wool pullover sweater over a long-sleeved shirt, fleece lined leggings and thick woolen socks. Her hair hung loose, curling naturally around her chin and down her back. "I brought my toque to keep my ears warm, and gloves that have those touch features built in so I don't have to take them off to film." She held them out for his inspection then looked around. He had already cleaned up the dishes and they sat drying in the dish rack. The countertop was clean and everything in order. "I never knew you were so domestic. You don't look the type," she said, without thinking.

Nicolas quirked his eyebrow, causing Evelyn to grin, then blush. "And what kind of type do I look like?" he said in a teasing, low voice.

"Oh... you know. The playboy type, that runs from one woman to the next, never settling down. A heartbreaker."

"I prefer to think of it as playing the field. Finding the correct mate shouldn't be trial and error. It should be a careful selection. I prefer to not make mistakes where love is involved."

Evelyn blushed again under his intent gaze. She hoped he would put it down to the warmth of the cabin and her heavy clothing. Grabbing her jacket, she put it on and said, "Time to get started! I will take this box," and picked up the one closest to her and headed for the door. Nicolas opened it for her then propped the door open with a log. He grabbed a second box and they carried them outside, and went back for more.

As Nicolas went back inside for his third box, Evelyn pulled her phone out and began doing some test shots of their surroundings, looking for the perfect back drop to frame their activities. She zoomed out on the sugar shack and pressed record, speaking aloud as she filmed. "It's set up day at the Jollie-Saint Christmas Village. A perfect day to decorate the village in preparation for our next viral Christmas fundraiser for the homeless. Santa's elves are busy inside with their various chores and naturally camera shy until the big day." She panned sideways taking in the path to the river and on to the bridge. "Rumour has it that Santa's sleigh will join the annual parade and we have inside intel that says it will make a secret journey along this very path before joining the parade in three days time. Needless to say, we are keeping an eye on this secretive trail, in hopes of spying St. Nicolas before he begins his annual journey around the world on Christmas Eve."

She panned back towards the sugar shack, and at that moment Nicolas walked through the back of the shot, carrying a live Christmas tree that he had evidently just cut down. He was dragging it by its trunk and waved at Evelyn, "I found the perfect tree!" and then continued on into the Sugar Shack, shouldering the door open and leaving it ajar. Evelyn zoomed in on the doorway, to show Nicolas busy setting up the tree in a tree stand.

"Let's go see what Santa's helper is up to, shall we?" and walked forward, still filming. At the door she paused to pan across the room, and then focused on Nicolas as he stood the tree up and balanced it, tightening the screws at the base. The camera was very pleased with Nicolas, capturing his fine, muscular attributes in a spectacular fashion as he straightened the tree. "Is this where you want the tree, Evelyn? Or do you prefer it over that way a bit more?" he said into the camera, as if prompted.

"I think it is perfect right where it is." Evelyn backed out of the doorway and then in a bright voice said, "This is Evelyn Christmas, counting down the days until Christmas. Stay tuned, as we stream live updates of the decorating of the Christmas Village fundraiser. You can watch it come alive before your very eyes! Remember your hashtags and share that Christmas spirit! The donation link is open. Happy decorating!"

Evelyn hit pause, reviewed the video and added music in the form of an instrumental jingle bells tune, added all the usual hashtags then hit upload to make the video live.

Smiling, she joined Nicolas inside the Sugar Shack, and together they began decorating the live tree. The wonderful scents of spruce blended with the maple scent embedded in the walls after decades of maple syrup making. Now that the woodstove had warmed the space, other scents joined in, woodsmoke and something that smelled like sandalwood. Evelyn pulled out a red garland strand and wound it around the tree, tucking it into place, humming jingle bells in a sweet soprano. Nicolas handed her the next strand and then wound it around the higher branches, the ones out of Evelyn's reach.

"You know, I never liked decorating the trees," said Nicolas. "Maybe it was my age. I found it hot, boring and a lot of work. I just wanted to go outside and build snowmen with my friends."

Evelyn considered his words and a shaggy, blonde haired little boy jumped into her mind's eye. She smiled at the vision. "Do you have any pictures of you at that age?"

"There should be a family ornament or two in here somewhere, unless my grand-mere has them stashed away somewhere. Let me look." He opened a third box full of ornaments and fished around in the interior for a bit, then pulled out a golden glass ball that had been faceted to catch the light, and in the center was room for a small portrait. He handed it to Evelyn, grinning. "I remember that photo. It was the year I decided to cut my own hair, because I wanted to look like a rock star."

Evelyn laughed, taking the ornament from him and peering at the proud face in the photo. She hung it on a sturdy branch where it was sure to be safe. "I think we should string the lights next, and then move to the ornaments." They wound the lights around the tree, tucking them in place then to make sure they were all working, plugged them into the outlet that was fed by the generator. The tree exploded with colourful lights, bringing a smile to Evelyn's face. The moved quickly through the rest of the ornaments, knowing that they needed to get outside and hang more lights before the daylight faded.

They pulled on their gloves and went outside. Nicolas had discovered a ladder in the Sleigh Barn and went to fetch it, while Evelyn untangled the light strands, straightening them out to be handed up easily to Nicolas on the top of the ladder. She could see him coming down the hillside, ladder carried on his back like a fireman. Just before he reached them, Evelyn's phone rang. Looking down at the call display, she saw that it was Natalie and quickly connected the call and put her on speaker.

"Hey there!" said Natalie in an excited voice. "Did you upload a video a hour or so ago?"

"Yeah, it was just a quick intro to the village. Why? What's up?"

Nicolas put the ladder down and started untying the rope that wound through the rungs, keeping it a compact size for carrying.

"Well girlfriend, the video is going viral again, that's what. Its already had 200,000 views in a hour," she squealed.

"What? Why? How? It wasn't that interesting. It was pretty basic really." Evelyn looked over at Nicolas and shrugged. He had paused is activities as their excited chatter caught his attention.

"Well, it seems your handsome Mr. Claus has caught the eye of your Vancouver fandom. They have started shipping the pair of you. As in matchmaking, kissy-kissy, shipped into an item. It seems that they recognized your leading man there. Check out the hashtag they have been reposting under: #SnowQueenAndGrinch"

"What?" said Evelyn, genuinely shocked. "How could they say that? Nicolas is not a—"

"Oh I know how," said Nicolas with a sneer, his voice full of anger. Evelyn looked up and took an involuntary couple of steps backwards as Nicolas towered over her, suddenly very tall and menacing. "What an idiot I have been. Taken in by a pretty face and a pair of lovely eyes. But you socialites are all the same, aren't you? Always on the look out for the next photo opportunity, for the next Socialbuzz moment where you can exploit the circumstances to your own benefit. I should have seen through it. You are manipulating me."

"Nicolas, no! No, I haven't been doing anything of the sort. I swear!" pleaded Evelyn, eyes bulging with hurt.

"You swear on what? Your fans? Your friends? Your dead mother? And what was she, other than a drug addict? No, Evelyn, you cannot swear on anything I would believe. You have been playing me, using me, using this—" he gestured at the village, "to gain what you needed. An audience. You have used my feelings and my family in the most disgusting way possible. You have pimped us to the world. All of this has been to gain followers and views. It was never about us or our community. I will not be a part of it," he snarled, taking her arm roughly and giving her a shake. Evelyn's teeth rattled, she was so shocked. ""This is exactly why I hate all this Christmas nonsense - it's all performance, all fake! Go home, Evelyn. This is over."

Nicolas spun around and strode over to the pickup truck with a furious stride and climbed in behind the wheel. He started it up and stomped on the accelerator, then to a spray of snow, drove out of the village and away from the Village... away from Evelyn... away from love.

Alone Again

"Evelyn? Evelyn are you there? Say something. Evelyn?"

Evelyn stared at the angry red tail lights of the departing pickup truck, with a stunned, frozen expression. Her phone was forgotten in her hand and she didn't hear a word of Natalie's urgent squawks, so overwhelming were her feelings of grief and shock. Hot tears slid down her cold cheeks but she noticed them no more than she did the rising pitch of panic in the shouts that issued from her frantic friend, left hanging in silence over the open phone connection.

"Evelyn Christmas, snap out of it and answer me THIS MINUTE, or I am calling the police!" Natalie screamed into the phone.

At the word "police" brought Evelyn out of her frozen panic and glanced down at the phone. "Natalie," she gasped in a broken voice, "Did you hear all of that?"

"I certainly did! I'm so sorry Evelyn, I didn't mean to blow up the situation there. I didn't know he was there right beside you. Why did you put me on speaker?"

"I thought it would be some good news about the factory. I thought to share it with him. And now look what I have done," she sobbed. "I've ruined everything."

"This isn't your fault, Evelyn. If anything, it is mine. I will call him and apologize. He can blame me—"

"No. Do not call him. He needs his space right now. He drove away."

"He left you there alone? What a jerk. You don't just abandon a woman in the depths of winter in the middle of nowhere!"

"It's not like that and you know it. I could walk back to the manor. It's not even as far as it is to my normal bus stop in Vancouver. And besides, I think... no, I know I am going to stay here another night." Her tears dried as she focused on the plan forming in her mind.

"You stayed there last night? Together?"

"Yeah, and it's not like that. He was the perfect gentleman. There are enough provisions and the woodstoves are already going. I am going to stay and continue to decorate. Georges sent enough food to keep me for a week. I even have running water. I will be fine. Besides, I just thought of something I want to do tomorrow. So yeah. I am staying put."

"Alright, you are the boss. You sure you don't want any company? Are you ok?"

"Yeah...yeah I am ok. I think I need time to think, too. Stay in town another night if you need to. No need to rush back now."

"Good plan. Alvin brought some fabulous finds over to the factory. Regardless of what the Grinch there decides, we still have a gala to through and that is not within his ability to cancel. That is Town of Noelville turf and he can't derail that."

"He's not a Grinch, Natalie. He's just...lost."

"Yeah, yeah. I get it. You are soft on him."

"Yeah... I think I am."

"Go and decorate. Sign into my Spotify and crank up my holiday mix. I will check in with you, in the morning."

"Thanks Nat. I am not sure what I would do without out you."

"Right back-atcha, girl. Be good."

"Bye."

"Bye."

The line disconnected and Evelyn pocketed her phone.

Wandering back to the Sugar Plum, she pondered his words. What *was* her motivation? Was she being as pure of heart as she thought? Or had she been using him and his family to gain followers? As a social influencer, it was the way of her kind. But she thought she was better than that. She'd never set out to be in the limelight. It was all an act for the cameras and her clients, to help them with their causes. That is what motivated her. *Are you sure?* a small, inner voice mocked. *So why did you film him without his permission?* Guilt reddened her cheeks, and for the first time she noticed the chill on her cheeks from her drying tears. She went inside and set the kettle to boiling, making herself a cup of tea, then carried it over to the couch and sat, sipping the tea and thinking.

What could she do to make it up to him? She looked around the cozy cabin and thought about his childhood that was cut short, and the bitterness of loss— lost time, lost familial connections, lost memories. Maybe she could make it up to him, by finishing was his parents had meant the village to be to this family. She glanced at her watch. It was just before 11:00 am. She would finish her tea, and get back to work, but with a different focus than she had had even a few hours ago.

It was time to make a Christmas miracle happen. And she knew just how to do it.

The one shop they hadn't really focused on was Santa's Toy Shoppe, arguably one of the most important structures in the village from a Christmas perspective. Evelyn pushed open the heavy door, her arms laden with logs for the woodstove. Three trips had brought in enough to keep the stove working all night and that was a good thing, because the cabin needed a thorough cleaning before she could even begin set up. She also needed to inventory, see what was actually here, so she could send Natalie shopping, armed with a long list to purchase.

Her phone pinged and she looked at the text message. It was from Natalie. "Views up to just shy of 400,000 now. I'm handling the replies and interactions. You do your thing. Spotify Play List!" followed by a Mrs. Claus emoji and a pair of bright red lips and a link to her playlist. Evelyn rolled her eyes, then tapped the link and hit play.

The list was full of male crooners from the 1930's to 1960's. She had to admit, the voices were comforting and warm, something she needed right now. She didn't look too closely into the reason, and instead just let the music flow around her like a warm hug, then got to work.

The woodstove took a few tries to get the damper draw correct, but after a few tries, she had a nice, warm fire going, then set to work. She put a metal pot on top of the woodstove, warming some snow from outside into melt water, and once it was warm, started washing the surfaces and cleaning the floor. She found some tallow soap in a cupboard which helped tremendously with the layers of dirt on the wooden surfaces. An hour later, she had the toy shoppe cleaned and an inventory list prepared. She sorted all the supplies into their proper location in the storage cubicles build into one wall.

Basically, she had all the parts to build a wooden train set made out of maple that likely had been harvested right here, during the building of the village. The engine was designed to look like an old-fashioned steam engine and was to be painted black and red. there were eight variations of wooden train cars with instructions for each. There was even a circus car with a whole in the top for a giraffe to stand tall. What she was missing was paint and glue, two items she located but long past being able to be used. Those went on the list to Natalie, with the quantities of each, plus brushes in various sizes. The other toy that the shoppe was set up to produce, was a maple rocking horse. Again, all the pieces were available for the production, but she was missing paint and maple stain and sealer. Also yarn for the horse hair. That also went on the list.

Standing back, she arched her back and viewed her progress. It was set up as a functional shop now with all the tools at the ready, cleaned and sharpened and ready for use. Satisfied with her work, she opened the decorations she had set aside for this building and got to work. An hour later, Santa's Toy Shoppe had come to life and was ready for his elves' arrival. She glanced at her phone, checking the time. It was about a hour before dark, and she was suddenly famished.

Retracing her steps back to the Sugar Plum Bakery, she checked the ice box and found an assortment of savory pastries. Selecting two of them, she set them on some tin foil on top of the cooktop and then added a fresh log to the fire box and also another one to the woodstove. She filled the kettle once more and set it on a burner plate beside the warming pastries, then sat down on the couch and called Marie-Claire. She answered at once, with a pleasant "Hello, Evelyn, what can I do for you?" Evelyn could hear the sounds of voices and realized the mayor must be at work.

"I am planning to stay overnight at the Sugar Plum in the Christmas village for an extra night. I have some more set up I am planning to do. I didn't want you to be worried, hence my call."

"Oh no worries, my dear. The cabins are cosy this time of year. Is Nicolas staying too?"

Evelyn swallowed the lump in her throat. "No...no he had some work to do and went back to the manor. I am fine here, do not worry."

"Ok, I can have Georges stop by with anything you need. Is there a message I can pass along?"

"No...wait, yes there is. Could you have him bring me coffee and doughnuts for one hundred people in the morning?"

"To the Sugar Plum?"

"Yes, that's all I need."

"If you say so, dear. I will send him over around 8:30am? Will that be early enough?"

"Oh yes, that will be everything. Thank you so much."

"Happy decorating, dear." Marie-Claire hung up the phone.

Next, Evelyn sent a text message to Natalie, asking her to pick up the supplies on the list and meet her in the park by the factory between 9:00 – 10:00 am. She received a thumbs up by return text.

The kettle whistled and Evelyn got up to make tea, then put a couple of piping hot pastries on a plate and carried it back to the couch. There was no internet in the cabin but there was excellent cell signal, so she settled down with her phone and turned on her hotspot, then fired up her tablet and settled in to get some work done.

She paused for a moment, then turned the camera on herself and began to talk, walking around the cabin and speaking of its history, the history of the village and the founding family. She had found some family photos on the walls and took still shots of those to be worked into the monologue. She had an idea for a Christmas present for him, one that only she could create. Once she was finished and satisfied with the results, she saved it and sat back with a sigh.

Regardless of Mr. Jollie-Saint's opinions of her, she had work to do. Pushing thoughts of his grumpy face and her growing feelings for the man out of her head, she opened the Vancouver campaign folder and got to work.

A Surprise Visitor

The morning dawned still and clear, with a crisp, fresh scent that put Nicolas in mind of his last trip to Whistler, skiing. It was as close as he could get to being home when living in a massive metro area of over 2.6 million people. He needed those escapes, to feel grounded. If he was honest with himself, he was not a big city person.

Yet the ghosts of the past that visited every Christmas season had kept him from returning to Quebec, as much as he loved his ancestral home.

This morning, he ate a solitary breakfast in the dining room. Georges had placed the food on the table, then left mumbling something about having to make a delivery, and rushed from the house. His grandmother had also left early, on some mission of her own. She was always assisting this charity or that fundraiser, and early morning appearances went hand in hand with being Mayor around Christmas. Come to think of it, this might be the morning of her television spot at the Quebec City television station, when she formally announced the upcoming fundraiser for the homeless initiative. He knew that this event was near and dear to her heart. She was driven to find a solution to all of this messy history, and put it to rest once and for all. Unfortunately, she had pinned all her hopes on Ms. Christmas.

Evelyn Christmas. She was a mystery wrapped up in an enigma. She had more layers than a mille-feuille. Sweet and delicate and yes, she was luscious. But there in lay the problem. Such women were never to be trusted. Her deception yesterday was a disaster just waiting to happen. And it did.

He was glad she had stayed at the village. He couldn't have handled facing her again so soon. He needed to rein in his feelings. Put up his barriers. Perfect the grumpy mask once again. It had served him well over the years. It was the only way to continue on.

At that moment the front door bell rang. Surprised, he lifted his head, wondering who it would be. He waited. The doorbell rang again. Cursing, he realized that Georges was not there to answer the door. He got up and made his way to the foyer then opened it. On the doorstep stood Sabine Perdue, decked out in an over-the-top faux fox fur, delicate white ear muffs and high heeled leather boots. The taxi driver lifted her luggage from the boot of the taxi and then hauled it up to the door, then walked back down to the car and drove away.

"Well don't just stand there like a frozen nutcracker! It's cold outside!" She smiled up into his face with rosy red lips, and stepped past him into the foyer. Nicolas automatically moved aside and then reached for her bags and brought them inside, closing the door behind him with one foot. Sabine stood in the entrance, looking around like an art dealer sizing up the value of a collection. He could also see the dollar signs flashing behind her sea green eyes.

"Sabine. This is a surprise. What are you doing here?"

"I came to visit you, silly! It is the holidays after all. Filming wrapped up yesterday and I just had to get away from the dreary weather in Vancouver. I thought about going to a hot spot, like Aruba, but I decided it would be nice to visit you in your family home, and meet your lovely grandmother. Is she here?" Sabine peered around, looking to see if she could spot the woman.

"No, she is at work."

Sabine pulled her Channel gloves off of her perfectly manicured hands and handed them to Nicolas, while she shrugged out of her coat. "Well, that is a pity. Where is your butler? I need to hang up my coat."

"He is out on an errand. He will be back shortly. Let me take that for you," Nicolas said, taking the coat from Sabine and hanging it up in a coat closet tucked away under the staircase. "Leave your bags. He will take care of them when he gets back. Come, have a seat in the library. Would you like a cup of coffee? Hot cocoa?"

"Coffee please. Black. I can't afford those extra calories, even at Christmas." She ran a hand down her designer jacket and hip hugging pencil skirt as though to emphasize her slimness.

Nicolas saw her seated then went to fetch a carafe of coffee and a pitcher of milk and some sugar cookies. When he returned to the library, he saw that Sabine was examining the pile of surveys from his and Evelyn's survey of the homeless. That morning seemed ages ago now. Seeing her touch the papers made him feel uneasy. He couldn't explain why, but it just felt wrong.

"What are these?" she asked, flipping through the responses.

"My grandmother is mayor of Noelville. She has commissioned Evelyn Christmas to conduct a campaign similar to the one in Vancouver, as a fundraiser for the mayor's homeless initiative."

"Don't tell me that woman is here too? Oh well, she won't interfere with our plans. Do tell me about the social events calendar. They do have parties at Christmas time here? I hear Quebec City is quaint. But I imagine Montreal is where the real fun happens."

"I wouldn't know," said Nicolas, his face unreadable. I left Noelville long ago, for Vancouver."

"Well, I will put out some calls. My manager will know all about the local elite and what parties are the best to get an invite to. They always make room for a star, you know." She poured herself a cup of black coffee and took a sip. "Don't you worry, I will have our activities calendar sorted in no time, darling." She put he papers down and returned to the comfort of the overstuff sofa.

Nicolas heard the front door open and then footsteps approached the library. Georges opened the door, still removing the scarf he had wrapped around his neck. "My apologies Nicolas, for not being here to greet your guest. Shall I make up a room?"

"Yes, please. This is Sabine Perdue. She will be staying with us for a few days."

"Shall I make up the room next to Ms. Christmas and Ms. Starr?"

Nicolas gazed at the old butler, paused for a moment and then said, "Yes, that should work out fine." Georges inclined his head and said, "Sir. Miss." and left the room to attend to the arrangements.

Sabine frowned at the door as it closed. "There is another woman here?" she asked, her town displeased.

"Yes, she is Evelyn's assistant."

"It's Evelyn now, is it? You wouldn't even speak her name at the SocialBuzz event." She studied him, trying to read his expression, but he kept his face carefully neutral. In all honestly, he didn't know what emotion would show if he relaxed his face. Annoyance, surely, but at Evelyn or at Sabine? Because he knew he didn't want her here. Yet, perhaps she could serve a purpose.

"I am sure you are tired from your trip. Would you like a quick tour of the house? Georges should have your room ready by the time we are finished."

"That would be lovely," said Sabine, getting to her feet and linking her arm in his.

Santa's Elves

Evelyn dusted off her hands, then picked up the two long ropes belonging to the two toboggans she had chosen, dragged them behind her and out into the bright sunshine. An SUV was just making the curve to the barn as she exited into the sunshine. For a moment her heart leapt, thinking that Nicolas had returned, but then we remembered that Georges was to meet her at this time. Sure enough, when the door opened, it was George who appeared. Reining in her disappointment, she put on a cheery smile and walked over to meet him.

"One hundred cups of coffee in an insulated dispenser, foam cups and one hundred doughnuts as ordered, mademoiselle." He looked around curiously, noting the absense of anyone else at the village. "Are you expecting company?"

"Oh yes. This is the day I go recruiting Santa's helpers, who I hope will become his elves. Here, help me load these on these two toboggans. I have a bit of a walk ahead of me."

"I could give you a ride, miss. You don't need to walk all that way."

"I think for this first trip, it should just be me. This is my quest, you see." She smiled up at him, anticipation dancing in her eyes. "It's not everyday that you get to meet Santa's elves. Besides, Natalie will be meeting me there. I will be fine, and the exercise will be good for me."

Georges nodded, smiling. "Then good luck. Give me your phone for a moment." Evelyn fished her phone out of her pocket and handed it to Georges. He pulled up her contacts and put his private cell number in her phone. "If you need anything, just message me."

Evelyn's smile widened, and she threw her arms around him and gave him a hug. "Thank you for everything!" then picked up the ropes and started walking back down to the village. She glanced back over her shoulder and saw him waving, before he got in his car and drove away. Silence descended once again. All was silent except for the crunch of snow under her boots and the occasional scolding from a blue jay disturbed by her passing. She walked though the village, studying her handiwork. It was coming together nicely, but there was still so much to do.

Her plan had to work. Recruiting the homeless was a stroke of genius. No one would ever give them this opportunity, not in a community where they saw them as the dregs of the earth. It was a commentary on humanity, that they assigned the label of lazy to people who had no work. There were so many reasons why people became homeless, and lazy was rarely the answer. People were more complex than that. She was going to prove it, by giving these homeless souls not only employment, but shelter and three decent meals. And not a penny of it would come out of the town's coffers that was not already being spent.

She firmly believed in a hand up, not a hand out. When you help someone up, you give them dignity. Give someone dignity and they will gain the confidence to take the next step. And the next step. And the next step. Much like the steps she was taking right now.

The village dropped behind and she entered the woods, absorbing the peace of the forest in its winter slumber. Her breath fogged around her and she spied the bright flash of a male cardinal, as he hopped from branch to branch, then flew away. A few more minutes of walking and she came to the bridge that crossed the river. Built of native stone and wooden planks, the bridge ran from one bank to the other in a gentle curve, wide enough for the sleigh. The snow was undisturbed. She was the first one to cross since the snow fell. She vowed she would not be the last before year's end, and hopefully not the only one to return tonight.

With a light step and even lighter heart, she crossed the river, pulling the toboggans behind her and headed in the direction of the makeshift camp. They spied her coming long before she arrived and was greeted with hands raised in recognition. The unofficial 'mayor' of the group came out to meet her, taking one of the toboggans off of her hands and walking beside her. Curious, he looked over at her.

"I don't think I introduced myself last time. My name is Francis. You bring coffee and doughnuts again. Thank you."

Evelyn smiled up into his whiskered face. "I assure you that I have a reason. The best way to discuss things is over a meal. I have a proposition for you all." She looked around. "I hope I am here early enough? I'd like to speak to everyone if possible."

"It's good timing. We tend to stay in our tents or blankets until the sun warms up the air. We have nothing but time, so it is more pleasant to move about when its a bit warmer." He paused beside a picnic table and unloaded the coffee urns onto the table top, the helped unload her second toboggan of the doughnuts. Then he hopped up onto the table top and shouted, "Gather round everyone, we have coffee and doughnuts for all, come get some breakfast."

People of all ages came out of tents, some wearing multiple coats, others wrapped in blankets. Most wore a smile, but there were also suspicious frowns and stares.

Evelyn took a deep breath and them smiled warmly and started passing around a box of doughnuts. "Hi again. I hope you remember me, Evelyn Christmas? Here, let me get on top of the table so you all can see me." She climbed up beside Francis, who helped her up with a steadying hand. "I have come with a proposal, that I would like you to consider. The reason that I have come to Noelville, is to assist the mayor with creating a way to assist all of you. My purpose in being here is to find a way to help you all stand on your own and find the shelter, food and employment that you need and want. We went through your surveys and we have an idea we'd like to share with you."

"I am sure you all know the Jollie-Saint family." Boos rose from those crowed around. Evelyn nodded, understanding. They didn't know the circumstances of why the factory closed. How could they? It had been kept very quiet. "I understand your feelings. There are some facts though, that I am sure you do not know, with respect to how and why the factory closed." She then told them in brief terms the circumstances that led to the factory being closed. The boos died away and they listened with rapt attention.

"Now, the mayor has authorized me to create a fundraiser to correct the errors of the past and to help compensate you all for what occurred, for what you lost. Will you hear me out?" She scanned the faces of the listeners. When no one told her to stop, she went on. "I have been working on the creation of a Santa's Village just across the river on the Jollie-Saint estate. The village buildings are already there, but there is no one to work them. I would like to hire you to become the elves of Santa's workshops. There is a North Pole post office, Santa's Toy Shoppe, a Sugar Plum bakery, the original Maple Sugar shack, and the Sleigh Barn on the hillside loaded with toboggans just like these."

"So what does that have to do with us?" shouted a man from the back of the crowd.

"Just this. I need help decorating and I also need help with running the village up until Christmas. If you are willing to move to the village, we can set you up in a space with your existing housing, and you can work the village during the daytime in exchange for meals. But I think I can do you one better, on the housing front. We have received permission to reopen the sugar factory which as you know is right over there—" she pointed to the right to where she could see Natalie in the passenger seat of a pickup truck, driving towards them with a truck bed loaded with boxes. Several town workers, including Alvin who was behind the wheel, completed the compliment. "And here come the town's representatives right now, to tell you the rest of the plan."

Evelyn crossed her fingers behind her back. She prayed this was going to work.

The truck pulled to a stop and out jumped Alvin, followed closely by Natalie. They walked up to the assembled homeless and then he took Evelyn's place on top of the picnic table. Grinning, he held up his hands and encouraged everyone to move in closer.

"Marie-Claire Saint, mayor of Noelville, wishes to extend an invitation for you all to take up residence on the third floor of the former sugar factory building." There was a moment of shocked silence, and then someone started clapping, and the rest joined in.

"The third floor was originally reserved for the executive offices in the old company, and it has some of the best views of the town that there are. There are balconies attached to several of the office spaces. We have been given a budget to complete the renovation of those office spaces into two-bedroom residential suites. This means that you will need to choose a roommate. The accommodations will be fully furnished and we will be reopening the employee kitchen on this level as a communal space, along with lounges and a recreation area that will double as a library and office center." Whistles hit the air, as they voiced their approval.

"There is no cost to you for the use of this space. Our only request is that you assist with Ms. Christmas' campaign in any way that she asks, as this campaign will be a direct benefit to you all. The space should be ready for occupancy by the end of this week, and we will be putting a pass code door lock on the front door, so that you all can come and go as you please without having to worry about keys. The sleeping quarters will be coded based on the oldest person's year of birth, something easy for all of you to remember. We would suggest you share this information only with your roommate."

"You are not required to stay in the factory, but we highly encourage you to do so as the weather is turning bitterly cold. Does anyone have any questions?"

A man at the back, clearly elderly raised a shaking hand. "Yes?" said Alvin, pointing at the man.

"My knees do not do stairs very well. Is there an elevator or some way to get to the top floor without taking the stairs?"

"Good question. Yes, there is an elevator in the building that we will show you how to operate. Its an older style, but still functional. We are having it serviced tomorrow to make sure it is in good shape, as we have furniture arriving and need it. It is a freight elevator, but it will get the job done." Chuckles met his words, and pleased smiles.

"What are we to do for food?" asked another person, a woman this time.

"Another excellent question. We have been speaking with the mission shelter staff and they are willing to set up for a cafeteria style bar where you can help yourselves at any time day or night. They will keep it stocked with food, and the hot meal will be the same as is being served at the mission. In time, we hope that you will be able to take over the running of the food bar on your own, but for now, we will be providing meals."

Alvin looked around, then glanced down at Natalie and smiled. She smiled back up at him and their gazes locked for a moment. Evelyn took in the exchange with a sad smile. *So that is the direction the wind is blowing,* she thought.

"What about bathrooms?"

"There are male and female washrooms already in place, but no shower facilities. We will be adding showers to those rooms in the near future, as part of our buildings renovation plan, but they won't be ready until the new year. There are two executive showers, which we will be retrofitting with doors to the main area. You will need to book a time for this room for now, and we will put a clipboard with 24 hours on it. Just block out the hour and the room will be all yours for that hour. All you need to do is write your name beside any free hour block."

Evelyn looked around, gauging the reactions of the ragtag group surrounding her. For the most part, the faces displayed uncertainty, mixed with a cautious hope. There were also disbelieving faces. She understood that look. Nothing had ever come easily to these people.

"As good as this sounds," Evelyn said in a loud voice. "It isn't free. This is a hand up, not a hand out. And I need your hands, your hearts and your help, right now. So I propose this. Come with me and help me decorate and set up the village, and then you can go back with Alvin and his crew and check out the factory before dark. I need as many of you as are willing, to run the Christmas Village for us, because it is going to be the fundraiser that puts a permanent roof over your heads. Deal?"

"Deal." The word moved through the crowd and expectant faces waited for the next steps.

"Then let's go!" said Alvin. "We will drive the pickup truck across the bridge and you all can follow. You can pack up and move over to the Village for the night if you want, or stay here, the choice is yours. By week's end, we hope you will all have chosen your room and roommates and moved into the factory penthouse suites!"

A cheer went up as Alvin jumped down and then he gathered up Natalie with a glance and climbed back into the pickup truck. She watched them drive away, the four-wheel drive having no problem with the deep snow.

"I need to head back now too. Meet me at the village as soon as you can. We have lots to do! Merry Christmas!"

Evelyn waved at them all and then grabbed both toboggans and began walking back to the village. She heard footsteps following and then felt one of the ropes being taken from her hand. Francois moved up to walk beside her. He was quiet for a bit and then he said in a lowered voice so the others wouldn't hear, "That was a very kind thing you did back there. Most of them will not say it, so I will say it on their behalf. Thank you for bring us hope."

Evelyn smiled warmly at the older man. "It is entirely my pleasure. I was once one of you. I was given a helping hand and that is why I am alive today. I owe a debt to the kindness of an unknown stranger, who picked me up out of the snow beside my dead mother, and brought me to a hospital. We all deserve a chance."

Francois nodded. "You have a lot of wisdom for a young woman. That only comes from knowing a life of struggle."

Evelyn glanced back once again. A long line of people followed her, grouped in twos and threes, possibly sizing each other up as roommates? The thought brought a smile.

One Christmas miracle down. Now to pull the second one out of Santa's sack.

The North Pole

B y the time that Evelyn reached the village, with her elves in tow, the boxes had been unloaded and carried into their respective buildings, waiting for 'Santa's Elves' to report for work. She peeked her head in the toy shoppe and found Natalie elbows deep in supplies as she sorted them by type and colour.

Evelyn closed the door behind her then walked over to Natalie and gave her a big hug. "Thank you so much for gathering all of this on such short notice. I don't know how you did it."

Natalie shrugged and then looked up as Alvin walked in with another box. "It was Alvin. He called the superintendent of the local school system, and got permission to raid their art supply locker. It was like being given the keys to candy cupboard. Most of what you see here came from there, and we only had to pick up a few things like wood glue and small nails and such from the local hardware store. When they saw what we were doing, they were curious as to why we would need so many, so we told them about the village reopening. They promptly donated everything we needed."

Alvin put the box down then pulled the tape and opened it up. "Once they realized that it was all part of the homeless initiative fundraiser, they called their head office and got permission to donate the beds that are going into the apartments in the penthouse. They are loading the truck in Montreal as we speak and they will be here by Friday. I think they are clearing out their clearance center and sending up anything they think we can use. It's pretty astounding."

"Leave that for now, Natalie. You need to get to filming. Our elves are arriving and don't we have some costumes to distribute?"

"Right. I have the box right here." Natalie pointed to the box and Alvin picked it up and carried it back outside. The first of the recruited elves were just arriving. As part of the housing initiative, the town was entering the names of those seeking housing on a tablet, along with their date of birth and age. A line had formed behind the first to arrive, while they took down the needed information. Where people had already selected roommates, that was also being recorded. Evelyn gestured at Natalie to start recording, then walked over to the line of people. "We welcome Santa's Elves to the Christmas Village, to begin their first shift, as we get set to rock around the clock. MusicMan, play me some carols!" As the keyword was spoken, Evelyn's smart speaker lit up and began to play "Rock Around The Clock" over speakers strategically hidden throughout the village.

The elves looked around in surprise then smiled. Evelyn took the first costume from the box and handed it to the woman standing in line. "Here's your costume. From tomorrow on, we will ask that you wear it at work. You are welcome to change now if you want, there is a bathroom in the Sugar Plum bakery." The lady nodded and walked off to the bakery, to change. Evelyn continued to hand out elf costumes until the line dwindled away to nothing. The line up to change was considerable, so some people stripped off their coats and put on the shirts right there in the street.

Once everyone had gathered back in the square, about fifty elves waited for instructions. Evelyn set the taller ones to stringing more lights on the surrounding trees and along the walkways leading back to the village and up to the sleigh barn. She then divided the rest into teams based on a show of hands, to 'elf' the various buildings. She took the teams to each building and had them elect a "head elf of the day" to manage their group, then set them to work.

In Santa's Toy Shoppe, the elves began assembling the toys according to the plans, setting up an assembly line process, from construction through to finish paint. There was a lot of trial and error at first, but by the end of the day they had worked out a process that was fluid and productive.

In the Sugar Plum bakery, Nicolas' mother's recipes were tested and tweaked until they could cook a batch flawlessly. Fortunately, one of the elves on this team had experience in cookie decorating at a former bakery and began to teach the others on the team the techniques used in flooding a cookie and creating faces. In no time at all test cookies of Santa's and Rudolph and Le Bonhomme de Neige were completed and ready for inspection and approval.

Over in the North Pole Post Office, the elf scribes read letters to Santa that the town workers had gathered from Santa's mailboxes scattered around town, and wrote out replies that included a candy cane treat, a coupon for a free hug from Mrs. Claus and the official stamp on the envelope from the North Pole.

The Sleigh Barn was swept and decorated and the toboggans cleaned and readied for the children big and small, who would soon be laughing and sliding down the hillside. A hot chocolate stand was set up at the edge of the slope along with a portable set of bleachers for parents and grandparents to sit, sip and gossip while watching their youngsters enjoy the sledding.

But the most interesting transformation to Evelyn, was in the Sugar Shack. As it turned out, the stainless steel boiler worked just as well for making large batches of maple treats. Soon it was pumping out maple caramel, cinnamon maple caramel, chocolate maple caramel, and blueberry maple caramel, for starters. Large vats of taffy bubbled away on the stove, all with a maple base rather than cane sugar and combined with flavours that would never have occurred to Evelyn, but which the elves seemed to understand intuitively.

By the time the sun was an hour from dark, the village had been transformed. The elves gathered in the center of the village and then Alvin and Natalie led them back across the bridge and on to the factory for their first inspection of the transformed executive offices in the factory, and to begin the initial registration for Friday's move in. Evelyn walked along towards the rear of the pack, conducting interviews with the various people and recording their impressions, and with their permissions, adding those to the library of live feed uploads. She had no idea how the actual campaign was shaping up as they had been focused on the momentous task of getting the Village ready for their grand opening also on Friday.

The idea was to have people enter the village by parking and walking across the bridge. There would be elves stationed at the entrance, ready to accept the donation of the guests as they came across, whether that be a donation to the food bank or a monetary donation. Once across the bridge, the refreshments and entertainment would all be free, with toys and gift baskets available to purchase, with all proceeds going to the fundraiser.

They had found one of the elves with previous department store Santa experience. Natalie had hit on the idea of creating a Santa photo opportunity in the sleigh barn, with the sleigh in the background, and so they decked the volunteer out in a Santa hat with his elf costume, then put a sign out front that read "Santa In Training". to complete the illusion. They took the broken toboggans and stood them up, crossed like a set of skies, then painted them in Christmas green and red, and put a comfy chair in front with a braided rug on the floor. That way they could add some more footage to the feed plus give everyone a photo opportunity that would hopefully translate into an avalanche of Christmas cheer.

All in all, she felt that they were ready to open. But all grand openings required a ribbon cutting and the Mayor had to be there to do that. Evelyn pulled out her phone and sent a quick text over to Marie-Claire, letting her know the plan.

They arrived at the factory as the sun was setting. It was lit up like a Christmas tree, all the light spilling out onto the snowy front lawn. Town staff had strung Christmas lights here too, which turned on as a dusk-to-dawn timer triggered. Natalie began to clap and was soon joined by the others in the crowd. Waving her hands to encourage everyone to follow, she went up the steps and she and Alvin opened the doors wide, holding them for the stream of elves to enter the building. Evelyn caught it all on film and uploaded the short clip with lots of hash tags and a special Donate Now timer button, that would automatically add a $25.00 donation to the fund. She was the last to enter the factory and looked around with genuine curiosity. The elves were following the city staff up the steps, being given a guided tour to their new home if they wished to stay.

The babble of voices faded away and Evelyn found herself alone with Natalie for the first time that day. Natalie touched her arm and said, "How are you hanging in there?"

"Me? I have been too busy to focus on my personal life. I have a job to do here, and that has to be my focus."

"Of course. You are a professional. But that doesn't mean you can just turn your feelings off. Have you heard from Nicolas at all?"

"Not a peep. I doubt he will be back." She sighed, then looked Natalie in the eye. "It's a good thing that Marie-Claire is the one that hired us, or we'd already be on the plane back to Vancouver. Our being here has nothing to do with romance. It's all about them," she waved a hand towards the empty staircase, "and that must be our focus."

"Agreed. Where are you planning to stay tonight? Are you going back to the manor?"

"No...I thought I'd stay in the Sugar Plum one more night. Tomorrow is opening day for the village and I am wanting to be up and at it early. Although I could use a change of clothes. Georges said to message him and he would bring whatever we needed."

"Then I will stay with you too. You had mentioned there were two beds in the loft. We can have a girl's night."

"That sounds wonderful. Are you sure though? You don't have to rough it with me."

"Of course, I am sure! We can do some sticker pricing of the items that are going to be for sale, to make things easier. Oh, by the way, I picked up that payment terminal you were asking for. And I upped our data for the hotspot so we don't get hit with overage charges. And we are borrowing Alvin's mobile satellite internet system for the duration of the village, so we will have reliable internet. He set it up this afternoon." She patted her pocket. "I have the password here. Network is called 'Jollie-Saint Village' in honour of Nicolas' mom and dad."

"Great plan. That's just what we needed. I had been worrying about that. You think of everything, don't you?"

Natalie grinned at her. "What kind of assistant would I be if I didn't figure out the cracks in the wall and plug them? Besides, you have plenty on your plate. Now you go sit on the bench there and message Georges while I scoot upstairs quickly to let them know we are leaving."

Evelyn gratefully sunk onto the bench, suddenly very weary. She opened her phone and sent a text message to Georges asking him to bring a basket of food and a change of clothing for both her and Natalie. She received his reply acknowledging the request. Then she sent a message to Natalie letting her know that all was arranged. With a sigh she pocketed her phone and let her head sink back against the wall, and closed her eyes for a moment.

The next second, she felt Natalie shaking her, and woke with a start. "Come on, sleepy head. We are done here."

Cutting Ribbons

By the time they returned to the Sugar Plum (which by this point Evelyn was beginning to consider to be a second home) Dark had truly fallen. A light snow fall accompanied them back to the village. The walk was magical, with Christmas lights twinkling everywhere.

A few of the soon-to-not-be-homeless had stayed behind to light campfires and cook stoves, and basically provide light for those returning. Tomorrow would be a new day for them, if they all chose to move. They both waved as they passed and walked on to the bridge that was now brightly lit in strands of white lights strung along both sides of the railing. It was a welcoming site and Natalie pulled out her tablet and began filming once again, commenting on the magic of the season and the hope of brighter futures for everyone. She then included a link to the schedule of events and also the hours and suggested donation, added the usual hash tags and then went on to the next video. She would upload them once they were in range of the internet connection.

"You know, this has been a truly magical adventure. I have never spent so much time in the snow, being born and raised in Vancouver," said Evelyn, looking around and taking in the beauty of the lights on the clean carpet of snow. "I think I could get used to this. I have always found the winter rain in Vancouver to be depressing."

"I know what you mean. Even though it's cold, somehow the dryness of the air makes it tolerable. The air smells so clean!" Natalie took a deep breath and then watched her exhale drift away on soft clouds. "I feel like Popeye," and she began making smoke rings with her breath.

Evelyn laughed. They walked down the trail, which acted as a tunnel due to the kaleidoscope of colourful lights strung across the opening. Evelyn looked around, thinking. "You know, we could make these into wishing trees. Sell ribbons to tie to the limbs and trunks. I know of this Irish tradition where they have fairy trees for Christmas wishes."

Natalie spun in a circle, taking in the lights and thinking. "You know what? That's a great idea. We can cut the ribbons tonight."

They exited the trees and into the village proper, and had to stop to take it all in. "Woah!" said Natalie, grabbing her tablet once again and hitting record.

The village was absolutely perfect. Breathtakingly perfect. Evelyn walked into the center and looked around, amazed at all they had done in the short time they had. The elves had outdone themselves and more than earned themselves the right to a decent bed and a hot meal. What they had done was mind-blowing. The lights she had strung had been efficient, yes... but the elves? They had made sculptured pieces out of the light. She could only guess, but to her it looked like they had tried to recreate the twelve days of Christmas on the evergreens in the square. It was pure magic. "Natalie, are you seeing this?" she called out, walking around the trees.

"Yes," said Natalie, still filming. "Tell me about it. What are you seeing, Evelyn?"

"It's a Christmas miracle!" said Evelyn, turning back to Natalie with tears of joy sparkling in her eyes. "I see hope, and love, and forgiveness. I see the downtrodden being lifted up, and the path to peace for all mankind. This is the reason for the season. That all mankind love one another, regardless of social status, or ethnicity, or orientation. The common denominator is our humanity. The elves here have shown they understand this, by pouring their hearts and energies behind their work today." She focused on the tablet in Natalie's hands and said in a clear, crystal voice. "Join us. If ever there was a cause that needed addressing, especially around the holidays, it's the issue of homelessness. The village opens tomorrow morning at 10:00 am and runs until 10:00 pm and we will be live streaming all day! And for those of you following our campaign from afar, know that your pledges will go to this initiative and other communities nearby who have joined in the efforts to eradicate homelessness. Share this campaign and remember your hashtags as we strive to end homelessness in Canada. Good night!" She waved once again and then turned around and started walking towards the Sugar Plum, the exhaustion of long hours of work and mental anguish causing her feet to drag.

Reaching the building, she saw a fresh set of tracks in the snow. She pushed open the door to see that Georges had set up a full hot meal station for them. The wonderful smell of roast beef and gravy and frites, and sweet peas and onions, made her stomach growl. Natalie was right behind her and they each took a plate and loaded it up with food before sinking gratefully onto the couch. Two packed bags were sitting at the base of the stairs and he had even heated up some mulled wine, which they poured from a carafe into mugs.

By the time they finished their dinner and the wine, they were both blinking sleepily, all thoughts of ribbon trees forgotten.

With a tired sigh and mutual agreement, they went to bed.

Evelyn was up before the dawn had pierced the trees, making coffee for herself and stuffing her fist in her mouth to stop the yawns.

The inflatable mattress was not the most comfortable place to sleep and despite the woodstove roaring below, drafts penetrated the cabin. It wasn't a place to stay for an entire winter, but for now, it was adequate. Besides, it was easier to get to work when you were already at work, something she had learned over many years of working from her home.

Her thoughts drifted to Nicolas as she filled the percolator with coffee grounds and set it on top of the wood burning kitchen stove. Would he come to the grand opening? This was his village after all. She was surprised that he had stayed away, if she was honest with herself. She had thought he was invested in the process. His grandmother certainly was. She regularly sent messages and words of encouragement, along with her promise that she would be there at 10:00 to cut the ribbon to officially open the Christmas Village. She had also messaged that the local news & press would be out in force, to record the event for the evening news. "So, make sure you are looking gorgeous for the cameras, my dear. They will be rolling."

Well, she certainly wasn't camera shy, that was for certain. She wandered over to the ice box (she noticed a fresh block of ice had been placed in the back, probably Georges' work) and opened it up to find eggs, bacon and hash browns waiting to be cooked. Smiling, she put the cast iron on the stovetop and began cooking breakfast. But the smile soon faded as thoughts drifted back to Nicolas. *Why hadn't he returned? It didn't feel right. Something was odd there.* And Marie-Claire's silence on the matter was unusual.

Maybe she should reach out and try to apologize. She really did want to show him what they had done with the village, how glorious it was. His mother and father would have approved of the transformation, she knew it.

At that moment, she heard Natalie coming down the stairs, irresistibly drawn to the smell of cooking maple bacon, like metal filings to a magnet.

"Yum. That smells delish! Is it ready?"

Evelyn poked the bacon, turning it over, then flipped the hash browns. The eggs were done and off to the side. "Two minutes and it should be ready. Just enough time to grab some plates. Do you want to cut ribbon while we eat?"

Natalie nodded and went to fetch to box of ribbon and a pair of scissors. "I think we should use this red and green plaid for the ribbon cutting ceremony. So festive with the silver threads."

Evelyn carried over two plates of food and set them on the table in front of the woodstove, then retrieved their coffee. They ate, and drank and cut ribbon for the next hour, as slowly they woke up. It almost felt like a Christmas morning, as she had shared several of them with her best friend over the years. The sun made its appearance known by striping the floor at their feet as they finished the last of the Christmas wish ribbons, then made a dash for the bathroom. Twenty minutes later they were dressed in their holiday finest for outdoor activities, Evelyn in her insulated leggings and tall thermal boots and long red coat, and Natalie in her jeans, hiking boots and short brown jacket with a snowy white scarf. They cleaned away all evidence of them staying there, and prepped the Sugar Plum for the day's sales then picked up the ribbons and headed outside.

First order of business was the set up for the ribbon cutting, which they tied between two trees at the edge of the village at the end of the path from the park. They pinned a huge silver bow to the center of it, creating a holiday present feel. They wanted to invite the community to unwrap the village and enjoy all it had to offer.

Soon the first of the elves arrived, skirting around the ribbon through the woods, and into the village, to take their respective places. Evelyn handed off the wishing ribbons to the female elf running the candy shoppe portion of the Sugar Shack, with instructions on their sale. The woman smiled and carried the basket back to the Sugar Shack. As the elves took their places and picked up their activities of the day before, soon the air was filled with the smells of baking, and candy making, and the woodsy smell of woodsmoke and wood working.

Evelyn felt a tap on her shoulder, and the same woman from the Sugar Shack stood there, with two steaming cups of hot chocolate in her hand. "Would you try this? We added maple and buttered rum flavouring, hoping to make a version of a drink made famous by a certain boy wizard." She grinned as she handed it to them and watched for their reactions. They took a couple sips and came away with a butter scotch flavoured moustache. The hot chocolate was smooth and buttery and very, very delicious. "Oh! That is amazing!" exclaimed Natalie, taking another sip. What are you going to call it?"

"With your permission, we will call it the Naughty But Nice Cocoa."

Evelyn grinned. "You have my blessing. Be sure to be handing out samples to passersby. And keep the recipe a secret!"

The elf nodded and walked back to the sugar shack where a festively decorated chalk board listed the items for sale inside. She added "Naughty But Nice Cocoa" to the list in two sizes.

Evelyn too another careful sip, and rolled her eyes in ecstasy.

Natalie glanced down at the tablet and suddenly noticed the time. "It's nearly 10. We need to go meet the Mayor. Come on."

They walked down the path to the bridge just in time to see a cavalcade of cars arrive at the parking lot across from the bridge. Evelyn looked around and was surprised to not see any evidence of the homeless encampment that had been there only hours before. Seeing her look of amazement, Natalie leaned over and whispered, "Alvin offered a ride in the pickup truck if anyone wanted help moving their things to the new location. After touring the set up, not one person chose to stay outside. We may still have some leave, but its a good start, right? And everyone had showers and a hot meal before leaving this morning. No beds yet, but that didn't bother them. They just set up in their rooms with what they were sleeping with here and were happy for the roof over their head."

"And that's the way it should be done. Congratulations, Natalie!"

The Mayor's entourage began walking towards Natalie & Evelyn, along with a couple of news reporters with cameras rolling. The mayor was talking to a middle-aged man with a short hair cut and dressed in a long grey wool coat. As they got closer, the words drifted to their ears.

"...been an election promise that has been way overdue. Your opponents have pointed out the lack of effectual progress in removing the homeless encampment from the waterfront and the eye sore it has created. People have openly complained about the trash and the filthy conditions that the camp has created. It has been a true eye sore for Noelville, driving people away from the enjoyment of this portion of the town. I ask, what are you going to do to resolve this urgent problem?"

The mayor paused, and looked around. "I beg your pardon, but what problem?" She spread her arms in a gesture of puzzlement, quirking an eyebrow in a manor reminiscent of her grandson. Evelyn swallowed hard at the now familiar family trait, struggling to keep her emotions in check and the welcoming smile on her face.

The reporter pointed over his shoulder. "That eyesore. We want to know what you plan to do—" he glanced over his shoulder once again and froze in mid sentence. There was no one there, and no sign of the previous occupants. His jaw dropped. "I apologize," he stammered, clearly taken aback. "I was unaware that they had been removed."

Marie-Claire waved one gloved hand nonchalantly. "It's no problem. It is a recent development, one that I am happy to go into, in more depth, in a later interview. But for now, we are here to celebrate the opening of the Christmas village with a ribbon cutting ceremony. Is everyone ready?" She looked around at the gathered media and nodded.

"As some of you older residents may remember, this village was built by my late son and his wife as a family present to their young son Nicolas. After their untimely deaths, the village was closed down and had never been used again, until now." The cameras rolled framing her in the shot with the woods and river in the background. "We wanted to change that, and also come up with a way to help Noelville's less fortunate. I happened to come across a SocialBuzz fundraiser in Vancouver, that was trending extremely high in the feeds. When I looked into it closer, I found this young influencer at the helm of the campaign with a passion for solving homelessness in Canada. She was brave enough to tackle the issue head on in Vancouver, which has a much larger population and by extension a much larger problem. Her campaign was staggering in what it was able to raise, and is still bringing in sponsors two weeks since it's peak. So, we reached out to this young entrepreneur and brought her to town. I would like to introduce you all to Ms. Evelyn Christmas and her assistant, Natalie Starr."

The cameras swung their way and they both lifted a hand to wave at the reporters. The mayor walked over to them and grasped a hand of each of them. "Evelyn, Natalie, please accept my warm thanks and gratitude in making the long trip from Vancouver to help us solve this problem that has been plaguing us for far too long now."

Evelyn smiled at the cameras. "I am very happy to come and lend my expertise in this area to your campaign. We truly believe that homelessness is a scourge where ever it is found and we can do so much better in providing a hand up for those who have fallen on difficult times."

"I am dying to see what you have done with the village, Let's cut this ribbon and open the village!"

Evelyn extended a pair of silver scissors to the mayor who stepped up to one side of the big silver bow, while Evelyn and Natalie stood on the other side. Alvin pushed through the crowd, gave Natalie and Evelyn and the mayor a nod then stood beside the mayor for the photo opportunity. She then proceeded to cut the ribbon, and as it fell apart, officially opening the park, the Carol Of The Bells began to play from hidden speakers around the bridge. Marie-Claire looked up, surprise etched on her aged features. Her eyes glistened with gratitude as the sweet arrangement by Nicolas' mother filled the air to gentle applause.

"Come, it's time to enjoy some Christmas!" and she turned on her heel and led the media across the bridge and into the village proper.

Mrs. Claus: Take Two

E velyn made way for the mayor and entourage to pass by and then turned to a couple of the elves standing nearby waiting to greet guests as they arrived. "Be ready," she said with a smile. "Christmas cheer forward! I can already see guests getting out of cars. I think the mayor has been doing some advance propos, getting the word out. We will be very busy between now and Christmas Eve."

"I believe we are about to earn our keep" quipped an elf named Charles. "Ever since I was a kid, I wanted to be Elf, like in the movie. Now is my chance to shine," and he promptly did a cartwheel through the snow and onto the bridge, waving energetically at the approaching crowd. His arm movements were enough to set the bells on his hat and shirt jingling merrily. A little girl pointed and laughed, then ran ahead of her parents, eager to meet the elf on the bridge.

Evelyn did a quick round of the village, checking on everyone to see if anyone was missing anything, Natalie at her shoulder, always filming. She was there to catch every special moment and upload it. It was a live stream and so content was paramount for this opening day.

Evelyn's phone began to ping in her pocket as responses came through. It felt like she had a swarm of angry bees in her pocket, there was so much vibration.

Eventually her feet found her at the Sleigh Barn. The doors were flung wide open and a man moved around the sleigh, looking it over. It was Nicolas. Evelyn stopped dead, her face turned away from the camera in Natalie's hands. Natalie caught sight of Nicolas and discreetly walked around the outside to do filming at the ski hill, leaving them to speak in peace with no camera's rolling.

Evelyn hesitated for a moment, then steeling herself for the conversation, she shoved her hands in her pockets, walked up the slope and into the barn.

Nicolas looked down from the sleigh when she entered. His face revealed no expression that she could discern. He paused for a moment, studying her, then went back to his perusal of the sleigh.

"Hi." she said.

"Hi," he said back.

"I was wondering when you might arrive. You stayed away longer than I thought you would."

"I had some urgent business come up."

Yeah, avoiding me, I bet, she thought.

"But I couldn't put this off any longer. The horses are being delivered today and will be hitched up to pull the sleigh over to the staging area for the parade on Saturday. They will stay in the stables starting tonight. So I had to be here." He glanced at his watch, checking the time.

"Your grand-mere has arrived. She is touring with the press at the moment. Have you had a chance to wander through the village?"

"No, I just arrived." Finished with his inspection, he climbed down. "The sleigh looks great. I don't know how you found all those volunteers on such short notice, but it looks like its going to be an amazing event."

"Thank you. We have been working very hard to make this event go off without a hitch. Would you like to meet them? I think you will be impressed with their work ethic."

"Yes, I would." He walked over to her, staring down into her face. She had forgotten how tall he was, and was embarrassed to feel her heart speed up and her face flush. His proximity, the masculine scent of him lit up her senses like nothing else could. It was a woodsy smell like fresh pine boughs and something that was uniquely Nicolas. "It will have to wait until after I have the sleigh moved. Do you think I should dress as Santa to move the sleigh or one of his elves? I have been trying to decide. There have never been people here before when the sleigh was being moved. I am thinking Santa. who else would move his sleigh? So, I brought along my suit—"

At that moment a vehicle swung into the yard. A pickup truck hauling a horse trailer announced the arrival of the horses. Nicolas went out to meet with the new arrivals and Evelyn tagged along. Seeing the new activity, Natalie reappeared, filming the arrival of the truck. The driver got out and greeted Nicolas with a cheery "Joyeux Noel!" and grasped his hand, pulling him into a bear hug. He was an older man, and jabbered away in rapid French, too fast for Evelyn to keep track of. Nicolas replied equally fast, slipping into the native Quebecois slang. After an exchange of a couple of minutes, they went to the back of the trailer and lowered the ramp, then disappeared inside. One by one they backed out some of the most beautiful horses that Evelyn had ever seen. They were tall, white with some dappled spots across their withers, and all wearing matching harnesses. Their tails and manes had been braided with red ribbon and even their hooves were painted red. There were four of them in total, and one by one they were walked into the barn and strapped into place.

If you can't have reindeer, then these are surely the answer, thought Evelyn.

Nicolas finished his conversation with the old farmer and he got in his truck and drove away. Evelyn walked back up to Nicolas, and patted the soft nose of one eager horse. "Do they have names?"

Nicolas grinned. "Of course they do. This is Dancer, Prancer, Cupid and Vixen."

Evelyn raised an inquisitive eyebrow. "No Rudolph?"

"Rudolph doesn't play reindeer games, which is what a parade is all about. He saves his strength for the main event." He grinned down at her, watching her reaction. Evelyn threw back her head and laughed. Nicolas' face went slack, watching her expression of sheer joy. He stared at her until it became uncomfortable.

"Well, at least we have these four. We have announced the moving of Santa's sleigh for noon, which is in about a half hour, so if you want your own little parade, you should get changed. Look," she pointed outside where red ribbon marked the route the sleigh would take. People were already lined up outside, waiting with cups of hot chocolate and elf bobble ears, for a first glimpse of Santa. "And yeah, I'd be wearing the suit. We will be live streaming this," she said loudly. "I assume you realize that but in light of recent events, I want to make sure you understand this."

"Of course. Could you stay with the horses? I will change quickly." He picked up a duffle bag and disappeared into a small room at the back of the barn. Natalie sidled up beside her, hit pause on her recording and whispered, "How are you holding up?"

"Better than I thought. he seems to be perfectly normal. I have probably been over reacting, as usual. I will sit down with him and apologize tonight, over dinner back at the manor. Are you ready to sleep in a proper bed again?"

Natalie chuckled. "I don't know. I kinda like it here. Look at those crowds!" They peeked outside the barn and the sidelines were now five people deep on both sides.

"Wow! Where did they all come from? And all the kids! It looks like some teachers brought their classes out for the day." Even as she said the words, she saw another thirty or so children crossing the bridge from the park." Good thing that Alvin brought over those portable potties this morning. I saw him setting them in place a few minutes ago," She pointed the driveway that was recently vacated by the horse trailer.

"I hope you are filming this. It would be good to interview a classroom and their teacher too. Keep filming, girl!"

Natalie grinned and moved back outside, to continue her work.

Nicolas returned, dressed in full costume. Bright red suit jacket and pants, trimmed with white fur, and a thick black belt with a golden buckle around his waist. He had acquired some padding to round out his form. Black boots shone as though recently polished, and he sported a long white beard and moustasche. White gloves and a red hat completed the ensemble. "HO, HO, HO!" he called, in a deep, rich voice. Evelyn smiled then walked over and straightened his beard with a tug, then smoothed his hat so the furry ball on the end hung over his right ear.

"You look the part. I hope the Mrs. Claus outfit is just as spectacular. And warm. Brrr."

Nicolas' eyes crinkled. "You will just have to see." He climbed up into the driver's seat of Santa's sleigh and too up the reins. "I think it's time to get this show on the road. Or on the slope." Evelyn checked her watch then stepped back from the sleigh and horse team, giving them room to depart.

Right on cue, "Santa Claus Is Coming To Town" blasted from the speakers and the doors of the barn were pulled wide open by a pair of elves. The slope down to the bottom was now lined with elves, who jumped and cheered and danced in place, as though greeting Santa's arrival for real. Evelyn grinned. She hadn't asked them to do that. They had thought of it all on their own. Nicolas urged the horses forward and a huge cheer interspersed with childish squeals of excitement, rose from the watching crowd.

Waving to the crowd, Nicolas urged the team to pull the sleigh out of the barn and down the slope to the base, to begin the journey to the staging area.

At that moment a horn sounded and Nicolas pulled the team to a halt.

A woman stepped from a limousine, dressed in a sexy Mrs. Claus outfit with fur muff and high heeled boots. She was assisted by two men, who escorted her to the sleigh. With a huge smile and kisses blown to the crowd, Sabine Perdue climbed up onto the sleigh and took a seat beside Nicolas. Once seated, he moved the horses into motion at a slow walk. Sabine waved and smiled at the crowd, then found a basket of candy on the floor and began throwing it to the crowd. The sleigh moved along the path, to the excited cheers of the onlookers.

But there was one person not cheering. That woman hid her face in her hands and cried.

Evelyn sobbed for a solid five minutes in the little storage space that Nicolas had changed his clothes in, hugging his shirt to her chest. Her heart was broken. *Why was that woman here?* No one showed up at a stranger's door without an invitation, especially from so far away. She must have been invited. Which meant that everything that she thought was happening between her and Nicolas was completely one sided. Like a fool, she had fallen for a sworn bachelor, one who was not likely to ever settle down. She had thought he was different, that he was changing. But she had fallen in love with an illusion. The realization did not make it any easier pill to swallow.

She threw down his shirt and stepped on it for good measure, then dried her tears and double checked her make up in the cracked mirror. A pale, slightly tear stained face looked back at her. She rubbed her cheeks to give them more colour then straightened her back, holding her head proudly. She was Evelyn Christmas, and she had faced worse things than being rejected by a man. And she had a mission to accomplish. Nicolas Jollie-Saint could choose whoever he wanted to ride on his sleigh. She had no say in the matter. And so, she would force it to not matter.

Feeling more composed, she left the storage room and re-entered the barn. The excited chatter continued outside, interspersed with cheers and applause as the elves capered ahead and behind Santa's sleigh, giving him the send off that the season demanded. She watched the crowds begin to break up and resume other activities as the sleigh passed them by, happy smiles in evidence everywhere.

Evelyn let out a steadying breath as she watched the sleigh enter into the forest and out of sight. She left the barn, smiling at the people who were obviously enjoying the activities. As she walked back, she saw the mayor conversing with a group of adults. The media teams had left to prepare their footages for publication and were no longer in site. For once Evelyn had no desire to be in front of a camera, so this came as a relief. She walked over to Marie-Claire and gave her a half-hearted smile. As always, Marie-Claire picked up instantly on her mood. A small frown flickered around the corner of her mouth before it returned full force, to reply to the woman at her elbow.

"Yes, we are establishing a new tradition for Noelville. From this year on, the Christmas village will be an annual event, as it was always intended to be. We are super excited for all the efforts that have gone into readying it for the enjoyment of your families. And look, here is Evelyn Christmas, who is the brains behind this year's launch. She is the one to be thanked for this incredible transformation and for kicking off the Christmas season with such flair!" Marie-Claire reached out and pulled Evelyn over to her side. "Without her help we would be nowhere. Why she has even been sleeping here to make sure that the village is a roaring success."

A tall, thin woman with greying hair smiled at Evelyn. "This is fantastic, Evelyn. I am so happy to meet you! Tell me, where did you find so many volunteers on such short notice? The elves are hilarious."

Evelyn smiled warmly back at the group. "I am glad you asked that. They are the people for which this village and the gala to come, were created. They are the homeless people of Noelville. But I am pleased to let you know that they are homeless no more. Thanks to the generosity of the mayor and the town of Noelville, they now have lodgings in the old factory. They are as excited as you all are, to be a part of this grand opening."

Murmurs passed around the group, pleased smiles, and some minor looks of concern. "They are your neighbours, the same as the ones who have bought a house beside you. This is not a hand out. It's a hand up. They are earning their lodgings by bringing Christmas joy. Is that not part of the reason for the season? Embrace them. They are doing their part," she said quietly.

The mayor nodded. "Wise words, Evelyn. We will continue to evolve this initiative you have started to make sure that those who fall through the cracks always have a way to get back up. As you say, a hand up is better than a hand out. Quiet dignity and pride go so much further than false smiles and posing." She frowned after her grandson, then said with a gentle voice. "You must be exhausted, Evelyn. I am sure Natalie and I can take care of the village for a few hours if you wish to go rest up."

"Oh no, I am perfectly fine," Evelyn said brightly. "We are open till 10 pm and I need to be here on this first day of operation to learn what we need to tweak."

"Fine. I will send Georges over to pick you both up just after 10pm. He will have late meal waiting for you. Now, go enjoy you guests."

"Thank you, that is very kind."

"It is the least I can do." Marie-Claire turned away to greet a new group of parents that were waiting to speak with her.

A Million Reasons

The rest of the day passed in a blur and quickly despite everything that was on Evelyn's mind. It was good that she would be late getting back to the manor, as she didn't think she could face Nicolas yet. And somehow, she knew that Sabine Perdue was staying at the manor. It explained a lot —Nicolas failing to return and inspect their work, and his sudden 'urgent' business. She was sure that urgent business involved Sabine and probably a host of party and soiree invitations, that a socialite could conjure up like magic.

She was thankful that she really only had to stay two more days in Noelville. Tomorrow was the date of the official move in, into the factory, and she knew that Natalie wanted to oversee that with Alvin, and make sure that everything was set up and running smoothly.

Saturday was the gala at the factory, an event that would start 4:00 pm in the ballroom as they had come to dub it, and run until midnight. The elves were being transformed into waiters and waitresses for the event and would be circulating with hors d'oeuvres that had been ordered and were waiting delivery. Natalie had found a catering company that could supply linens and everything needed on sort notice and the would be setting up tomorrow while the furniture donation arrived and was unloaded.

Tomorrow, Natalie was needed at the factory so she had arranged for Alvin to pick her up and bring her over for the day.

That left Evelyn on her own in the village tomorrow. But somehow, she couldn't stomach it, so she decided it was time to put one of the elves in charge. She wandered through the village until she found Francois, who was busy in Santa's Toy Shoppe, overseeing the train production. When he spied Evelyn, he grinned and walked over to shake her hand.

"Everything is going great! We have sold over half of our production already. At this rate, we will need to double our production. And the elves are getting a kick out of this too. We given each other Christmas names, because the buyers were asking us to sign the toys! Can you imagine that? My elf name is "Sugar Daddy Darling" because I can't stop eating those sugar cookies!" He made a swooning face and grinned at Evelyn who grinned back.

"I already have a Christmas name, but just to double down I am "Christmas Eve Snow Queen". She high fived him, laughing. "Don't tell her I told you, but Natalie is 'Natalie The Noel Starr' as her middle name is Noel."

"Well then, the tradition is set. I don't think you came over to chat about Christmas nick names though?"

"No. I would like to promote you to Village Coordinator. Natalie will be busy over at the factory tomorrow, and I am feeling the need for a break. What do you say? Are you up to running the place for a day? Or possibly longer?'

"I am honoured that you consider me capable. I would love to do it."

"Great, come with me and I will walk you through everything."

They spent the rest of the daylight hours identifying where all the key components were located; power switches and wood lots and spare propane tanks. Evelyn grabbed a third tablet and enabled it for Francois' use with his own password. "Keep this for now. That way you can message me if anything comes up or if you think of something that's needed. And you can do your own video if you want. It's set up to automatically upload when you stop recording." She walked him through the process and he grinned like he'd just received a new toy... which Evelyn supposed he had, even if it was only temporary.

As dusk descended, the lights winked on all over the village and the magic of the season kicked in. It was fully dark by 4:30 pm and with the clouds that had moved in later afternoon, a light snow had begun to fall. The toboggan hill lit up with solar powered flood lights that would last just long enough to allow night tobogganing until close. If anything, the crowds swelled even more, as people got off work and collected their families and went off to see what the buzz was all about.

Evelyn felt a twinge of guilt, wondering if this was taking away from the sales of the vendors in the main town. She vowed to find out, as she had decided she was going Christmas shopping tomorrow. She would wander the stores, chat with the shop owners, and get a feel for their sales. She didn't want to negatively impact the sales of the regulars, who depended on this season to finish out their year successfully.

When the evening finally came to a close, Evelyn and Natalie thanked the elves, and sent them on their way home. Weary smiles of thanks were returned, and they shuffled off to get a hot meal and some much needed rest.

As promised, Georges was waiting for them with the car running. They carried their luggage to the SUV, placed it in the back and climbed gratefully inside. He looked back at them through the rearview mirror, gauging their level of exhaustion. What he saw there convinced him. "Go straight up to your rooms and into the jacuzzi for a hot soak. I will bring up your dinners to your rooms. You can relax and rest. The rest of the family has already retired for the evening, including Ms. Perdue."

There it was. Positive confirmation. As if Evelyn had needed it. "Thank you, Georges. That would be very much appreciated. And please do not bother with breakfast for me in the morning. I plan to sleep in a bit and then go shopping in town. I will eat there."

"I will grab a quick bite and then will be leaving early. Alvin is coming to pick me up by 8 am." said Natalie.

"As you wish, ladies."

The drive home was quick and once they were inside, they headed straight to their respective rooms. Evelyn immediately noticed the smell of botanicals, which meant the jacuzzi was already full and waiting for. She almost ran into the bathroom and closed the door, then quickly stripped down and lowered herself into the bubbles with luxurious sighs and moans of pleasure. Tension she did not realize she was holding, melted away as the warmth soaked her bones. She felt her eyes drooping as she let the cares of the day melt into the water. She thought she heard the door to her room open and close, then all was silent. She ignored it, as she relished the relaxation. When she could no longer keep her eyes open, she crawled out of the tub, dried off and crawled into her coziest pair of pajamas.

The tray on the table in front of the window held a bowl of salad greens thinly cut vegetables in a light dressing, and a crock of chicken pot pie. It was warm, delicious and filling. She ate it a lot faster than she had thought she would, then pulled the maple Creme Brûlée over in front of her. When she moved the bowl, a note was revealed tucked underneath the bowl. Curious, she picked it up to read it. She unfolded the paper and read the masculine handwriting.

"Evelyn,

"I wish to thank you for your efforts with the Christmas Village. It has turned out far better than I could have expected, for so short of time period. You have worked miracles. It is truly spectacular.

Which is why I hope that you will forgive me for inviting Sabine Perdue to ride on the Christmas sleigh beside me in the parade on Saturday. She has made a good point that her superstar fame can expand awareness of our campaign far and wide. I think it's the best decision given the circumstances.

Sincerely, Nic "

Evelyn stared at the short note, read it again, crumpled it in her fist, then crawled into bed to cry.

Evelyn woke, bleary eyed and feeling ill. She had tossed and turned for hours before finally being able to drift off to sleep, but sleep had not been any release. She had dreamed of riding in the sleigh with Nicolas on Christmas Eve, flying to all homes around the world and delivering toys right up until they had reached the park where she had been born. But instead of delivering toys, he had asked her to get out, that she wasn't good enough to be Mrs. Claus, and had left her abandoned in the middle of the night, in the heart of a wet, Vancouver downpour.

She shivered, pushing herself to a sitting position and looked around. It couldn't be much after dawn. Yawning, she got up and took a hot shower to wake fully. She had no interest in going back to sleep. She came back out, wrapped in a towel, to see a pot of coffee and some morning pastries sitting on the table, the previous night's dinner having been cleaned away. Silently thanking Georges, she wrapped herself in her house robe, poured herself a cup of coffee, added some thick cream and then opened her laptop. It was time she got some work done.

She selected a raspberry cream cheese pastry, took a bite, then signed into the SocialBuzz network.

The blast of responses hit her like a tidal wave. Blinking, she looked at the number of viewers for their current campaign, and the numbers were staggering. They had another viral sensation on their hands, with over two million views and counting. "Oh my gosh," she breathed, and then went to the crowdfunding platform that was gathering pledges and whistled. The pledged amount sat at over $1,000,000 and counting. Over a million dollars pledged in less than a week. None of this took into account the proceeds from the actual village, or the gala that was still to occur. She noticed a few new hashtags had been created around their campaign, but the ones getting the most traction were #dancingelves and #toyshoppeelves and #maplecandyChristmas. Also, a new one #grinchandmrsclaus. Evelyn privately hoped that was for Nicolas and Sabine, and not a reflection of her. Whichever way it was intended, it no longer applied to her.

She started reading the replies and the cheer and good wishes that were pouring in online warmed her heart. She gratefully accepted the encouragement, as it helped her focus beyond her heart ache to what was really important. This campaign was going to forever change the landscape in Noelville and she hoped it would provide a road map for other communities to follow. One super successful campaign could do that, which is what attracted Evelyn to doing influencer type activities.

A knock sounded at her door, and with her "Come in!" Natalie poked her head inside and seeing that she was awake came to join her at her laptop. "I was just coming to give you the good news. We are blowing this campaign not only out the door, but off the roof. Can you believe it? If our last campaign is anything to go by, we should end up around the $5,000,000 mark when all pledges are accounted for. What are they going to do with all that money?"

"Well, I am sure there are plenty of programs that need assistance. But if I were you, I'd be putting together a plan to reopen that factory. Think about it. You could house a lot of support services there, and employ many people that society considers "unemployable" due to disabilities, or other issues. Maybe something for you and Alvin to discuss over dinner?" Evelyn waggled her eyebrows at Natalie, who giggled.

"Well, we will see. I am heading out. By the way, I think Nicolas is looking for you. He's roaming around downstairs."

Evelyn frowned. "Well, that is too bad. I don't want to talk to him."

"I don't blame you. I just wanted to give you fair warning. There's the doorbell, See you tonight." She gave Evelyn a quick hug, then bounced out of the room to meet Alvin.

Evelyn did some more work on the computer, made some notes on things to follow up on, then got up and got dressed. She looked at the clock by the bedside table. It read 9:30 am. Gathering her coat and purse, she headed downstairs.

As Natalie has predicted, Nicolas was waiting in the lobby. As soon as he saw her descending the stairs, he said "I am heading into town and can give you a ride."

Evelyn frowned at him. "Don't you have someone else to shuttle around? A starlite like Sabine doesn't normally drive herself."

"She's already gone. She hired a driver to take her shopping for a dress for the gala."

"That must hurt your pride, to be dispensed with so quickly," she said in a snide tone.

"Actually, I told her I was unavailable."

"The plumber stand you up, too?"

He frowned at her. "What has gotten into you?"

"I am perfectly fine, thank you. And I can take myself shopping."

She went to move past him but Nicolas grabbed her arm, halting her.

Natalie looked up into his earnest face, keeping hers blank.

"I wanted to spend time with you. I don't care where you are going.

I'd like to come." Evelyn studied his face for a moment, then looked away.

"Why?"

"Why?"

"Yes, why? I dislike being a third wheel. You have a girlfriend. So, why do you want to come with me?"

Nicolas raked a hand through his hair, looking completely confused. "I owe you this much."

"You owe me nothing."

"Look, I want to apologize for my earlier behaviour. But in private. I don't want to do it here. Please, let me accompany you."

Evelyn let him sweat, saying nothing, merely looking at him. It felt good to make him squirm, even as she knew she was going to capitulate.

"Fine." She buttoned up her coat and marched past him into the snow.

Another Million Reasons

N icolas opened the passenger door of the SUV and saw her seated inside, then climbed into the driver's side.

Evelyn fastened her seat belt and waited. She wasn't going to make any of this easy for him. Why should she? It was torture for her. She took a deep, steadying breath and gazed out the window.

"So, where to first?" he asked, in a voice that tinged on timid. If she didn't know better, she would say he was embarrassed.

"I have a list of supplies needed for the toy shoppe to pick up. Natalie has already ordered them. And then I wanted to walk the village and check in with the shop keepers. It suddenly dawned on me that we might be negatively impacting them by drawing people away from the markets. Certainly not something that I intended to do. I am not used to small town dynamics and how sensitive their ecosystems can be."

"Alright, what is our first stop?"

Evelyn told him. Nicolas drove straight there and they picked up the bundles of wood ordered from the machine shop, already cut to size and ready to assemble. Natalie had emailed the dimensions a few days ago and they now had a twenty-four hour turn around time for restocking.

The second stop was for more baking supplies, so they stopped in at the local bulk supply store. Boxes of baking supplies were carefully packed into boxes and again placed in the back.

The third stop was for paper supplies, and this pretty much filled the SUV. They made a trip over to the village and dropped the supplies off just before opening. All ready there were long line ups to enter the village. Nicolas looked around and then said, "What are all these people doing here?"

"They are waiting for the Christmas Village to open. Hours are 10 am to 10 pm."

"All of these people are here already?" he whistled, amazed.

On the other side of the bridge, the elves came out to greet them and carry away the various supplies, Francois there to direct traffic. He shook hands with Evelyn and with Nicolas, wishing them a Joyeux Noel, then whistling jingle bells as they walked away. As they got back in the car, he glanced back at the village, already humming with excitement, and then at the eager crowds in front of them.

"We are going for an early lunch. I know just the spot. We need to talk."

Evelyn looked at him but stayed silent. Butterflies rolled over and over in her stomach as she tried to supress her feelings of anxiety. Nicolas drove a little way out of town to a quiet diner located towards the edge of town. From the outside, it didn't look like much but as soon as she walked inside, she could see that they had been in business for a very long time. Hand made wooden tables, polished to shine like a mirror were set with baby blue plates and cutlery, and wine glass tumblers. The warm smells of Greek cuisine filled the air, spice and lamb and citrus. When Nicolas entered, the proprietor greeted him by name.

"Nicolas, and lady, welcome. I have your favourite table right over here, Come, sit."

He led them to a table in a corner behind a tall screen that gave a measure of privacy. "Would you like wine?"

"Yes please. We will be here a while I think." Nicolas looked at Evelyn. "We have a lot of catching up to do."

The owner left to fetch the wine and soon returned with a carafe of wine and a basket of rolls. Nicolas looked at Evelyn. "Will you allow me to order for you?"

"Sure, I like almost anything."

Addressing the owner, he said, "Please bring us your Greek platter for two."

"Absolutely. I will prepare it at once."

Nicolas poured wine into the tumblers in front of them then lifted his in a toast. "To Evelyn Christmas, and her success with her fundraising venture. From what I have seen so far, it has been a roaring success." He clinked glasses with Evelyn and then took a sip and put it down. "Now, I want to know more. grand-mere says I have been neglectful and have missed out on some very important developments. In actual fact, I thought she was going to box my ears. She certainly told me to smarten up. So, Evelyn Christmas, *what have you been up to?*"

Evelyn took a sip of the wine, weighing if it was a high-level summary he wanted, or if he wanted to know all the deep facts. "There is a lot to tell. What is it that you are interested in?"

Nicolas sat back and studied her, as though trying to peel back the layers and expose her true self. She had her guard up and it was rock solid.

"Don't shut me out. I sincerely want to know what has transpired."

"You promised me an apology."

"So I did. So here it goes. I apologize for my beastly behaviour the other day and for ignoring you over the last few days. It was wrong of me, I know that now. You had no intention of causing harm or hurt, and I reacted like a child. As for my absense, I was distracted by the arrival of Sabine, who as you know is a demanding woman both emotionally and with her time. I thought it best if I humour her and take her where she needed to go, which as it turned out, was to Quebec City. So, I was literally out of town."

Evelyn shrugged. "Your romantic life is no concern of mine. I am here simply to do a job."

"I disagree. I think you are here for your passion, which it appears you excel at, and that is providing solutions for the homeless. Will you tell me what you have done and how it has all been arranged?" Nicolas sat back, sipping his wine, and waiting.

The food arrived and was placed in the center of the table.

And Evelyn began to talk. She stared off into space, not brave enough to look directly at him, and started her recounting from when he had walked away. Evelyn told him about their idea to bring in the homeless and have them operate the Christmas village as Santa's elves and become part of the Christmas miracle transformation. She told him about the factory and his grandmother's permission to reopen it, about the local business's donations and the support of people throughout the community, about the campaign taking hold and going viral, and now the latest news about how the homeless will be permanently sheltered in the old factory and the donations pouring into the campaign every minute.

"So, you see, the village has taken on a life of its own. I hope you are not disappointed. It can no longer be just your childhood memory. It was always meant to be more, to be shared. This is the legacy your parents wanted, I think. They meant it to be the spot that brought not only your family, but the whole community together over the holiday season. They meant it to live in everyone's memories."

The retelling had taken almost two hours, with Nicolas only adding the occasional prompt. Evelyn looked down at the platter in front of them and was amazed to see they had eaten nearly all of it. The wine was nearly gone too. She looked up at Nicolas and surprised a look of shock on his face. "You did all of that in three days?"

"Yes, but it wasn't just me. It was Natalie, and Alvin, and Francois and the town workers and the elves and Noelville's parents and school teachers, and media personnel and even Georges had his part to play. And the mayor, of course. And now the country is watching and donating and it looks like there are requests for interviews. Your grandmother's office has been overwhelmed with media requests and the outreach from mayors of other cities."

"This venture has taken on a life of its own, which is what it means to have a viral campaign, and this is when I step away. This is when I hand over the reins to those that have hired me. In this case, it's physical as well as virtual reins. Your course as Santa is set, and I will not be needed any further. Which is why," she lowered her eyes, unable to look at him, "I will be taking a flight first thing on Saturday morning back to Vancouver. I booked it this morning."

Nicolas looked shocked. "You are leaving? Why?"

"I told you. My job is done here. There is no reason for me to stay. All the pieces are in place. Natalie will stay behind for another week to make sure everyone knows what they are to do. But that is it. It's time I went home."

"I thought you'd be here for Christmas," murmured Nicolas in a soft tone. Evelyn looked up and met his eyes, then glanced away.

"Despite my name, my memories hold no more Christmas traditions than yours do. I have no family. It is a day on the calendar. Nothing more." She looked around the restaurant and saw that it was nearly full, something else that surprised her. "Now if you will drop me off at the market, I would like to complete my final survey of the local vendors and make sure we are not negatively impacting them."

"I will accompany you. It would be good for me to know what they have to say, too."

"Fine. We should go then."

Nicolas squared the bill then they drove back to the village market center. Parking in the lot which was the closest they could get to the closed off streets, they climbed into one of the waiting horse and carriages. Nicolas pulled a blanket from the other seat and spread it across their laps while the driver clucked to the horses to get them moving. Horse hooves clattered and the bells on the bridles jangled. Nicolas stretched out a arm behind Evelyn's back to rest on the top of the seatback.

It was almost a romantic ride. Quiet. Peaceful, but with an underlying sorrow for things that could have been and weren't. He tugged at her in ways she couldn't explain. All she knew was despite the hurt she felt, she loved him, deeply. Evelyn peeked a look at him, to find him staring at her with a far away gaze. What was going on behind those beautiful eyes? He lifted his left hand and drew a strand of wind-blown hair out of her eyes, tucking it back behind her ear. She shivered at the contact, searching his eyes. Nicolas leaned forward, and Evelyn was mesmerized by the stormy blue eyes staring into hers, growing larger...

The carriage lurched to a stop, breaking the spell of the moment. They broke apart with a start and Evelyn awkwardly got to her feet and climbed down from the carriage. Nicolas came up beside her and took her left hand, tucking it in the crook of his arm while he led her down the sidewalk. As they walked, heads turned and people started calling out. At first Evelyn wasn't sure what they were saying but then the words reached her ears. They were calling her name. "Joyeux Noel, Evelyn Christmas!" and "Bonne fête, Evelyn!" That they recognized her birthday was also Christmas day warmed her heart, for the term had two meanings in Quebec.

As they walked down the street, people stopped and waved, and some whistled, then a crowd started forming and the people started clapping, almost as if she were a celebrity. Evelyn came to a halt, confused at all the attention. Where they stopped was out front of a bookstore, and the owner came out, smiling from ear to ear. he took her right hand and shook it, beaming. "Thank you for stopping outside my humble store. I have wanted to meet you for days, to thank you."

"Whatever for?" she asked, bewildered. She noticed the store owners on either side of the bookstore had also come out, joining the balding bookstore owner.

"Your inspired campaign has tripled our sales over the previous year. There are tourists here in record numbers. I think that people visiting Quebec City for the holidays have heard of the Christmas Village and are adding it to their holiday plans. There are actual bus tours arriving daily now, all with one wish on their list. To stroll the village and visit the Christmas village. Word has spread like wildfire. Look behind you, there. See? Another busload has just arrived."

Evelyn and Nicolas looked down the street to where the man pointed, as a large group of people, led by what looked to be a tour guide, walked down the center of the street and obviously giving a guided tour. Evelyn blinked, trying to take it all in. Phones were pointed in her direction and the crowd pushed forward, some holding out pens and paper, and asking for autographs. Evelyn shrank back, not sure how to respond to the press of people. She wasn't used to crowds. She worked alone for the most part. Overwhelmed, she shrank back against Nicolas, her anxiety kicking up to new levels.

Seeing her distress, Nicolas stepped forward to stop the press of people. "Evelyn is very grateful and warmed by your caring. She is not available for direct conversations at the moment." He looked over the head of the crowd and spied the perfect distraction. "But if you are looking for a celebrity to approach, I see Sabine Perdue is out for a stroll today also, and there she is!" He pointed back the way they had come.

Sabine was walking down the sidewalk towards him, her regular entourage of security surrounding her, waving at Nicolas as if asking him to wait for her. The crowd turned and seeing the famous actress, moved off in her direction. The wall of people was the perfect distraction needed, and Nicolas pulled Evelyn into the bookstore, followed by the pleased store owner. They went to the back of the store, where he asked the shop keeper if there was a rear exit to the building. Evelyn stood trembling beside him, and the shop keeper, seeing her distress nodded for them to follow. "This way. It will put you out back of the store in the alley and you can walk the entire length back to the car park. Thank you for stopping, and Merry Christmas!" he said, unlocking the rear door and letting them out.

Once clear of the crowds, Evelyn let out a long breath and tried to calm her racing heart. "I'm sorry for the panic attack there, Nicolas. I am not used to that kind of attention. Crowds focused on me make me nervous, a hold over from the childhood bullies. I don't like the limelight, which is why I do things remotely, with a camera. Can we get out of here?"

Nicolas nodded and then put his arm around her and guided her back to the car. His presence was a comfort and his warm arm calmed her and made her feel safe. As they exited the alleyway, Evelyn looked around carefully, pulling up the hood of her coat to hide her face, then followed Nicolas to the cark as fast as her legs would carry her.

Once safely ensconced in the car, he drove them back to the manor, not speaking a word, but occasionally glancing at her, check to see if she was ok. Evelyn gave him a weak smile then focused her attention on the passing scenery. The gates were a welcome sight, and with a pang she realized that she was beginning to see them as home, which they would never be. Her eyes roved the now familiar outlines of the manor, trying to commit the images to her mental memory. Photos and video were great, but nothing captured the smell and feel of a place like your own memories.

Nicolas parked, then helped Evelyn out and up to the steps. Georges met them there, and Nicolas gave him hurried instructions about delivering the supplies to the village then took Evelyn inside. He hung up her coat and then took her by the hand and pulled her along behind him, entering the library, where he let go of her hand and poured to glasses of whisky. Pushing one into her hand, he made her sit down.

Evelyn took a shaky sip and let the liquid do its work, warming her. Nicolas sat down beside her and pulled her over so that she fell against his side, head resting on his shoulder. She froze for a second, then melted into the security of the embrace. "It's ok to be afraid in pressured situations like that one," said Nicolas. "Crowds can be overwhelming. That is why famous people have security around them, like Sabine. You are not used to that level of intense focus, but you had better to get used to it. You are a celebrity now, whether you want to be or not."

Evelyn considered his words. "I suppose you have become used to it by dating all those famous women."

Nicolas frowned. "Some what. But I've been in the spotlight one way or another my entire life. Not enough to need security, but I suppose that is changing now too."

Evelyn thought of his relationship to Sabine. There was no question that he would need security if they were to be married. The thought saddened her. She took another sip of the whisky. She felt the liquid burn and her eyes watered. At least she thought it was from the whisky. "I have no intention of hiding in my house the rest of my life. Once I am back in Vancouver I will be back to being an nobody again. Big cities are easy to hide in. Speaking of which, I need to go do some work on my laptop and I should probably pack." She pushed away from Nicolas with reluctance. She wanted to stay cuddled in his arms, but they weren't her arms, were they? And if she couldn't have the whole man, she wanted none of it.

She put the glass down on the table and stood up. "Thank you for the pleasant day. I am glad we were able to talk at last. Have a good night, Nicolas."

Evelyn turned away and walked to the door. She did not see the sorrowful look in Nicolas' eyes as she left the room.

The Charity Gala

I t was the ringing of her cell phone that woke Evelyn. She rolled over and groaned, then fumbled for her phone. "Hullo?" she mumbled sleepily.

"Wake up, sleepy head. I let you sleep as long as I could," said Natalie, "but the Gala venue opens in two hours and I need you to get your butt over here, so we can finish the set up. The caterers will be delivering everything in about thirty minutes time, and prize donations are stacked outside the doors. So come on!"

"What time is it?"

"It's noon, you ninny. You might as well bring your dress and change here."

Evelyn sat up and yawned. "Ok, I will be over in thirty minutes. Save some work for me to do."

"Oh, there's no fear of running out of things to do. See you in a few." The line went dead.

Evelyn forced herself into the bathroom, dragging her feet. She had a raging headache and was not looking forward to the day at all. That was unusual, as it was these key events that usually set a campaign on the path success or failure. Having the campaign already exceeding all goals was deflating in a way. She had peaked too early and now her endurance was waning.

The heat of the hot water soothed her tense muscles. She stayed in the shower longer than she might normally, but today felt like a day to do that. She let the hot water wash away her anxiety and then locked away her heart. Nicolas was her past. There was no sense focusing on it. She was on a flight first thing tomorrow morning, and this day was half over. She could do this.

Squaring her shoulders, she decided that she would dress for the Gala right now. It was opening in two hours, and it would save her a trip back to the manor later on. She had packed everything except her formal dress and a set of casual clothes, last night before going to bed.

She sat down in front of the make up mirror in the bathroom and proceeded to complete her make up and then twisted her hair into an elegant updo that left the nape of her neck exposed. The silk emerald green dress that Natalie had packed, shimmered with a silver undertone. She chose her favourite strand of pearls to wear around her neck and some diamond drop earrings that were surrounded by emeralds. They had been a gift one Christmas from her step mother, and had belonged to her mother. She spent an hour dressing. She viewed it as putting on her war paint, creating a sophisticated mask behind which she would hide until she returned home. When she was satisfied that she looked cool, aloof and in total control, she pulled on her heeled boots and coat, then picked up her purse and left the room.

She walked down the staircase, head held high and back straight. She could feel a pair of eyes on her as she descended, but when she turned her head to see who it was, no one was there. She could have sworn that Nicolas had been watching her. Maybe it was just her own desires coming to the fore. She shoved the thought away and locked it behind her cool facade.

At that moment Georges arrived in the foyer, as he was acting as chauffeur for the family members for the day. "Good afternoon, mademoiselle. Are you ready to go?"

"That would be lovely, Georges. If you could drop me off at the venue, that would be perfect."

"Of course. The others are all gone. What time should I pick you up? You will want to change again?"

"No, I will be staying there until the evening festivities are complete. I should be ready around 8 pm or so."

"You are not staying for the dancing? The band they have hired is very good."

"No, I have an early flight in the morning and I will need to get so bed as soon as possible. I will send you a text when I am ready to leave."

"Very well. The car is waiting outside." He opened the door for Evelyn and left the manor.

Nicolas watched Evelyn descend the stairs with a pole axed expression. She took his breath away. She was the most beautiful woman had ever seen. He closed the door to the dining room as she glanced his direction, then peeked the door open again when George appeared, to watch the exchange.

Once they left, he went upstairs to his room, to change. Standing in front of his closet, he chose his formal suit and white shirt combo and dressed quickly. Sabine was expecting him to pick her up from the hairdresser's around 4:00 pm and then escort her to the Gala event. It wasn't the first time he had done this. Over the past year that they had been dating, he had picked her up and escorted her to the celebrity events that she loved. Frankly, he was surprised that she even bothered with Noelville's fundraiser. It was a nothing event as far as social events went for celebrities, especially this time of year. Which meant that she was attending for him. He tried to rein in his annoyance. The simple truth was that she wasn't the one he wanted to go to this event with.

Evelyn had made it very clear that she had no interest in being Mrs. Claus. Ever since he'd walked out on her that first day down at the village, she had been cool and aloof. She'd refused to come back to the manor, which was just as well, as Sabine had kept him busy with her events, so there had been no time to worry about apologizing for the fight.

And then there were her notes, telling him that she no longer needed his help, that she could take care of the Gala and Marie-Claire's wishes without his help. He'd wanted to go and apologize, but the right time had never seemed to be there, until yesterday. His apology felt like too little, too late. Besides if she was really that shallow, why should he bother to apologize further? Everything she had accomplished had truly stunned him. She really didn't need his help. That was the sad truth of the matter.

At one point, he had thought she felt the same way about him, as he felt about her. He had nearly found out, there in the carriage. If only the driver had gone slower.

If only....

Nicolas gave his head a shake. He seemed to be saying that a lot lately. *If wishes were kisses, how happy I would be...* that had been his mother's favourite song. She would have approved of Evelyn. He knew that deep down. Nicolas pulled open the top drawer of his dresser and lifted out a ring box. He opened the box and inside, nestled in a velvet bed, was a woman's diamond solitaire. His mother's engagement ring.

He stared hard at it, then snapped the lid shut and put it deep in the pocket of his suit jacket.

He put on his outer coat and headed out to the BMW. He needed to do some shopping of his own before picking up Sabine. It was time that he got off the proverbial fence and proposed. The Gala would be the perfect setting.

"There you are! Wow! You look gorgeous!" Natalie took Evelyn's hand and pulled her into the transformed ballroom, taking her on a quick tour of the set up. A central platform has been built in the middle of the room for the band, who would play light music for the cocktail hour from 3:00 – 6:00 pm and then for the dancing that would start around 8:00pm. Around the outer walls, blind auctions were set up. Ticket stations were set up at every table to process orders and then purchasers could put their tickets into whatever box they wished, as many as they wished, in the hope of winning that prize. The prize draw would be held between 6:00 – 8:00 pm while everyone conversed and enjoyed the caterer's selections of hot and cold.

"Here, you can set up the ticket stations. We have a box of rolled tickets and each prize must have a gift box in front of it, with a slot to place the ticket. You might need to make up some more boxes quickly (she pointed to a flat pack of Christmas boxes) as donations keep arriving."

"How many people are you expecting to come?" asked Evelyn.

"If the line up outside is anything to go by, I think we will see upwards of a thousand people by the time all is said and done."

"Are you sure we will be able to fit that many people in here?"

"Oh, no, that is why it will be spilling out into the main floor of the factory. We are going to have more tables set up in the food court and along he sides of the hallway. There will also be a sealed cash donation box, that is dressed up to look like a mailbox to Santa, but the chute goes down into the basement to a metal safe. It's over here, come look."

They inspected the cash donation box. It was a bright red mailbox on a metal tube painted to look like a fence post. Christmas lights wrapped around the post and up onto the mail box, blinking red, green and blue. A sign was attached to the post, announcing the purpose of the mailbox. "That's a great idea, Natalie."

"Thanks, but one of the elves suggested it. I can't take credit for this one." Natalie's eyes scanned the crowd and picked out Alvin. "There's Alvin. I need to speak to him quickly. Are you all set?"

"Go, I will get to work."

Evelyn returned to her task of setting up the ticket boxes, and accepting new gifts as the donations arrived. Soon all the boxes were used up and yet more donations arrived, which she stacked off to one side, deciding they could raffle them later on using the boxes over once again.

Before she knew it, the doors opened and people flooded into the hall, laughing and talking with excited voices, as waiters began to circulate with trays of beverages. The band arrived and marched up onto their stage. Christmas carols filled the hall, adding to the ambiance. Evelyn was happy to remain seated at her ticket station and watch the people mingle. The line up in front of her grew, as she sold tickets and gave instructions for the tickets. Two elves appeared, joining her at the table and between the three of them they were able to process the crowd much more efficiently. The time flew past and just as the crowd in front of her thinned, a buzz of excitement ripped through the room.

Across the hall, security guards moved in a box pattern in front of an impeccably dressed woman in a shimmering, figure hugging, cream sequined gown with a plunging neck line. A cream faux fur boa was wrapped around her lovely throat, and diamonds sparkled in her ears and on her fingers. Her hand rested on the arm of a tall, handsome man, who walked beside her and smiled at the crowd. Nicolas escorted Sabine into the room, while people clapped for their arrival, and a few wolf whistles pierced the air.

As soon as the band saw the pair, their music slowed and the lights lowered. Nicolas held out his hand and Sabine took his and together they moved onto the dance floor. They were soon joined by others until she could no longer see the pair dancing, but that did not stop Evelyn's treacherous eyes from trying to do so. When she realized what she was doing, she got to her feet. The line was gone, all the tickets sold and there was absolutely no reason for her to stay a moment longer. She reached into purse and pulled out her phone, and started a text to Georges.

Before she could finish the text, he appeared at her elbow. "Mademoiselle, would you permit me this dance?"

"Oh!" said Evelyn, blinking. "I was just messaging...never mind. Yes, I would love to dance with you."

Georges bowed properly over her hand, then led her to the dance floor. They circled for a moment, and then he said, "As pleasant as this dance is, the truth is I came looking for you. I came across some disturbing information recently, and in light of recent events, I thought it was important that you have all the facts."

Evelyn stared back at him. For some reason, her treasonous heart leapt into action, frantically galloping within her chest. "What information?"

"Well, it seems that a certain house guest has been playing a game of charades. You know that in my capacity as butler, I am often asked to relay messages. Apparently the messages that one Simone Perdue asked me to relay, contained some falsehoods." He stared at her, looking intently into her eyes so that there could be no misunderstanding. "Specifically as it relates to my employer Nicolas and his relationship with you. It seems that she has a jealous streak and that her visit here has been nothing more than a ploy to make sure that the two of you never got together."

Evelyn laughed a bitter laugh. "She was wasting her time. Nicolas doesn't even know I exist and he was very happy to fire me and then replace me with Sabine for tomorrow's parade."

"Do you think so? What if I told you that he received a note from you shortly after your misunderstanding, stating that you no longer wanted to be involved in the parade? I have the note right here in my pocket. Would you like to read it?"

"What? I never sent any such note!" said Evelyn, pulling away from Georges. He tightened his hold on her and continued to slowly dance.

"I know you did not. But Nicolas thinks so. He thinks you have pushed him away, and want nothing to do with him. He believes that you can't stand to be in the same room as him. Sabine has been playing a clever game and she is about to win it." He looked deeply into Evelyn's wide eyes. "What I want to know is, do you love him? And before you answer, think carefully. You are out of time. If your answer is that yes, you love him, then it's time to fight for what you want. What is your answer, Evelyn?"

Fear flooded Evelyn but at the same time she felt a surge of anger at this woman who thought she could manipulate the world to her own desires, with no thought for the feelings of others. She looked over at the pair, dancing on the floor. She could tell in their body language that they did not love each other. But she did. She loved Nicolas with a terrible hunger, with a deep thirst that a lifetime of being with him could not quench. She tore her gaze away and looked back at Georges, who was waiting patiently for her answer.

"Yes. I love him. Deeply and truly." Georges smiled down at her, relief flooding his eyes. "Then it is time to fight for him. In a few seconds I am going to interrupt their dance and we are going to change partners. It will be up to you to speak to Nicolas, right here, right now, and convince him of your love. Fight for him." Evelyn stared up at George, then gave a tiny nod.

Georges carefully maneuvered them until they were side by side with Nicolas and Sabine. Sabine looked over at Evelyn with small, cruel smile then dismissed her.

"Excuse me, Nicolas. Sabine, would you honour me with a dance?"

Sabine smiled at Nicolas, patted his cheek, and then they switched partners. Evelyn shivered as Nicolas' arm came around her waist and her slender hand was swallowed up in his.

The band ended their song and then started into a new one, "If Wishes Were Kisses" by Perry Como.

"If wishes were kisses, I'd still be kissing you

I'd hold you in my arms again the way I used to do..."

"Hi," said Evelyn nervously.

"Hi," said Nicolas, softly, staring into her eyes.

"Did you get a note from me saying that I didn't want to be Mrs. Claus?" She stared back with equal intensity, drowning in his eyes.

If wishes were kisses, how happy I would be

I'd always have you close to me to thrill me through an' through

"Yes, it was the next morning after we had our fight, or rather I should say I walked out on you and accused you of horrible things that I later deeply regretted."

"I didn't write that note," breathed Evelyn, watching his reaction.

Nicolas faltered a step, then recovered. "You didn't write it?" he asked, surprise mingling with a sudden suspicion.

"No," whispered Evelyn, her breath washing over Nicolas' lips that were suddenly near as he pulled her closer.

If dreamers were schemers, I'd make my dream come true

If wishes were kisses, I'd still be kissing you!

"How do you know this?" asked Nicolas, although he suspected the answer already.

"Georges just told me." Nicolas looked over to Georges, who nodded his head in confirmation, as he whirled Sabine away from them, giving them the privacy they needed.

Nicolas spun Evelyn closer to the stage to make sure they could not be overheard.

"So does this change anything?" he asked, is expression intense. "Are you saying you would like to be Mrs. Claus?"

Evelyn looked up into his face and knew that now was the moment. There would never be another chance.

"I would love to be your Mrs. Claus. I would love to be your Mrs.— I love you, Nicolas."

The band noticed that something important was happening, and the music softened even further.

The look of fear left Nicolas' eyes at Evelyn's words, and love bloomed in them. He let go of Evelyn and went down on one knee, right then and there. He fished around in his pocket and pulled out his mother's ring box and opened it, holding it aloft to Evelyn.

Looking up at her, at the tears swimming in Evelyn's beautiful eyes, he said in a loud voice, "Evelyn Christmas. I love you with all my heart. Will you become my Mrs. Claus? Will you marry me?"

If wishes were kisses, how happy I would be!

I'd always have you close to me to thrill me through an' through

If dreamers were schemers, I'd make my dream come
true

If wishes were kisses, I'd still be kissing you!

Evelyn looked down at the face she loved more than any other, and
with tears spilling down her face, she said, "Yes! Oh yes, yes, yes! I
love you so much Nicolas!" Her words burst into the suddenly silent
hall as everyone had stopped dancing and were watching the event
with complete absorption. Nicolas pulled out the ring and placed it
on Evelyn's finger, then rose and swept her into his arms and kissed
her...

A glass shattering as it hit the floor caused them to jump apart
and come back to the present. The crowd roared their approval and
clapping and whistling filled the hall. All except for one person.

Sabine Perdue gave them a look of disgust then left, taking her
entourage with her.

Nicolas and Evelyn laughed, then went back in for a second, longer
kiss.

Hand in hand, they left the hall for some much-needed alone time.
They had plenty to discuss, and they might even get around to it,
between kisses.

If Wishes Were Kisses by Perry Como

If wishes were kisses, I'd still be kissing you
I'd hold you in my arms again the way I used to do
If wishes were kisses, how happy I would be
I'd always have you close to me to thrill me through an' through
If dreamers were schemers, I'd make my dream come true
If wishes were kisses, I'd still be kissing you!

If wishes were kisses, how happy I would be!
I'd always have you close to me to thrill me through an' through
If dreamers were schemers, I'd make my dream come true
If wishes were kisses, I'd still be kissing you!

Words and Music by Larry Stock
And Milton Drake

https://genius.com/Perry-como-if-wishes-were-kisses-lyrics